Dear Reader:

I am so excited that you have chosen to read *Take Two and Pass*. This is one of my all-time favorites from an author who takes real life and makes it ten times deeper to get his point across. Nane Quartay is a visionary; he wants to make an impact with his writing and he drives that point home in this novel.

Tokus Stone, the main character, is like many inner city young men who want to get out of the predestined horrible future determined only by their ZIP code. He wants to have a better life than his family members who came before him and decides that slinging dope for a living is a means to an end. He uses the money earned to pay for college and for basic survival. Just when he is ready to end the "street life" and move on, everything changes.

Pause is a confused young lady who only knew pain and abuse as a child. She has developed a cold and callous outlook on life and, in particular, does not have a high regard for the male species. Quartay shows us that "a pause can kill" in the most unique way.

Nane Quartay's books—*Take Two and Pass, The Badness* and the upcoming *Come Get Some* are not your typical "urban fiction." They are so realistic that readers will be caught up in every single, poetic word.

Thank you for supporting this author and Strebor Books in general. If you are interested in making extra income, please email dante@streborbooks.com to be sent an "Opportunity" packet. Now sit back in your favorite chair or, better yet, chill in the bed, and be prepared to be tantalized by yet another great read. Meanwhile, come check out my blog on http://myspace.com/zaneland.

Peace and Many Blessings,

Zane

Publisher
Strebor Books International

www.simonsays.com/streborbooks
http://myspace.com/zaneland
www.planetzane.com
www.eroticanoir.com

Other books by Nane Quartay
The Badness

ZANE PRESENTS

TAKE TWO
AND PASS

NANE QUARTAY

A

PUBLICATION

STREBOR BOOKS

NEW YORK LONDON TORONTO SYDNEY

Published by

Strebor Books International LLC
P.O. Box 6505
Largo, MD 20792
www.simonsays.com/streborbooks

Previously published as *Feenin*

ISBN 13 978- 1-59309-105-7

LCCN 2006928396

Distributed by Simon & Schuster, Inc.
1230 Avenue of the Americas
New York, NY 10020
1-800-223-2336

Cover design: © www.mariondesigns.com

First Printing November 2006
Manufactured and Printed in the United States

10 9 8 7 6 5 4 3 2 1

ACKNOWLEDGMENTS

To all of my friends! Those who helped me with encouragement as I dreamed a little dream of a novel. You helped keep the ebon in my flow. Thanks to Bernard Moseby, Linda, Terry T, Carolyn Corbin and Lisa Cannon for being the first to read my story, even when it was raggedy. To Stephanie Kelly, Cheryl R, Kendall Rhodes, Norma Chapman, John, John and John for letting me flip the script whenever I wanted to trip. It was mad fun!

I also wish to express my many thanks to the writers for allowing my words to wander in their intellectual space. You all helped me dot the "i's" and cross the "t's" of my imagination. I owe you all. Black Inkwell, Albany Writer's Group, and my fair and honest backbreaking critics at Barnes and Noble.

It takes a village to raise a child. It took a tribe to raise mine. There are going to be friends that I have missed but just know that it wasn't my intention.

Peace!
Nane Q

PROLOGUE

Tokus Stone stood looking out the window at nothing, wondering what would happen next…and he wanted to say good-bye. "Peace" to the violence that lay outside, on the desolate streets below. "Later" to the hunger that plucked at his insides, that gnawed at him until his soul went raw. "See ya" to the cold harshness of people, to their salty numbness that dripped like bitter syrup into their eyes and mouths. He felt them all…and he dealt with the barren landscape as hell. An entity that was very, very real. He brought the binoculars to his eyes and looked down at the street from the eighth-floor apartment. A people watcher in the ghetto. All the despair of a sixteen-year-old, saddened by abuse and devoid of love, arose in him as he watched his people and listened to his drunken stepfather rage at his mother.

"You just a lyin'-ass ho," his stepfather spit out. Tokus' fertile young mind conjured images of the hookers he passed downtown every day. They wore outfits that stirred his imagination into hard places. They'd let you feel 'em up and everything for two dollars, but Tokus kept that to a minimum. That wasn't his mother though, and he could gladly kill his stepfather whenever that word came out his lying, drunken mouth. He looked down at the people crawling on the street far below.

The nothingness of the big city glared back at young Tokus, invading him, filling him with emptiness. *I'm gonna get outta here,* he thought. Education would be his rescuer, his lifeline out of the ghetto. One day he wanted to own his own business, be his own boss. Take care of his mother and help her cast off the line of losers she always seemed to reel in, present husband included, and leave this street life behind them. Soon he would enter his junior year in high school, and if he kept his grades where they were, he was sure he would be able to get a grant to attend the university. Yes, he would "learn" his way out of the projects, and nothing could stop him.

The usual suspects were hanging out on the corner. A coarse sky loomed over the drab neighborhood, spreading dreary light over the mundane existence known as the slums. There was a corner store with bars on the windows, and various colored brick buildings lined the rest of the block. Morning, noon and night the desolation was the same; poor people crammed on top of poor people with the only common denominator being pain and hunger and devising a means to get beyond and above the cycle of sleeping and waking. With no hope in between. *Everything is fair when ya' living in the city*, Tokus mused.

He watched through his binoculars as a Black Jesus stumbled around the corner, running down the street as if the devil were after him. He wore a tattered pair of shorts and a tiny vest a few sizes too small. On his back was a cross made of cheap wood and printed in big, white letters on a placard attached to the top of it was the word "America." His eyes bulged in fear as he pumped his fists, snatching at momentum, frantically reaching for speed to add to his cumbersome frame. Black Jesus wasn't made for running. A carload of teenagers came screeching around the corner after him with automatic weapons pointed out the windows. Tokus watched the usual suspects sprint for cover as rapid gunfire spit forth, showering the sidewalk. The first shot caught Black Jesus in the leg and spun him around as the car pulled up beside him. The second shot pierced his side and slammed him against the wall. The third bullet hit Black Jesus in the chest, and he danced, dead, against the cold, brick building. He slumped to the ground, lifeless. "America" was stained with his blood.

"Why you always got to wait till you get drunk to come in here with your mess?" his mother asked the drunk. She didn't yell. "Crazed people yell," she had once told Tokus, "and I ain't crazed!" Tokus loved her for her understanding, but he just wished she would leave her husband and move on. He had long ago stopped asking his mother why she stayed, and at some point, Tokus had stopped caring. She had chosen her path and she walked it with determination. She could walk it alone as far as he was concerned, but something, somewhere had to change.

The harsh reality of his stepfather's wrath was an early lesson for Tokus. From the age of four until he was nine there were savage belts and wicked belt buckles. From ten to twelve there were stinging electrical cords and big, thick-handled straw brooms. But at fourteen, Tokus developed into a strong, muscular banger, and his stepfather resorted to using fists. He delivered solid heavyweight punches that overpowered the boy, laying him out, leaving him flat on his back, looking up at a twisted face, flared nostrils and bulging jaws that snorted air with a twisted disposition. Sweat poured angrily down the wild man's face. Yellow teeth showed unevenly as he sneered, standing over the fallen child, cursing the day of Tokus' conception. Tokus had taken many beatings, but as he grew in mental and physical strength, a lifetime of fear was replaced by a burning desire for payback. He waited. His time would come.

A piercing scream, a chorus of pain came down the hallway. Tokus winced inside and ran toward its source. He came to a stop in the bedroom doorway, catching his breath in horror. His stepfather knelt between his mother's legs. Her skirt was hiked way up over her thighs and her blouse was ripped open. Her breasts flopped out lewdly, exposed as the man reached out and pawed them. Then he slapped her in the face.

"You don't tell me 'no,' you lying slut!" he screamed. "You! Don't! Tell! Me! No!" he growled, punctuating each word with a backhand. "You just open your legs and get ready!" he finished. His chest heaved from mixing alcohol with physical exertion. He never saw Tokus charging toward him with his shoulder aimed like a battering ram.

Tokus saw his chance and hit harder than he had ever hit anyone on the football field and sent the man sprawling, face first, into the nightstand near the bedside. Tokus sprang to his feet in a defensive stance. The fading afternoon sunlight streamed through the window behind him, bathing him in ninja shadows. The stepfather rolled onto his back. The skin on his face puckered where he had been cut. The blood leaked down his face as he climbed to his feet, wobbled a bit, then threw his head back and screamed like a banshee. Tokus waited as his stepfather rushed toward him, a bulldozer with bared teeth.

Reality slowed for Tokus and he entered the "zone," a place where everything and everyone moved in surreal, slow motion. As his stepfather covered the few feet between them, Tokus realized that pound for pound, body-to-body, he would get steamrolled, so he went low, throwing his shoulders at the older man's knees. The stepfather went sailing, flailing into the curtains behind Tokus and crashing through the window. He grasped a handful of curtain and clung, pulling the fabric behind him and ripping the curtain rods out of the wall. The thin, aluminum rods wedged into the corner of the window and held for a second but the weight of the stepfather quickly snapped them in half. Tokus heard a desperate scream before the rods went clattering out the bedroom window, eight stories to the ground below.

Tokus looked at the window, shocked! For a second. Then he went over to the window to see where the creep had landed.

"Help!" came a panicked cry.

Tokus looked down, surprised to see that his stepfather was hanging on the window ledge. Shards of glass were biting into his fingers and blood leaked out onto the ledge. He was holding on with both hands, but Tokus wondered, for how long?

"Help me!" he screamed at Tokus.

"Help me, who?" Tokus asked.

"Help me, Tokus!"

"Mr. Tokus."

"Mr. Tokus! Mr. Tokus! Mr. Damn Tokus! Now pull me up! Please!" The glass bit deeper into the tender flesh of his fingers. Tokus' mother hurried over to the window, saw her husband hanging there and got frantic.

"Oh, my God!" she shrilled. "Oh! My! God! Tokus, pull him, pull him up!" she ordered and began to cry, her fingers dug deeply into the soft flesh of his shoulder.

Tokus leaned his head out the window. "You gonna die."

"Please, Tokus! Please?" The dangling stepfather kicked frantically at the building, his fingers pressed farther into the bits of glass as he fought against the fall.

"You know," Tokus began. "When you fall? Before you hit the ground? You gonna feel like I feel when you hit me. When you hit Ma."

"I won't do it no mo'!" the stepfather cried. His fingers slipped a fraction, and tiny squirts of blood shot against the windowsill. He moaned in pain and his arms tensed, tightening, gripping against the gravity that was pulling his body toward the hard concrete.

"Never no mo'! Promise! I promise! Please, Tokus!" the dying man cried for his life.

"A feelin' of nothin'," Tokus continued. "Nothin' you can do about it. As you fall. Nothin' you can hold on to. Nothin'."

"Tokus! Pull me up!" the stepfather begged.

"Tokus, help! Pull! Help him up!" his mother sobbed and collapsed to the floor, whimpering.

"Tokus, don't kill me! Don't let me die!" his stepfather yelled. Then he lost his grip.

Tokus lunged forward and caught his stepfather's hand. The momentum almost pulled Tokus out the window, but he held strongly to the wall with his free hand as the flailing, screaming man struggled against him. It took all his strength to pull the big man back up. His stepfather seemed to be fighting his efforts, twisting and turning, screaming and crying, but after a minute they both tumbled inside and sprawled on the floor, exhausted.

His mother rushed to her husband and fussed over him, ministering with a soft, gentle hand while she cried with relief and happiness. Tokus sat opposite the pair and looked into the man's eyes, surprised at the anger and fear he saw there. His stepfather was a changed man. There would be no more abuse.

The next day passed uneventfully. On the contrary, not a single word was exchanged in the strangely quiet, dysfunctional household. Hollow silence echoed ominously off the thin, plaster walls within the tenement as the three of them avoided each other in the small, two-bedroom apartment.

Nothing mentioned, nothing gained.

Two days later, Tokus' mother and stepfather went away forever, leaving him alone in a man's world to fend for himself.

Tokus stood looking out the window at nothing, wondering what would happen next.

MISTRESS OF IT

S he stood, deliriously trembling, at the entrance to the park. The young girl searched frantically; her addiction screamed out for satisfaction and her flesh moved in chronic surrender. Long gone were the days when drug use was recreational fun, a fad. Times were now hard-core bouts of having and not having, getting and getting got over, even worse, acts that were once theatric drama were now hellish scenes in which she starred. Control of her life had been violently wrested from her and abused by a blizzard of white powder that enslaved her mind and spirit. Yet she loved her master. Her deeds were the proof. So she searched, following a voice only she could hear. The call of yearning.

She had to feed It. It was her habit. A greedy insatiable monster who stomped across the landscape of her soul. It talked to her often. It knew where the drugs were and was well versed in all the ingenious ways in which to procure the precious substance.

The park loomed before her, threatening in the darkness of the late hour, sinister in its rolling, grassy slopes. An alarm went off somewhere in her mind, warning of danger, but that was drowned out by the thunder of It.

"Go," It said and she obediently shuffled down the man-made pathway as It grew heavy with urgency. The sights of the park held no interest to her. The beauty of nature's multicolored leaves of the tall trees, the picturesque shores on either side of the Hudson River were a mere blur, as she set about her mission. She passed the small, outdoor amphitheater with hillside seating and the area known as The Shade, where tall trees stood with their leaves clasping together overhead, casting cool, shadowed refuge during the burning midday hours. The park was deserted—not a soul was in sight—but It guided her. She blindly obeyed. A monument saluting the Buffalo Soldiers was around the bend, hidden from her side of the path by the sloping land. The statue was huge. One soldier stood tall, rifle at the ready, while another kneeled to help a fallen comrade. This part of history meant nothing to her. It only had eyes for the three men who leaned against the tall, stone wall encrypted with the story of the all-black regiment known as the Buffalo Soldiers.

"Look!" It exclaimed as she rounded the curved pathway. She saw a light-skinned man with a big nose put a crack pipe to his lips. Reflexively, she inhaled with him and It pinpricked her brain with a glimpse of false euphoria. She put on her best sexy, crack smile and floated over to where the men stood between the soldiers and the wall.

The big-nosed smoker started rapping:

"Take two and pass,
take two and pass,
take two and pass
so the rock will last."

A dark-skinned man had the pipe. He took two hits and passed the pipe when he spotted the girl approaching.

"H-h-hold up! Waitaminute!" one of the men stuttered, looking the girl over. He recognized the type. "W-w-we got us a trick baby here. Y-y-you out here trickin', baby girl? Huh?"

The big-nosed man broke out with another rhyme:

"All men are created equal.
That's why corrupt governments
Kill innocent people.
With chemical warfare
They created crack and AIDS.

Got the public thinkin'
These are things that Black folks made."

"Ask!" It commanded.

"Let me get a hit?" she asked.

"You t-t-trippin'," came the reply.

"Give me some," she said seductively.

"Yeah. You out here trickin'," the man said.

"Well," the big-nose spoke up, "I don't need no pussy, so get on, trick! I don't need no pussy."

"That's cause you smokin' that shit!" the dark man said. "You don't need no orgasm cause in your brain you already done got off. Skeeted ever' which-a-way!" He turned back to the girl. She could feel It agitating her. The hunger in her eyes was deepening. Her skin...her blood cried out for cocaine.

The dark man pulled a pebble-sized rock of crack cocaine out of his pocket. It's heart skipped a beat.

"You want some?" the dark man asked. She nodded her assent, mute with It.

"I give you some...if you take all your clothes off."

"No!" she shouted without consulting with It.

"What?" It said.

"No! No! Hell no!" she sang. It got angry. It was real ugly when provoked.

"Let me show you something," It said and began flashing scenes across her mind. Scenes from another time, another life. She was on her knees in the back seat of an old abandoned car with three teenaged boys. She'd spit them out the window. Then a German shepherd hunched over her, the dog's paws on her back, its hot breath on her neck. A group of men stood around watching, drinking beer and laughing at the girl who would do anything to get high.

"You will," It said and suddenly she felt the call of cocaine pulling, tearing at every fiber of her being.

"We outside," she said to the man, fighting It.

"Ain't nobody out here but us," the man and It replied in unison. Slowly, she looked around the park. In the thick stillness, she felt eyes everywhere. But there were no other people, not a one.

"Where at?" she asked.

"Here," the dark man replied, mirthfully. He leaned back against the stone wall with a knowing look.

"Go ahead," It said. "Do it. Now!" A blinding high pushed through her flesh, beamed directly into her brain that sent her mind on a spinning, flashing plateau that was miles above the cosmic reach of common thought, a teasing glimpse that quickly dissipated. She sobbed aloud and with trembling fingers, she peeled off her dirty, ripped shirt, exposing the holey, rusty bra underneath.

"Yeah!" It shouted. The three men smoked as they watched, eyeing her small pointy breasts as she removed her bra.

"The rest," said the dark man, wisps of smoke escaping from his lips. She stepped out of her pants and stood naked before them. She extended her arm, palm outward, seeking payment.

"Naw!" the dark man said. "Naw, you got to do more than that, baby!"

"You said naked," she cried.

"I know what I said!" he barked. "But let me see you crawl. Crawl to me. On your hands and knees. But sexy though! Like on TV," he finished. It brought her to her knees. She was openly crying now, and she began to crawl.

"Be sexy!" It warned.

Her sobs were alarming as she fought It. Cries of pain racked her body and she shook with the effort of trying to control herself—to lift herself from her knees, get up, get dressed and escape. She was fed up. It surged to life in response, shocking her with the overpowering need for crack, but she had reached the point of emotional saturation. She collapsed in a heap, mourning her searing desires and the pain It had wrought. The agony of living the white lie.

"She buggin' out," the big-nose said.

"Yeah," said the dark man with a mischievous grin. "Let's take her clothes." The three men gathered up her clothes and ran, laughing with chemical glee, leaving her naked and alone in the park.

Tokus was taking the shortcut to Heath Street when he spotted the naked woman, shivering in the shadows of the old abandoned bridge that passed over the park. She huddled there, soaked in tears, another victim of the rock laid bare by the addiction to the altered state of mind. Her pain, her shame was something that no longer touched Tokus. He had seen her condition many times in many guises, but he attributed their plight to weak-mindedness. *Some people just have addictive personalities,* he reasoned.

Life had forced Tokus into a lifestyle that suited his need to survive, a lifestyle just outside the word of the law. He hated the effect of drugs on people and the victims beyond the addicts. But drugs were a crutch people sought with a need, heedless of its impending, destructive effects. *No matter,* Tokus thought, *'cause I got dreams.* Sadly, he looked at the naked girl, turned and walked away, headed back to his favorite street corner. The best drug spot in the city. He fingered the plastic-wrapped pieces of crack in his pocket and mentally prepared himself for a night of selling drugs in a world where dreams die first.

WALL STREET

Tokus emerged from his office, a dark, dilapidated alleyway that stank of urine and spilled wine, into the still night air on Heath Street. With a wad of money hidden in his underwear, taped to his thigh. The distinct sounds and smells of the money market washed over him in waves. Traffic was heavy as customers moved from broker to broker—curious, inquisitive and careful. Now this, Tokus thought, is a seller's market.

Mentally, he checked the stats of the Underground Index.

Crack cocaine was at twenty dollars a share. A real keeper. Crack has a bright future in America. It feeds on itself.

Marijuana was strong and holding. A solid investment with good returns. This commodity suffered a minor setback when crack burst onto the scene but has since undergone a full recovery.

Alcohol was deceptively steady, an old blue blood's legacy to society. Liquor stores, which endured the ups and downs of economics, stood on both ends of the block. A few doors down from the package store was the neighborhood church. A fortress of God in a sea of iniquity.

These were the numbers, the real numbers, on the poor man's Wall Street on Addict Aisle.

Buyers lined the street. Their need, popping in their veins like popcorn, was as real as water is to life. But they were cautious, scared that their future was dependent upon today's decisions. The buy. That's what it was all about. A bad choice, like buying a piece of soap or a white pebble would leave a buyer in no-man's land, alone and abandoned, with no help in sight. So addicts worked hard at being good, knowledgeable consumers.

Tokus spotted a couple, a man and a woman, coming down the Aisle.

They looked tired. Both wore torn jeans and T-shirts run over with multicolored dirt, their eyes alight with anticipation. They started across the street toward Tokus. The couple stopped in the middle of the street, purposeful, oblivious to the traffic and the crowds. The nappy-headed, dirty-faced man unzipped his pants and urinated, blind to the world. It was only fair. The world was blind to him. He stood back, zipped his pants and admired his work with the woman beside him, rapt, intent, as the liquid ran along the ground. A finger trail pointed in the direction of a young hood off to Tokus' left and, armed with this inside information, the buyers went off eagerly to purchase their shares.

"It gets wild," Tokus muttered as he scanned the Aisle for his regulars. He saw Fiction lounging in the doorway of one of the old abandoned buildings across the street. Fiction was a skinny fella who wore Coke-bottle glasses that seemed too heavy for his face. He was called Fiction because only the truth could be stranger than him. There was a girl with him—Tokus guessed she was sixteen, seventeen tops—who didn't care for truth or Fiction, only the nether world to which she sought entrance. Tokus imagined they were discussing stock options when they turned and disappeared inside the building. It seemed they had agreed on a merger when they appeared silhouetted in the shattered window. The girl went down on her knees, groping for Fiction's zipper. Ah, Tokus mused, insider trading. Services for shares.

A group of buyers turned the corner from Highwater Street onto the Aisle, coming to a halt on the perimeter of the frenzied activities. They stopped to observe the action while passing a joint and a forty ounce of malt liquor among themselves while they plotted and schemed.

The bedlam surrounding Tokus registered as normality. Addict Aisle was a body with the heart cut out, open and bleeding with desperation. He reflected on the drug industry and its place in every society, every city and its thriving, flourishing future.

"We need two bumpies."

Tokus was startled out of his fruitless mental wanderings, automatically reaching into his pocket while checking out his customers. He withdrew his hand, empty, upon seeing the two children who were trying to buy crack to get high.

"Get outta my face." Tokus dismissed them.

"Two!" the other kid said.

"No," Tokus answered.

"We want two bumps," the boy demanded.

"You get shit from me." Tokus turned on them. "Now get the fuck outta my face, kid!" he yelled menacingly and the two youngsters scampered down the street. Damn! Tokus shook his head ruefully. Farther down the Aisle, a dealer took the kids' money and discreetly passed them the coke.

"Damn!" Tokus exclaimed again. He looked at his watch. He usually quit dealing at twelve on school nights, but Tokus had decided to put the "closed" sign in the window early, permanently shutting down his business. Tonight was the first night of the rest of his life.

Usually his schedule had never varied. It was a discipline that had gotten Tokus through high school, after his mother and stepfather had abandoned him, and that structure served him well in college. The university had been a lot tougher on his abilities and his resolve, but in a few short weeks it was finally "G" day. Graduation. The whole idea of graduating from college and moving into the legal way of life brought a smile to his face. But he needed his nights free to concentrate on studying for the final exams. He had enough money saved to sustain him for a few weeks, so Tokus had decided to stop dealing. In a few minutes he would be free. His days of selling drugs to functioning zombies would be forever in the past. Tokus smiled inwardly. *A few more and I'm outta here.*

An old man pushing a shopping cart ambled over and gave his bottle and can collection money to Tokus for the phantom dream.

"Quit," Tokus said as he handed the man the rock. The old man looked at Tokus with disdain. This was his last night on the corner so Tokus was going to tell everyone to quit. The looks he received indicated how far over the crack edge the users had fallen. The old man snorted derisively and hobbled off slowly as he groped in his pocket for a pipe.

A shiny, jet-black Lexus drove up to the curb with a distinguished-looking gentleman behind the wheel. Tokus wondered what the story was with that guy. Obviously, the man had money; yet success didn't seem to fulfill him. As high as he had climbed, he still needed to fly.

"Quit," Tokus said.

The rock was piped and lit before the car pulled away from the sidewalk headed back to the suburbs—the nice part of town.

A bum ambled over to him, smiling, shuffling, doing his best Chris Rock, begging for free dope. He was the worst kind of crack head—a broke one. Tokus chased him away.

A well-dressed older man with a secret came to Tokus for a vial of poison. Tokus knew his secret. She lived on Barrett Street, three blocks east of the Aisle. Minutes away from the church where this guy preached. His name was Deaugood.

"Let me have one," the man said simply.

Tokus' eyebrows arched in a question. "How many?"

"One."

"For who?"

"Myself," the man said to the sidewalk. Tokus shook his head in wonder as he felt around in his pocket for a rock of crack.

"Quit," he said, placing the pebble in the preacher's hand. The preacher looked at Tokus, wide-eyed, with a comment just behind his lips. Instead his teeth clenched and his look went from one of incredulity to one of intense pain. His hand clenched around the crack cocaine in a fist that suddenly clutched at his heart. He swayed a bit, a rickety swoon that led into a stumble as he staggered into Tokus "office." Tokus' brow furrowed in alarm. *Oh, no*, he panicked, *not tonight. I just wanna get outta here*. The preacher was leaning against a building trying to breathe, catching air in raspy wheezes.

"What's wrong, old man?" Tokus asked from the sidewalk, determined not to get any nearer.

"You better not die here, preacher," Tokus whispered harshly, as he quickly glanced up and down the Aisle. No one was paying the incident the least bit of attention.

Tokus glared back into the alley.

The preacher was slouched against a building. His body trembled while his lungs hacked for air to feed his drumming heart. The preacher's body was spewing up pain and panic in his face, but Tokus didn't see any fear there. The preacher had danced with this convulsion before and he knew the intricate steps. Soon the coughs eased and Deaugood slowly began to gather himself.

When Tokus saw the preacher straighten up, he regarded him with a twinkle in his eye. "You know, preacher man-ah," Tokus began in his best Southern, Sunday go-to-meetin' voice. "You got to hold on to God's un-changin' hand." Tokus hopped toward the preacher on one foot with one finger raised in the air. The minister, who was now standing with his fist closed around the rock, looked on, stunned, as Tokus went on with his sermon.

"He can be your Kryptonite-ah, when the woman-ah, with the cooty-cat-ah. Come round. I say the cooty-cat-ah, with the cape-ah, with the silver 'S' hanging out of it come round."

The two men stood face to face. Serious.

Finally Tokus said, "Quit."

The preacher walked away, head bowed. Lust chased him down the street and around the corner to the house where his mistress waited hungrily.

Midnight is the hour of sin and pain on Addict Aisle and Tokus decided to leave and be rid of both. Glancing up and down the Aisle, he silently said good-bye to what had been his life, before turning his back and walking away from it all. With a smile.

When he turned the corner onto Highwater Street, Tokus ran headfirst into hell. Dressed in black.

NEMESIS

On the corner of Heath and Highwater, Bug Minnon's life was changed forever. On a warm, cloudless night he came face-to-face with his enemy. A nemesis who had been a lifelong companion, a monster who stomped around the landscape of his soul, leaving a poison that seeped into his heart. Sometimes it even showed its hideous face for all the world to see.

"I can read miiiinds, man!" Bug crazily exclaimed.

Moose stood with his head turned skyward, an upturned nose sniffing the air.

"You smell rain?" his voice wafted down to the smallish man. Bug was so zooted he simply floated himself up to where he could hear better.

"Naw, man," Bug answered. *But yo' ass always smellin' rain*, he thought, *'cause of that metal-plated brain you got.* If Bug ever told anyone about Moose's weakness they would both be dead. First Moose would kill him and then someone else would kill Moose. Hell, people would fight to draw straws to see who'd get the first shot at the big man. Bug's mind twirled the idea around in the haze of his stupor, toyed with the notion of betraying his best friend, of having power over a giant. But then he discarded the idea, tossing it into the mushy mist of his smoke-filled brain. Moose kept him fed. With brain food. Mind candy. Manna. Because of Moose, Bug could look into people's thoughts.

"I can read miiiinds, man!" Bug repeated. Moose stopped sniffing the air and arched an eyebrow at Bug.

"Here we go," Moose groaned.

"For real!" Bug said. "One rock! If I smoke me some…I can read people's minds. Tha's right. That's the kind of high I gets," Bug finished triumphantly.

Moose was quiet. He was in one of his moods, Bug determined. Danger! Danger! The thought flitted across Bug's mind making him giggle fiendishly. Boy, he felt good! Moose turned to him and raised his arm, pointing across the street.

"What's that man thinkin'?" Moose asked with a devilish glint in his eye.

"Who?" Bug squeaked.

"Him," Moose thundered, jabbing his finger in the direction of a man in a wheelchair. Bug squinted in the darkness, focusing, channeling his powers. The old man sat in his wheelchair. Both his legs were amputated at the knees and he was filthy. He sat facing a water fountain fashioned of stone angels and granite doves spouting dirty yellowish liquid. Behind him was a playground with two children playing on the swings, laughing carelessly and living young. Their laughter washed over the grim, crippled figure as he stared blankly at the large structure of intended serenity. A large dog sat behind the man, steadily chewing on the rubber wheel of his chair. The man sat motionless, a living statue, hardened, transfixed, with a mongrel gnawing on his "leg."

Bug went into a trance. "He's thinkin'," Bug droned. "If I could crawl around inside the inconsequential, the indignities of life would hold no meaning." Bug turned to look at Moose. "And I could stab this dog in his eye," he finished. Moose regarded Bug, surprised.

Told you!" Bug exclaimed. Moose's eyes clicked before he turned and began walking down the street.

"Come on," he called over his shoulder. "Let's go down to the Aisle and cop."

Bug hurried after Moose, and they headed for the red-light district; the best stuff was down there.

Drug traffic on Heath Street was like shopping at the mall but without the ornamental finery. Heath Street was a collection of rundown, abandoned buildings. The gutted houses had no windows, just black holes that beckoned, no—dared one to enter. The streets were littered with the used paraphernalia of chronic drug use—needles, pipes, rubber straps and such. There was even a version of a drug drive-thru as dealers did their business from open car windows.

The dealers themselves were bold and brazen, kings ruling over all who reside on the Aisle of Addicts. They all wore similar expressions, a defiant look that dared and a scowl that warned. Expressions that became a part of their lives as card-carrying chemical distribution reps. The citizens of Addict Aisle shuffle around obediently in their empty, lifeless husks of bodies, their very existence like wisps of smoke born of their habit. The men, bedraggled and beaten, in search of the next fix. The women, some old, some decrepit, having sold the last of their material goods are now selling the one commodity left to them. The drug denying them the ability to see what they have become—walking sperm banks with a habit.

Numbed to the elements of street life, Moose and Bug looked neither left nor right. Sights of the city made some people cry but, for them, it was emotionally effortless. As they hurried down Highwater Street, Bug took a moment to consider the man he called a friend. Moose was frightening. He cut an imposing figure, in dress as well as in manner. He was clad in a tight, black T-shirt with the word "Hell" splattered across his chest in red, burning letters with the evil image of the devil hidden in the flames. Moose was a roughneck, one of the roughest necks around and he always seemed anxious for a fight because he thought there wasn't a man on the planet who could handle him.

And with good reason. Moose's chassis was built on a massive core, an eighteen-wheeler with sledgehammer fists powered by steel ribbon biceps. A big, strapping, brooding man with a fast-burning fuse, Moose was the image of a man on a dark mission, to be avoided, or failing that, appeased at all times and at all costs.

Earlier in the evening, Bug and Moose had been up on Judson Street getting high on some shit that Moose boosted from a corner hood. The young pusher had been frightened into bravado until Moose put his finger in the middle of the kid's forehead and pushed. Hard! Then the thug dropped all pretense and offered Moose everything that he had on him. Moose took it, and then punished the hood with raging fists to the head, twice when the boy was knocked out.

Moose was a fearless man, but like other supermen, failed to take into account the infirmities of mere mortals. Bug was snapped back to reality as they rounded the corner onto Heath Street when a young hood went crashing, face first into Moose's chest. Bug gasped.

The man stumbled backwards onto Heath Street and looked up to see what he had run into.

"'Scuse me, my man," he pardoned.

Oh, hell! Bug's mind set off an alarm. *That's Tokus. Tokus the drug dealer.*

"'Scuse me, hell, bitch!" Moose spat.

Tokus' eyes went dark-dead, dead like the sea, dead like death, and the darkness of the night surrounded him like a comforting blanket. Tokus glared at Moose.

"I said 'excuse me,'" he replied flatly.

"You gonna 'scuse me' what you got in your pocket, little man," Moose said.

The two men eyed each other, assessing, measuring. Moose was much taller than Tokus, yet they met eye-to-eye, neither man flinching. Tokus reached into his pocket, took out a large baggie full of white powder and smiled at Moose. A dangerous smile.

"You want this?" Tokus asked. "Take it."

The street grew eerily silent as they faced each other. The air grew heavy with tension. The night pulsed with the quickening of the crowd as they gathered around, drugs forgotten, chemical euphoria delayed.

"That's mine," Moose stated, laying claim to the big bag of cocaine while he took his shirt off, revealing a heavily muscled chest. Bug counted the scars of two gunshot wounds and at least three knife wounds.

"Oh, yeah," Moose cried. "That's mine, little man."

Tokus, who had been taking his shirt off, paused, dropped his shirt to the ground and stepped toward Moose, his body tensing, his face clouding over with midnight madness. Moose suddenly reached out with both hands and grabbed Tokus by the head, pulled him close and noisily kissed him on the lips. Then he shoved him roughly away. "Bitch," he sneered. Moose assumed a boxing stance, his eyes aglitter with the excitement of a veteran prizefighter. Tokus just looked mad.

They circled each other until Moose moved in, fast and fierce, rushing Tokus with all his weight and power behind a vicious right hand. Bug had seen many a man fall victim to that blow. Moose called it his money punch, but Tokus dodged it with ease. Instinctively, Moose followed with a sharp left. Again, Tokus avoided the blow. Going with the momentum from the misguided left, Moose shot his foot at the side of Tokus' head. Tokus sidestepped as Moose stumbled past him, tried to regain his balance and failed, falling hard and landing on one knee. Tokus came in swinging, landing a thundering right, complete with thunderclap, to the top of Moose's head.

"Ahhhh, damn!" Tokus screamed and clutched his fist.

The big man crumbled into the street in a heap while Tokus winced and cradled his hand as if a worm of pain was wriggling up his arm. Tokus shook his fist as if it had hit a solid metal brick and his fingers seemed to swell with pain. His fist had hit something harder than bone. Moose wasn't getting up.

Tokus stepped back, breathing heavily. The rise and fall of his chest echoed loudly into the silence of the night as the fiends of Addict Aisle looked on.

Sensing that the fight was over, a few of the druggies got brave. Moose had victimized most of them at one time or another.

"Get up!"

"Come on, you ole punk ass! Get up!"

"You pussy man!"

"Strictly butt!"

"Strictly dickly is what you mean!"

"Yeah!"

Amazingly, Moose got one hand underneath himself and began struggling to his feet. His eyes rolled crazily in his head and one side of his face ticked madly. Tokus stepped toward Moose, his fist curled and cocked, when Bug leapt between them.

"Naw, man! Naw!" Bug cried. "My man is out! He's out! You can see that! He's out, man!"

"Not if he gets up," Tokus growled. Moose had made it to one knee, but his entire body was shaking. Saliva trailed in a long string from the corner of his mouth and his eyes had turned a bright red. Specks of blood dotted his head where Tokus had punched him. Bug turned back to Tokus.

"He's done. Why you gonna hurt him again, man?"

"He kissed me," Tokus roared.

"So kiss him back then!" Bug replied desperately. Moose moaned.

"Get out of the way or take his place," Tokus warned.

Bug looked at Tokus and knew there was no question of his intent. Here lay his best friend and Bug had a decision to make. Unbidden, memories came rushing at him like scarlet ghosts and the ugly monster reared his head and roared. Ninth-grade study hall. A football player, a senior twice his size had stood over him, threatening. His heart had raced in epileptic spurts. Like now. A thin sheen of sweat had broken out on his brow. Like now. His body had felt fragile, as if one touch would send it bursting into bloody, boneless pieces. Like now. Then, horribly, he had bowed his head, turned and run away. Like now.

Bug didn't wait to see if his best friend made it to his feet or not, but the sound of Moose screaming followed him down the block and around every corner for the rest of his life.

His nemesis had won again.

NEW STILES

Bug scurried from the painful screams that coursed through his brain and reverberated inside him. Growing in intensity instead of fading with the distance that he put between himself and the horror of his life—he was a coward in flight. He slammed into the park, past the Shade and the Buffalo Soldiers into the darkness under the bridge. His soul found comfort in the dark. A place where he could become invisible while he shed real, bitter tears. And the tears came in torrents. His high from the crack was gone and he felt it. It was a thing called reality, a hard cold thud of an unclouded mind whispering with conscience and crying with shame.

He collapsed against the brick wall and slid to the ground with his face buried in his hands, his heart wrestling with the flow of thin blood that coursed through its chambers. His chest heaved from exertion from the hurried flight he had taken down Highwater Street as he tried to outrun an intangible part of himself. The need to run a marathon crept upon him and Bug shrieked out loud as he realized that the race would require a few additional miles and he would still lose. This demon wasn't even a thing of the past. It was horrifyingly now.

Moose was far from the best of men, but he and Bug had called each other friend. Leaving him when he needed help desperately was the ultimate in cowardice and Bug knew it. Felt it at the core of what pure heart he had left. But morality had no meaning in his life. He had given that away the minute he sucked on the glass dick and inhaled the newest of poisons: crack. Rat poison, rubbing alcohol and cocaine stirred together into a coarse paste and married by flame to the hungry walls of Bug's brain. He cried at his weakness.

Time was immaterial to him and Bug had no sense of how long he had been under the bridge when he noticed a subtle movement in the dark. The thick blackness in the air seemed impenetrable but Bug hadn't been paying any particular attention to his surroundings. The bridge spanned a narrow finger of the Hudson River but from underneath it arched largely into the night. A parking lot was tarred under the bridge and connected to parking lots on either side. The hard, black surfaces stopped short of the shoreline, which had been paved with a walkway, interspersed with well-kept plots of grass. This was one of the safest places outdoors to get high and publicly intoxicated.

Bug often did both.

Alarmed, Bug squinted to focus in the darkness and when his eyes adjusted he almost jumped at the sight. There was a naked woman huddled in the darkness. She sobbed and inched away from Bug in fear. That was when he saw her eyes. And in her eyes Bug instantly knew what the deal was. Why she was outside buck-assed naked. He had seen it before. A nasty, crackhead ho that had run into a brainblasted smoker who didn't want her services. Trickin' a trick.

But Bug had his own pain. His pain came from an internal wellspring that just kept gushing and frothing. An affliction that knew no mercy. Just like hers.

So who was he to judge?

"Hey," Bug gently called her. "You gonna be alright?"

She screamed hysterically at him. Stupid question.

"Listen," Bug stood up and began unbuttoning his shirt. She screeched again. "I know," Bug said softly. "I know. Look, just take my shirt and cover yourself up, girl. Here." Bug tossed the shirt to her without approaching her. She made no move to catch it and it floated to the ground. Bug paused as a truck passed noisily overhead. The still, night air amplified the rumbling of the big rig as it pounded over the bridge, and as Bug waited, he heard the gears shift before the truck picked up speed.

"Come on, now," Bug pled. "How you gonna get home all naked and everything? Just put it on and you can run straight to your house."

She eyed Bug warily, but some of what he said seemed to have reached her. Slowly she reached out and pulled the shirt to her.

Bug stood, waiting while she buttoned up the shirt. As the girl slowly covered herself, Bug pondered the meaning of the simple act of clothing himself. Of having fabric, a barrier, between his naked self and the world, hiding the imperfections because, after all, they were his faults and not for the world's prying eyes. Of protecting what was his and his alone, to be bared only at his discretion. Life could be like that sometimes. Life could be a shirt with no heart or brain or any other vital organ adorning the sleeves.

"You know what?" Bug asked her as the girl buttoned the shirt up. "I ain't smokin' no more. Fuck it. I'm leaving that shit alone. Look what it did to me. Fuck it." Idly he pulled at the sleeve of the ragged tee shirt that he wore as the girl stood and watched him.

"Fuck it," she repeated, her voice sounding small and defeated.

Bug nodded his head. "You live around here?"

"No," she replied. "I don't live nowhere."

"Oh," was all Bug responded. He looked at her. Standing there wearing his shirt, she didn't look that bad. Her hair was nappy and filthy, and her face was streaked with tear-tracked dirt. But underneath all that, Bug saw something. Maybe it was time to hope.

Bug looked up at the bridge that ran overhead, linking one side of the city with the other. He remembered reading a book about a man named Stiles. His name meant "a bridge between two pastures," a point of crossing over to a new land. It was time for him to seek new stiles. A better way. A better life.

Another truck rumbled overhead and Bug listened expectantly for the shifting of gears that would signal a change of speed. When he heard the ratchet of the engine, Bug made a decision.

"You want to 'fuck it' with me? You know, quit this smokin' shit?"

She paused for a moment, regarding Bug. Then, slowly, she nodded her head in agreement.

"First things first. What's your name? I'm Bug."

"Pharren," she said softly. "My name is Pharren."

"Pharren." Bug tried the name on for size. "We really got to do this. 'Cause I'm serious. Okay?"

"Okay," Pharren answered.

"Okay," Bug agreed. "I live over on Orange Street. You ready?"

"Yeah. I'm ready. Let's go."

"My son lives with me," Bug told her as they began walking. "His name is Monday."

Together they went off. Halfway there, he took her hand.

WE IN HERE

Tokus sat down and ordered barbecued ribs and collard greens with a distinct disregard for cholesterol counters and heart monitors. This was soul food at its finest; food for the spirit. That's what fatback seasoning and ham hocks meant: a gateway to the cure for what ails ya'. A balm in the season of discontent with a dash of hot sauce in case your vision got watered down and led astray. Death weighed heavily on his soul, so Tokus needed a stain lifter, a vanisher to let him know that he was still real. A solid commodity that needed to be given succor in the throes of being alive and striving.

His plate came with a flourish—black-eyed peas on the side with a dash of black pepper gently caressing the tops of the pods. Steam was still rising from the plate so Tokus looked around at the surroundings, hoping to spot something new, something to signify the dawn of a new beginning. All he wanted was a life without murder and avarice to feed upon so that he could begin anew in a world of justice. That was all he wanted. A world in which he could receive all that was meant for him. Love and happiness.

Tokus recalled a movie he had seen called *The Best Part Yet*. It was about a guy who had spent his first twenty years waiting for the best part yet, the shining moment of his life. He thought he saw it a few times: once in a job that paid him lots of money; once when he learned the joy of the slots; and again in the arms of a woman and her body with its love melting all over him in tides of pleasure. But they were just fleeting glimpses. The slots cost him his job and the woman took her body away…along with its allure. In the end the desperate man had held a pistol to his head as he wondered aloud, to no one at all, "Now this is the best part yet," before he pulled the trigger.

If he only knew, Tokus mused.

His thoughts were interrupted when the tall, white cop walked in the door. The cop stood in the doorway for a moment, looking over the customers with an unsettling stare, searching. His haunted, gray eyes settled on Tokus for a split second too long before he went over to the counter and placed an order. The hum of conversations died down when the law walked in the door; all talk faded to whispers. It's never known what is expected when a white cop bothers to invite himself into a world where he fits like rat hair in a hot dog.

Lika's Place was a neighborhood restaurant with good food and reasonable prices. Usually this meal was a splurge for Tokus, spiritual spending, so to speak. After dining on some good down-home cooking, he was always left with a full stomach and a sense of contentment. It was quiet and peaceful at Lika's. Lika herself had an unusual sense of drama. She had decorated the dining area with an African motif: paintings, drawings and even a small sculpture of a falling African with a heavy chain around his wrist. There were also photos of great African-Americans affixed to the wall. They were all dead now. Malcolm X, Martin Luther the King, W.E.B. DuBois and Richard Wright.

Tokus fixated on a poster of an older black man that hung directly in his line of vision. Thinning, gray hair was dotted with blood on one side of his head, his lip was busted, and one eye was swollen shut. Small streaks of blood flowed from the intrusions to the man's flesh and his open eye cried in pain as it swelled with hatred. The caption underneath read, "Thirty years of police force."

The night's events crept back into Tokus' thoughts, frightened memories that fluttered here and there, causing panic wherever they fled. He ate a forkful of greens and forced himself to look up at the television screen that hung from the ceiling over the serving counter.

It was playing an old seventies flick, one of the many blaxploitation films that happened to be a hard-core, action movie that touched the grit of life. An old man was sitting in a chair with a shotgun nestled in his arms talking to his young nephew who was hiding from the cops. The old man stood up and peeked out the window. The nephew shook his head and said, "But, Big Daddy, they don't even know that we in here." Big Daddy frowned scornfully at him. "We in here. They out there. We don't know what they know…and don't know!" Seconds later, an amplified voice blared out, "This is the police. You have five minutes to come out—or we're coming in."

The face of Five-O blocked the television when he came over and said with an evil grin, "Tokus Stone. The man. Ruler of Zamunda. King of the streets. Can we talk?"

Five-O didn't wait for an answer. He put his plate down on the table, opposite Tokus, and pulled up a chair. He sat heavily and reached for the hot sauce in the middle of the table to sprinkle over the fried chicken and macaroni and cheese piled on his plate.

"Did you hear about what happened up on the Aisle the other night?" Five-O asked Tokus.

Tokus didn't answer.

Five-O paused with the bottle of cayenne pepper in mid-shake. "Did you?"

A look passed between them.

"Let's make this simple," Tokus replied. "Just what in the hell do you want from me, Mr. Joe P. Law? Ruler of the Blue Klan. Scum of New York."

Five-O sprinkled the red sauce liberally over the heaping plate of food and put the bottle back on the table before he spoke.

"Aah," he answered. "Direct. I like that in a slave. And believe me, Tokus, that is exactly what you are…my slave. From this point forward you will do exactly what I tell you, exactly when I tell you to do it. When I say, 'shit,' you say, 'what color?' Is that straight with you?"

A phone rang. Five-O gulped down a mouthful of the macaroni and held up a finger to Tokus as he chewed. He reached into his pocket, pulled out a cellular phone and barked into it.

"Yeah!"

Five-O listened and his face grew dark.

"What! And how do you know that?"

He listened longer this time.

"Well, I'm taking care of that. If you let me!"

Another pause.

"At this very moment," Five-O growled and fixed Tokus with his stare.

"Give me a fuckin' break, will ya! What are you doing, watching me through your precious glass wall?"

As Five-O listened, his mouth twisted into a sneer, an angry curl. He gripped the phone tightly and closed his eyes before he responded.

"Yeah. Yeah. Yeah. All right. It's done." He punched the button to hang up and turned to face Tokus.

Five-O knew about Moose. There was no doubt of that now. Tokus realized it when the cop seated himself and spoke to him by name. Now it was time to find out precisely what Five-O had in mind. Calmly, Tokus regarded the policeman who was sitting in a soul food restaurant, eating fried chicken, in front of a poster indicting a police state. He looked up at the poster again. The red spots of blood that dotted the coarse gray hair; the bloody, busted lip; and the dark, swollen, angry eye. Was that face the result of taking life head-on?

"Excuse me," Tokus said softly. "It's probably my fault. I probably didn't ask the right question. Let me rephrase. What, exactly, do you want from me, you fucking dick?"

"Simple," Five-O answered, picking up a chicken leg from his plate. "I want you to kill a man."

Tokus tried to hide his shock.

"Now why would I kill someone for you?"

Thirty years of police force, the poster screamed.

"Because I checked your resume," Five-O replied. "And I see you have experience in the field."

"No, I don't," Tokus responded. "Who told you that? Noooo!" Tokus had learned a long time ago to never admit anything. Even when, deep in your brain, you knew that you were "it," you always "tag off." "It" was always someone else. Deny, deny, deny!

"Who's bullshitting now, huh?" Five-O groaned with his mouth full of chicken. "What do you need...pictures? Or will an oral report be good enough for you?"

"Tell me...something!" Tokus said.

"No, no, no," Five-O swallowed. "I'm the master, remember?"

Five-O stood from the table, his meal unfinished. "Meet me tomorrow at the church up on the Aisle. Make it around noonish, okay? See you later, buddy."

With that he turned on his heel and walked out the door.

Tokus heard his future fade away with the hollow echoes of the cop's dying footsteps.

EXORCIST MARBLES

The church stood out like a pimple against the face of the ghetto, an unwanted sentry with evil at its doors. Holiness Baptist Church was carved into the façade in a holy arc above the doorway, reaching out in both directions, gathering lost souls into its bosom. A muted, soft light shone through the stained glass portrait of a Black Jesus with open, welcoming arms.

From across the street Tokus studied the building ruefully, fighting the urge to turn tail and run. His life would be changed forever if he walked through those church doors. Tokus felt it. Was certain of it. What was even more certain, and more immediate, was what would happen if he didn't go inside. If the law wanted him in church, Tokus knew, he had better be in church. Helplessly, he crossed the street and went through the tall, wooden doors.

Once inside, Tokus saw that it was indeed a "holiness" church. Rows of benches formed a funneling aisle that led to the pulpit. The pulpit itself was raised a few steps from the floor, with room to the left for the choir, room to the right for the piano, and in the middle, the dais from which the ministers flung the "word" at the congregation. Directly behind the dais was a big, soft chair with two smaller ones on either side. This was church! He could almost feel the many Sunday sermons, the hand clapping and the joyous shouts echoing from the walls. They floated over Tokus like alien ghosts, which he shook off with animosity.

Spirits had no place in his life.

All his life had been a bitter taste that he kept spitting out into the wind.

And now the devil himself wanted to meet him in a church.

Tokus slid into the nearest pew and waited.

Five-O wanted Tokus to kill a man. Tokus was determined not to do it. Not that he was a stranger to the many faces of death. He had seen it in various forms, and it no longer impressed him with the fear of what would come next. Death was just a void. Something he would live through when he got there.

Death had spoiled him from God. Tokus didn't flee God; he just didn't know Him.

A side door that Tokus hadn't noticed opened slowly and out stepped Reverend Deaugood, head bowed, reading the Bible. Deaugood hardly looked up as he made his way to the pulpit and Tokus stretched out on the pew—a caustic observer. The aged, wooden pew emitted a loud squeak, causing the Reverend's head to snap up at the sound. Smiling, he began walking toward Tokus with a greeting. "Brother! Welcome to Holiness…" Deaugood's voice trailed off as he recognized Tokus.

Tokus smiled and folded his arms across his chest. "Hello, Reverend Deaugood! Can I call you Reverend? Well! You sure look different than you did the other night. Bent over in the alleyway with a rock squeezed tight in your hand and having a heart attack. You was snortin' air like the devil was trying to get out!"

Tokus stood from the bench.

"That was you, wasn't it, Reverend?"

It was more a statement than a question and Deaugood took it at its value. He looked at Tokus carefully, then turned and looked at the pulpit for a moment before turning back to Tokus. When he spoke, his voice was calm, rational. "Listen to me, young man. The fact that you judge me; that don't bother me. You're young. You think you got it all figured out anyway. The fact that you think that I'm not a man of God, couldn't be a man of God…" Deaugood groped. "Well, that…that kinda dismays me a bit."

Deaugood paused and fixed Tokus with a stare. "No matter what you think I do, don't ever assume that I can't do this," he finished, indicating the Bible he held in his hand.

Tokus snorted in response. "You know what, Deaugood? Long time ago, I knew this man. He was an older dude…about your age. He ain't have no kids so he became a big brother to this little knuckle-headed boy. But soon the man became a father figure. He provided discipline, morality and respect for a little boy who was looking for a father to teach him the meaning of these things."

In the front of the church, a dark figure emerged, unseen, and slid into a shadowy corner. He peeked around the corner at the two men and listened.

Tokus went on. "One day the man passed away. You know what the little boy said at 'dad's' wake? He read a poem: 'His life was an extension of his God—in its livelihood and in its meaning. Inevitable in his life was the specter of death with its claim on his last breath. Between the first breath and the last, the first day and the last, the first joy and the last; he rose above the small and became the epitome of God's intentions." Tokus looked meaningfully at the pulpit, nodded his head in agreement and sat down. "Now that is what *you* are supposed to be, Deaugood—the epitome of God's intentions."

Five-O stepped from his hiding place. "Very nice," he said. Both men turned as Five-O sauntered toward them. A cigarette dangled from the corner of his mouth, unlit. His face was all angles and hard lines. Straight-back eyebrows clung to a sharply angled forehead that off-ramped into a slightly tilted nose. His eyes looked like the devil had been playing with exorcist marbles. They jellied before they turned evil.

He tilted his head at Tokus with a reproving look. "Don't you know you never get a second chance to make a first impression?"

Tokus waited.

"All right," Five-O said finally. "I don't have much time. You two…sit down."

Neither man moved.

"I said sit down!" Five-O barked. They sat.

"All right," Five-O said as he fished a lighter out of his pocket and lit his cigarette. Angles and lines danced over his face through the flickering flame.

"Now," Five-O began. "Reverend, this guy over here…is a drug dealer.

But you already know that, don't you? Anyway, I want Tokus here to do something for me...a favor, you know! But he doesn't want to do it. Can you believe that, Rev! Astounding, right? But Rev, you heard about that guy who was found dead up on Highwater Street? Guess who did it? Go ahead! Guess! I'll give you a clue. The killer is in this room. Now Rev, I'm a cop. If I kill someone, it's not murder, so it had to be one of you."

Five-O looked from Tokus to Deaugood. "Did you guess? Do you know? It was Tokus Stone! Mr. Man here. Yes, sirree! Hit that big black buck in the top of his head..." Five-O turned to Tokus. "Didn't know that guy had a metal plate in his head, didja? You hit him so hard that you drove that metal right into his brain. It was a slow, painful death. Painful."

The tip of the cigarette glowed as the cop took a hit and spoke to the preacher. "Tokus could go away for life. Would you like that, Reverend? Probably, right? But I've given him an out. All he has to do is poison someone for me. Put the poison in a rock of cocaine, sell it to the mark and the guy will go away, way up high. He probably wouldn't even know he was dead till he came down."

The cigarette glowed again.

"So basically, Reverend, it's take a life or do 'life.' And make no mistake, Tokus, I'll push hard, very hard, to make sure that you never get out."

Five-O let the threat hang there, deadly in its silence.

Deaugood clutched his Bible, cleared his throat and looked questioningly at the cop.

"Excuse me," he said. "But why do I need to hear all this? It has nothing to do with me."

Five-O puffed on his cigarette as if it were bubble gum-flavored.

"Because...you have a story to tell, Reverend, and I can't wait to hear the ending."

USELESS FREEDOM

"**Y**ou know, everybody in America, this great country of mine, has freedom. But the way you people live, it's a useless freedom...and that's when shit happens."

Five-O paused to take a drag off his cigarette, dumping ashes on the church floor while Tokus and Deaugood waited. Five-O's presence shattered the serenity of the church. He corrupted the spirit with his manner, his stance and the stale, pungent smoke that wafted from the cancer stick in his hand. He did the devil's work and cloaked it in a blue uniform—smile. Joy in other's pain; pain in other's limbs—that was his motto.

The wooden pew was becoming uncomfortable to Tokus. He shifted to the left, wishing that this twisted nightmare would hurry to its conclusion.

"So Rev," Five-O said. "You gonna tell us the story of your useless freedom?"

Deaugood looked exasperated, as if he didn't have the slightest clue what Five-O was talking about. Tokus wanted to choke him.

"Come on," Five-O urged.

"What you mean?" Deaugood cried.

"What you mean!" Five-O said mockingly. "What you mean!" He dropped his cigarette on the church floor and ground it out with his foot. He walked over to where Tokus sat and leaned against the raised back of the bench. Tokus glanced at the cop, hoping he would slip and fall on his ass. A smile played at the corner of Five-O's lips. "You know, 'back in the day,' as the local coloreds would say, when I was a teenager, my brother was a cop. That's why I'm a cop...'cause of my brother. See, my brother was a man. A man with power. A man with a badge. So sometimes he would blur the lines. You know, mix the black and the white and make gray. Everything was gray to him. But he had this badge, so gray was good. My brother also had this thing for black women."

Five-O paused to look at Deaugood. "By the way, is that a myth about black women?"

Deaugood didn't respond.

"All right," Five-O went on. "Well, then my brother took a fancy to this young girl. She was only about sixteen but that didn't matter to him. See, back then there wasn't no such thing as raping a nigger girl so he could do whatever he wanted to. He could take it or leave it."

Tokus shifted in his seat again, irritated. The way that Five-O was objectifying black women were getting under his skin.

The soft, muffled ringing of a telephone echoed through the church. Five-O held the two men with an upheld finger as he reached into his pocket for his cellular phone.

"Yeah!" he barked. He listened for a minute.

"What is your malfunction, mister?" Five-O roared. His face had turned a dark crimson before he turned away and began whispering harshly into the phone. "Look, I've been doing this for years. It's my job, for Christ's sakes! I know what to do and I know how to do it. So I don't need your shit and I don't need you on my back."

Five-O listened. He didn't utter another word into the phone. He just grunted and punched the button to hang up. The devil was playing with those evil marbles again. His eyes jellied as he glared.

"Is this story going anyplace, you fucking maggot?" Tokus spat at Five-O. A slow silence followed and hung in the air, oddly, by an evil smile that spread slowly across the cop's face.

"Sure," Five-O sang. "Sure. See, my brother had a problem."

"No shit!" Tokus pitched in.

"No shit," Five-O answered. "Yes, yes, yes. See, his problem was that a young, black buck beat him to the punch. Boy was somewhat like you,

Tokus. He was out on the streets peddling dope. Marijuana at first…that was the thing back then. Then he moved up to heroin and LSD. Chemicals."

Five-O paused to light up another cigarette. Tokus glanced at Deaugood. The Reverend slouched on the bench, eyes downcast and nodding his head almost imperceptibly. Five-O puffed on his smoke a few times to get it burning good and resumed his tale.

"So one day, my brother answers a call for an assault and when he gets there…it's the girl. She's sitting on the street corner…just sitting there. Doesn't look like anything's wrong except her dress is all ripped up. She doesn't have on any underwear, and she's a basket case. My brother tries to help her but she won't say a word. She won't even acknowledge his presence. So he reaches out and helps her to her feet. He puts her in the squad car and as he gets in, he sees bloodstains on the ground where the girl had been sitting." Five-O walked across the aisle to Deaugood. "See, Tokus, the girl had been raped. By the drug-dealing punk. My brother found out who did it, but the girl still wasn't talking."

"Stop!" Deaugood leapt to his feet and the word came out with a hard edge. Five-O ignored his plea.

"That drug dealer…"

"Please! God! Stop!"

"Was the good Reverend Mister Deaugood."

Tokus tried to hide his disgust. "Surprise, surprise."

"That's not the real surprise though," Five-O crowed. "There's more, there's more, there's more! The girl got pregnant! The day my brother found out, he went looking for Deaugood. Caught him with a stash in his pocket. Deaugood was hot. He had heroin, LSD and cocaine on him. The good Reverend went away for six long years—hard time. That's where he met Jesus and he came out of prison a Holy Roller."

Deaugood dropped back into his seat, apparently stunned by Five-O's knowledge and the shameful revelation of his past. He looked sorrowfully from Tokus to Five-O and back to Tokus.

"That was over twenty years ago," Deaugood said apologetically. "It's not real to me anymore. That's not me now. It's not real."

Five-O sneered. "It was about twenty-three years ago and it was—and still is—very, very real. Okay? See, 'cause that girl had that baby, a little baby boy, dropped out of school and lived with dead insides for the rest of her life." Five-O turned to Tokus. "Now this is as real as it gets. The girl's name…was Rosetta Stone."

Tokus' jaw dropped and his life went slack.

"Your mother," Five-O roared with laughter.

THEN SPEECHLESS

Five-O faced the two men, intently watching as they squirmed under his jaundiced eye. The diaphanous sounds of life seeped inside the church as he waited. He smiled as he waited for the explosion that accompanied unexpected, painful revelations.

Tokus sat on the hard bench and listened to the tear roll down his face—a tear for himself and the man who had fathered him. He heard the harshness of the years roll away into oblivion. The echoes of childhood reverberated painfully in his soul and then cascaded away in a wash of painful renewal. This is it, he reflected. This is me.

Deaugood sat across the aisle from Tokus, watching and waiting, unable to voice a comforting word that would compensate for a lifetime of non-existence. No words would suffice. No voice could encompass, and no actions could speak to the darkness of what now existed. Tokus looked into the preacher's eyes. For a sign. Guilt, shame, hypocrisy—anything that would help him gauge the lunacy of Deaugood's actions. The preacher's eyes held no remorse. In fact, there seemed to be a hint of defiance, a smirk of daring, a glint of dangerous liberation from the constraints of his religion. Sin.

Deaugood laid his Bible down.

"I didn't...," he began.

"Didn't what?" Tokus barked.

"I mean..."

"Mean what?" Tokus growled. Deaugood was standing with his hands held outward, imploring.

"Look here, old man," Tokus said bitterly. "There's only one thing you can say to me. Say that it's a lie. Tell me I'm not on this earth because you decided to rape my mother! Say it!"

"I...I...I can't," Deaugood sputtered.

Five-O laughed loudly and stepped forward, the devil's enjoyment written all over his face. "As much as I enjoy these little family reunions, I think I'll leave you two alone. Give you some quality time together. But Tokus, you have forty-eight hours to take care of that little assignment I gave you." He pulled a small plastic bag out of his pocket and tossed it to Tokus.

"Here," Five-O said. "That's strychnine. Melt it down and rock it up and give my friend a dose. Remember. Forty-eight hours." Tokus stared numbly at the package in his hand.

"Why?" Tokus said in a raspy voice.

"Yours is not to question why," Five-O answered as he began walking toward the door. "Why do I have to go all the way out to the mall to get my girlfriend some body oils when my wife buys it from the corner store? Why! Why! Why!"

Five-O bustled out the door.

The church filled with a silence that bristled with anger and anxiety. Neither man knew how to break it yet were apprehensive about filling the void. Tokus started for the door.

"Wait," Deaugood cried.

"No," Tokus stated calmly.

"Let me explain," Deaugood pled.

"You know, Deaugood," Tokus answered. "I should just punch your face in. That would give me such joy. Just to watch your face break, watch you drop. Like a piece of rotten ..."

"Would you please...just give me a chance to explain."

"Look here, Deaugood," Tokus said. "The only explanation you owe will be the one you have to give when you open your eyes in hell. The hell that your Bible has ready for you."

Tokus walked to the door, opened it and paused to look back at Deaugood. "You don't owe me a damned thing," he said and stepped out of the church.

Deaugood went home that night with a heavy heart. A weight had been thrust upon him. For years he had carried it inside until it had become a silent episode of a long-gone dream gone bad. Now it blossomed full weight and everything inside him bowed in an attempt to bear the freshness of the scars. His wife noticed it upon his back, too. When she asked him what was wrong he said, "Nothing," and kissed her. What would she say if she knew? What would she do? What would his congregation do?

Deaugood looked in on his daughter. Doria looked up from the book she was reading and smiled at him. The smile faded when she saw the worry etched into his face. When she asked him what was wrong, he smiled and said, "Nothing, baby girl, nothing," and went to his room and closed the door. He wondered where his son Bug was. He wished that he could see him right then. Maybe they could talk. Find answers. Forgive and forget.

Deaugood lay down on his bed. He was weary.

His heart twinged. Deaugood closed his eyes.

His chest tightened and his heartbeat gathered speed. Deaugood clenched his teeth and rode the wave of pain that gripped him. It hurt. He had never felt the pain like this. Deep inside, somewhere, he felt calm...and joy! The pain took him, his vision blurred, his heart pelted against his chest but Deaugood simply hissed. No one could hear him.

"Father, forgive me," he prayed. A light beckoned to him from beyond and Deaugood followed it forever. Never to return.

ZERO TO INFINITY

The color and the detail of the small African warriors on the shelf caught Pharren by surprise, holding her in their stare as she examined them with delicate fingers. Bug's apartment was small but it was comfortable compared to some of the places she had laid her head to rest. The furnishings were sparse with barely the necessities, but it looked lived in. She could make it better...in time. She sat on the well-worn couch with the tiny figurine standing gingerly in her palm.

"That's an Undamo Warrior," Bug said from the bedroom doorway. He had a blanket in his hand for Pharren. She would be sleeping on the couch.

"Things from the past," Pharren said, a bit sadly.

She had taken a bath, cleaned off the dirt and grime, and now wore a long gray shirt and an old, baggy pair of Bug's pants. All of his clothes were too big for her, making her seem small and timid. She was in unfamiliar surroundings and her nervousness showed in her face. Bug walked over and sat next to her on the couch. He said nothing, just looked intently at her face. He found her face interesting. Soulful. She blushed beneath his stare.

"What's wrong?" she asked, her eyes downcast.

"Nothin'," Bug replied. "This is just the first time I really got to look at your face. All I saw at first was your eyes."

She looked up at Bug. He touched her cheek. Pharren's hair was combed straight back and tied in a ponytail, pushing her face to the fore. She had passionate features. Bug could imagine enjoying them. Touching them. Kissing them.

"Your skin is smooth, and I like the way your face is made. Your lips, the shape of your face, cute little nose and a round forehead. I like the round forehead."

Pharren giggled.

"I'm serious. You look like the kind of woman that I could have somethin' with. That makes it all better. If you want somethin'."

"You know you inspectin' me like I'm a piece of meat," Pharren said lightly.

"No. I handle you like a piece of art."

They were silent for a moment.

"Anyway," Bug said. "Things from our past...are our past. We live now. For now on. Okay?"

"For now on," Pharren repeated.

"Plus, we can do this. Together. Draw strength from each other. And my son, Monday. He's eight years old now."

Pharren looked around the room. "Where is your son? Can I meet him?"

"I don't know where he's at," Bug replied. "He'll be home soon though."

"He might be with his mother?" Pharren asked. Bug regarded her for a moment before answering.

"I never met his mother."

"What?"

"I never met his mother," Bug stated. "Long time ago, before I started smokin', I was hustlin'. You know, whatever I had to do to get some dead presidents. Benjamins, Washingtons, Lincolns, whatever. Well, one day I was gonna rob this store, so I hid in the back, near the trash thing...the dumpster...'bout closin' time. Right when they started turnin' the lights off in the store, I heard some noise. I ain't quite hear it at first 'cause I was all hyped up and everything, but I knew I heard somethin'. I had to see what it was before I did anything else. A rustlin' noise. Like paper movin'. I ain't know what it was but right then I heard somebody at the back door of the store. So I lifted the lid of the trash thing and climbed in. So I was bein' real quiet, listenin' as the man from the store came out the back door and walked around outside. And that was when I saw him."

"Saw who?"

"The baby. He was layin' on top of a trash bag. Naked. He couldna been even a few days old. So I'm all stooped down, hopin' that he don't start cryin'. And you know what he did? He smiled at me. I swear! He smiled right at me! Like we wasn't in the stinkin'-ass garbage together."

Bug paused and looked away. Pharren gently touched his hand.

"I chilled there for a minute. Just lookin' at him. Then he reached for me. I never did rob that store. I took him home with me."

"So you named him 'Monday.'" Pharren prodded gently.

Bug nodded his head. "That's the day I found him."

"He better be glad you didn't find him on Sunday." Pharren smiled.

Bug laughed. "Right!" he agreed. "But I gotta set some new rules for him. He can't be stayin' out late like this. Not anymore."

Pharren looked down at the figurine she still held in her hand.

"These are pretty," she said.

"Undamo. They were assassins. In Africa."

A knock at the door interrupted Bug as he was about to launch into the history lesson that he had given to Monday many times. It was rare for anyone to come knocking on his door and never at this time of night. Instantly, Bug thought of his son and wondered where he was and why he wasn't home. He crossed the room to the door, tossing the blanket to Pharren before calling out. "Who?"

"Police. Open up."

"What is it, officer?" Bug yelled out.

"This the police. Open the door."

"For what, officer?" Bug asked.

"I have your son out here." The voice boomed. "Now open up."

Bug opened the door. Five-O was standing there with Monday, Bug's eight-year-old son, glaring with the intensity of "right." The law. Bug was familiar with Five-O and his tactics, and he knew this wasn't good. Five-O was a snake, a devil. Someone to be avoided, someone who couldn't solve most problems without a violent or otherwise painful solution. Monday came in the doorway and threw his arms around Bug, holding him tight, scared.

"This yours?" Five-O asked, pointing at Monday with his nightstick.

"My son," Bug replied.

"We found your son outside," Five-O said, motioning toward the open door. Harsh moonlight framed Five-O as he stood with his baton in his hand.

"He was hustling a little earlier in the mall parking lot, collecting money for charity. Probably you," Five-O continued.

Bug started to protest but Five-O shut him down with a raised voice. "Just where were you, crackhead, while your son was running the streets?"

Bug flinched under the accusation, clutching Monday even closer to him as Five-O began his cop stroll, back and forth, taking in the surroundings and slamming the nightstick into his palm. Bug watched the baton apprehensively. He was very familiar with the stick and the sickening joy Five-O derived from swinging it. Five-O had beaten him once, behind a building over on Clinton Avenue for peeing outside.

"If I ever catch you pissing outside again, I'll rip your dick off and show it to you from the other end," Five-O had told him as he lay in a quivering heap with blood steaming from cuts in his head.

The memory of it was painfully vivid.

Five-O turned to Bug. "You know I hate people like you," he spat. Pharren got up from the couch and went over to Bug and gently took Monday's hand. She looked to Five-O for permission. Five-O waited as she led the child from the room.

"People like you give humanity a bad name," Five-O continued. He began slapping one end of the baton into the palm of his hand, punctuating sentences with loud slaps.

Slap! Slap! "You know what that means, smoker? Humanity?"

Bug tensed at the harsh sound.

Slap! "It means taking care of you and yours."

The pain and the threat of Five-O echoed off the walls.

Slap! Slap! "It means knowing right from wrong."

Bug's eyes narrowed defiantly. He knew it was going to happen. The hurt.

Slap! "It means manhood. Being a man."

But not the shame. Not this time.

Slap! "Are you, you little rock monster?"

Bug sputtered, "Am I what?"

"A man!" Five-O barked. The bedroom door squeaked open a crack and Pharren peeked out, wide-eyed, at the two men.

"Yes, I am," Bug replied.

"My ass, you're not!" Five-O bellowed. "A man takes care of his own. Where were you tonight while your son ran the streets? I know where you were. Fiending. Smoking."

"Fuck you, Five-O! Fuck you!"

Five-O bore down on Bug until his face was inches away. He spoke in anger and spittle. "Actually, you wasn't smokin', though. No, you wasn't. In reality…you know, reality that place that you try to escape all the time… in reality you were at the bottom of nowhere on a springboard, mister. Borderline bitch!"

Five-O paused. He seemed to be struggling within, fighting the good, the bad and the ugly. Finally he spoke, "You are zero to infinity. The real nowhere man."

Slap! The baton started again.

Bug cowered.

Slap! "If I find your son like I found him tonight! Once! Just one more time again; I will lock you up and find someone who will take care of the kid. Someone who gives a damn."

Five-O turned for the door. He paused to glance back at Bug. Pharren, and now Monday, were both watching.

"You got me, stupid man?" Five-O hissed.

Bug lowered his head. Five-O didn't see the tear in Bug's eye. Nor did he notice his clenched fist.

MIND POWER

Anger pelted Bug in a harsh shower in his darkness. His personal unending pit.

Five-O had left something rancid behind when he had slammed his way out of Bug's house. Something that remained inside Bug's heart. Something that hardened and reached and exploded and damaged. Bug felt himself go black. A soft click accompanied the carefully closed bedroom door as Pharren and Monday left him alone with his anguish.

They had seen. They had heard it all.

Bug's home, his domain, had been shattered, burned to the ground by stinging, fiery arrows that Five-O had thrown at him.

In front of Monday. His son.

Monday was the anchor in Bug's life, the laughter in the rain, the innocence in a spotted world. In Monday's eyes the sun rose high in the sky so that they two, father and son, would have a place together. Two against the world. For Bug, there was nothing so precious in a cold world than having a warm hearth waiting for him when he came home from the war called survival.

Five-O had brought frost to a warm heart.

Bug knew he needed to talk to Monday—maybe explain, as best he could—about the policeman's visit. But any explanation that came to mind was only a pathetic excuse for not being there. Briefly, it occurred to Bug that maybe he should try telling Monday the truth about what happened that night. That he had gotten high off crack with Moose and that they were going to get another fix when they ran into Tokus. That Tokus and Moose had fought until Moose was seriously hurt. That he had run away in fear, leaving Moose to suffer.

Bug discarded that idea.

He stopped with his hand on the knob of the bedroom door, steeling himself with a resolve he didn't feel when the sound of muted sobs echoed from within. It was Monday. Pharren was soothing him.

"It's all right, baby. Shh. Shh."

"But I ain't try to…"

"Shh, baby. Come on now. Shh."

Bug backed away from the door. This was supposed to be a new beginning for him. A new start. A chance to start all over. Five-O had no idea. No one did. His change had come from within, from his heart and now he couldn't share it with his son. He had been emasculated. Yet he wore the cloth of hope for a better life. One that Five-O could never enter with his stick of intimidation and pain.

Bug looked at the front door and his bravado abandoned him. Five-O could come into his home at any time and tear it apart any time he desired to spill dark blood. Whup! Whup! That's the sound of the police.

Anger welled up in Bug. At his helplessness. At his vagueness. Bug moved away from the door to the mantel where the tiny Undamo warriors stood, the miniature wooden figures he had collected to teach Monday about that part of his heritage. The Undamo. Assassins.

It had taken Bug months to amass his collection of the Undamo tribe. He had found each one of the dozen figurines in the most unexpected places. He had felt as if each one had been calling to him. One under a pile of knick-knacks in a bookstore. Its vibrant earth colors caught his eye and its red, black and green mask appealed to him with meaning. After his initial discovery, the remainder of the tribe seemed to gather at his will: at garage sales, flea markets. He even found one at a swap meet.

Bug whispered to them.

"Lies! They lie! They lie like they know," Bug ranted. "But they don't know. They don't know."

He paused to pick up one of the Undamo Warriors and spoke directly to it. "I am a man. A father. For my son...I gotta step up. Stand tall." With a sob, Bug flopped down into a chair.

"Shit," he exclaimed. Scenes from that night crept into his thoughts. Tokus and Moose. The fearful flight down the street. The pain of cowardice. Pharren under the bridge. Five-O in the doorway.

"Why do lies have to be so...so...real?" Bug asked the Undamo. "Something inside me ain't right. Some cold where I should be strong. Some weak where there's supposed to be fight. 'Cause if I can't fight this...shit! That's what it is! Shit! Then I can't fight for Monday. I gots to get my life back."

Bug leaned his head back and closed his eyes. "I gots to," he mumbled. Soon he fell off the ledge of consciousness into sleep.

"Your life will not tremble."

A voice in the darkness called out. Bug had heard voices in his sleep before, but they would always be gone in the morning.

"Look to me, Undamo."

That word got his attention and Bug felt his vision search the blackness for the calling voice. Suddenly, there were colors—red, black and green— but Bug knew he was dreaming. I ain't answerin', Bug thought fearfully. Hell, no. Nope.

"Look to me, Undamo."

Who would mistake him for an Undamo! The darkness shifted and Bug saw. It was the warrior he had held in his hand, the one he had talked to. The Undamo's eyes looked into Bug, inside his soul. The place where he lay hidden, away from the world, huddled in close, cramped quarters. There was strength and compassion in the assassin's eyes, a comforting sense of surety that gave Bug a jolt of clarity. The Undamo held his hand out to him, palm upward. Small replicas of Bug floated above the Undamo's splayed fingers, revolving slowly, bathed in a soft, blue light.

"This is T'challa," the Undamo spoke.

"No. That's me," Bug heard himself say.

"You are T'challa," the Undamo stated and motioned toward the replica's forehead. Bug's body jerked in response. The head of the replica began to glow a bright orange, and Bug felt his brain begin to burn as he watched. The Undamo made another movement over the front of the tiny head, over the cerebrum, the center of judgment and emotion. Bug felt a hot slashing in his head and calmness washed over him: He wasn't afraid. It was liberating. Then the Undamo really went to work, paring and rein-forcing. Shearing off the useless, inhibiting pieces of Bug's psyche, while placing bundles of ambrosia at the doors of the once hidden fortress of his mind. The pons varolli, which controls sensations, speech and vision; the cerebellum, which coordinates movement; the medulla oblongata, which monitors breathing, heartbeat. They were all reborn and made better, stronger. When the Undamo was finished, a new man was made.

"Thank you," Bug whispered. The Undamo nodded his head once and made another motion. This time it was over the replica's heart. The oper-ation was complete.

"Your life will not tremble," the Undamo commanded.

"As a man," Bug replied and resumed his sleep.

Pharren gently shook Bug, trying to wake him.

"Bug," she called. "Get up. Wake up."

His eyes opened.

"Bug," Pharren said.

"My name," he stated, "is T'challa."

POISONED AMBROSIA

The loneliness of Tokus' apartment was good company, compared to the friends he didn't have, and the life he wasn't living. The thoroughness of it all, from birth to manhood, sadly amused him. There was his stepfather, an electrical extension cord with teeth and the power of the world, who stung Tokus with unbridled anger and pure hatred. There was the death of Moose on his hands, all over his fingers and up under his skin, vibrating with the reminder of living. Then along came Five-O, a bastard in a prick suit with an assassination and a death warrant all rolled up in a bag of poison. Surely, Tokus thought, this was a full plate. With a bag of chips on the side.

His father was a rapist.

Settling back on the couch, Tokus reached for the remote control and hit the power button. The sound came in before the picture fuzzed to life, bathing the living room of the small apartment in an eerie, alien light. Tokus had the normal bachelor's pad. A medium-sized bedroom was located just beyond the tiny, thin kitchen. A moderate pile of dishes was stacked in the sink but otherwise it was relatively clean. The bathroom was in a little nook off to the left, exactly one step past the hall closet. It was functional and reasonably well kept. The front room was comfortable with the basic living room set—matching couch, love seat and chair. It was strong, comfortable furniture. He really didn't want to buy any more, and Tokus tried to be as neat and as careful as possible. The walls were bare. There were no pictures or giant posters or cheap art or paintings—no, just the plain white walls and a battery-powered clock that Tokus bought at a garage sale for fifty cents. It worked perfectly. He didn't need much. A forty-ounce of malt liquor sat on one of the two end tables that Tokus had found on the sidewalk one day. Next to the bottle was a bag of weed, killer ganja, that he fully intended to smoke and get high and away from earthly troubles. He needed to escape. Get zooted.

It should be so easy.

Deaugood was dead. Word traveled at light speed in the ghetto. The much-adored Reverend Skellum Deaugood had passed away in his sleep. A man whose good works would live on as he watched from up above.

"Hell is up there, too," Tokus growled as he lifted the forty-ounce of beer from the end table to his lips and took a good, solid swig. A nasty thought rushed down his throat, pursued by the ale, taking form as it went to the bottom. He belched.

The wake was being held today.

Tokus wondered if Deaugood's family knew that the great Reverend was a rapist. Smiling, he took another swig. The picture would be perfect, the drama complete. He had the power to hurt and destroy an entire family in the blink of an eye. It would be so nasty to walk up to the microphone and look out at the mournful, expectant crowd and prepare to shock them out of their sadness and into angry denial. Together maybe they could all go over and spit on Deaugood's casket.

There came a knock on his door.

A voice blared out. It was Peanut, a neighbor from across the hall.

"Yo, man," Peanut said. "I got that for you. I got it from the store."

Tokus rose and opened the door. Peanut stood in the doorway with a cigar in one hand and a beer in the other, waiting for Tokus to invite him in. Peanut was alcohol, and alcohol was him. It was in his red eyes, his drunken conversation; it was even his walk.

Tokus took the cigar from Peanut, paused and said, "Come in."

Peanut limped into the room, looking around with a herky-jerky motion of his head. He sniffled his nose a few times, emitted a loud screech and turned to Tokus. Tokus shut the door, pointed Peanut to the couch and went over to sit in the chair. It was best to keep distance from Peanut sometimes. Peanut relaxed on the couch as he watched Tokus unwrap the cigar, a blunt, and then slice it down the middle with a small knife that he pulled from his pocket. He dumped the tobacco out on the tabletop, laid the tobacco wrapper beside the pile and reached for the bag of weed. After prying the bag open, Tokus poured the marijuana evenly into the tobacco skin and rolled it up nice and snug. He wet the edge of the rolled cigar with his tongue to make it adhere, and the blunt was complete. Peanut popped the top of his can of beer, took a sip and sniffled a few more times before he spoke.

"Yo! You know you and me gonna be all right…when I get my money."

Tokus eyed Peanut while he lit the weed-packed cigar. Peanut was crazy. He had a lawsuit against the three major networks for contributory negligence. According to Peanut, the sound of rapid gunfire, which each television station broadcast nightly, had given him breast cancer. Ten million dollars would cure it just fine, but he would settle for two million. When that money came through, Peanut and Tokus would get amazingly high and stupidly inebriated. Peanut's treat.

Breast cancer! Tokus shook his head. Peanut was crazy.

The combination of tobacco and weed produced a strong smoke that bitterly relaxed his mind to the point of uncaring fun. He took a long pull of the blunt, held the smoke in and passed it to Peanut.

"Peanut, if you smoke a strong blunt…your breast cancer will be gone," Tokus said without exhaling. "You know cannabis is medicinal."

"Naw, man, naw," Peanut replied. "Blunts just get you high, man." He took another hit. "You heard about that preacher who died yesterday? Heart attack." He passed the blunt.

Tokus nodded yes. Peanut went on.

"I bet that shit hurt! Man, your heart just gettin' all tight on ya'…then your lungs ain't workin' right. Then you probably die with your eyes open. Tryin' to take some light with ya."

Peanut shook his head ruefully, "I ain't gonna go out like that. Peaceful. That's how you go. Peacful."

Tokus' thoughts were elsewhere. He pondered confronting the Reverend's wife and family at the funeral and making the announcement. Maybe tell them of the two lives that her husband ruined. About his mother, a torn woman, both mentally and physically, who suffered so deeply that she would abandon her son to follow a man whose only love was the power of pain. Or maybe he would take the grieving widow down the spiraling pathway of the life that was created on a lonely, violent day. The day his mother was taken away forever. He would tell them! Loud and clear!

Deaugood's life was poisoned ambrosia; may it rot the ground where it lay.

"Ha!" Tokus laughed aloud, a short bark that held no enjoyment. Peanut sprang to his feet, startled.

"Whew, boy, I thought that was some gunfire or somethin'."

"Peanut, you are flippin'."

"For real! I felt my cancer actin' up. Don't bust out like that, baby! Laugh like regular folks."

Tokus passed the blunt to Peanut, smiling at the "regular" man. Peanut sat down, happily puffin' on the cigar with one hand held over his chest. Tokus took a long drink of beer, slammed the bottle down on the table with a loud "bang" and reached for the remote control. Peanut sprang to his feet again.

"So you got breast cancer, right?" Tokus asked.

Peanut nodded his head. "Yeah."

"And you got it from the evening news?" Tokus prodded.

"Yeah."

"From the 'bang-bang' of gunfire?"

"Yeah. And I got proof, see…"

"And gunfire is all over the news…right?" Tokus cut off the reply.

"Yeah," Peanut replied warily.

"So I could kill you," Tokus said as he grinned drunkenly. "Right now."

"What you talkin 'bout…" Peanut stammered.

"Because," Tokus paused to beer burp. "I…I…I got cable. CNN. News, twenty-four, seven." Tokus aimed the remote control at the television set. He was smiling but Peanut was shaking. He was afraid. Tokus watched him, realizing that the fear was real and the emotion was strong as Peanut dropped the blunt and began to plead. His pleas fell on deaf ears as Tokus began racing through channels. Peanut shrieked.

Tokus reeled as he weighed the experience of feeling power, of having someone in his grip, under his thumb without mercy. Manipulation of the powerless reveals the weakness of truth and the touching and feeling of men's souls. There was at once the satisfaction of lust spent and the tainting of a heart in this vindictiveness.

Peanut was crying.

BIG MA

Tokus stood way back, behind a huge, scarred oak tree, watching the pained procession of the bereaved at the shattered funeral. Deaugood's family, his wife, his son and his daughter stood in a grieving line with pain settling differently on each face. The mother was sadly stricken. Hers was a face that had seen many a black horror—the dogs of the civil rights movement, riots and Jim Crow—but this agony seemed to come from a different place. The difference could be heard in the wrenching sobs that rang out into the stone garden. Her cries put a pall on the still grayness of the day. A sadness hung about her.

Tokus thought about his mother. About the good things. Then he wished. On the good things.

The daughter stood next to her mother, holding the older woman's hand, offering a sad comfort and haunted warmth. She wore an expression of shocked disbelief that her father was gone, as if the naked soul of Reverend Skellum Deaugood wasn't sprawled inside the steel blue coffin that rested on slats above its six-foot-deep destination. To her, his spirit was alive, moving with warmth that said "father." Always would. She pulled her mother closer.

The son was different. Tokus looked closer at the young man who stood apart from the grieving family. A hint of recognition bothered Tokus as he studied him but he couldn't put a name to the passing twinge. He knew that face. From somewhere.

Tokus moved in closer. He caused no undue attention as he stepped forward. His intentions were still unclear, yet the angry motive was harsh and driving him mercilessly. The Reverend must have been a good man, Tokus thought, as he took note of the large crowd attending the service. They looked sad. Tokus felt bitter.

An elderly woman walked over to Tokus and stopped him. She looked into his eyes with the kindness of age.

"What is it?" she asked, taking his hand in hers. "You look so hurt, young man."

Tokus looked down at the aged hands that held him so kindly, so safely and he couldn't speak. There was only one purpose for Tokus at the funeral: to announce to the congregation that his father, the rapist, was being buried. Dirt forever. He wasn't prepared for compassion.

"The Reverend was a good man," the old woman said. "He taught me how to see the heart of a person. Their spirit. And you know what? I see yours."

"Come on." She patted Tokus' hand. "Come with me."

She pulled Tokus through the crowd of people, past the well-dressed men and women who murmured in hushed, mournful conversations, to a spot with a clear view of the casket and the grieving family.

"Some would question why the good Lord would take a man like Reverend Deaugood from us. From the church and from his family." The old woman indicated the bereaved with a nod of her head.

"Some might not," Tokus blurted and the old lady recoiled a bit. Tokus instantly regretted his outburst but could see no way to reach out and pull the hurtful words back.

The woman paused a moment, as if contemplating the full weight of death and circumstance, of life and challenge, of struggling to overcome the tangible and the intangible, only to end up in a casket, waiting to be lowered slowly into the earth.

"Young man, the Reverend did a good work with his family, seeing as where he came from," she began. "And he came a long ways…yes, he did. He had to reach, I mean reach high, 'cause he didn't have no example. You know, nobody to follow. What they call role models nowadays. He did good."

Tokus looked at the old lady, indecisive with his secret, hesitant, but realizing it still had power. I should tell her about the nastiness of drug dealing, rape and jail, Tokus mused.

But what purpose would be served?

This woman was dear to life—the world was a better place with her in it. Someone like her was what was missing from his frame of reference for family. A nurturer. A grandma to visit, to be pampered by. The one woman who would always make everything all right. Gently, he squeezed her hand in understanding. She looked up at Tokus.

"Baby," she began, "I know…"

"Big Ma," a small voice softly interrupted. "Bianca keep pinchin' me. I tol' her to stop but she keep on pinchin' me."

Big Ma was gentle. "Hush, child. Tell her I said she better behave 'fore I have to come over there. Go on, now!" The little girl hurried off to deliver the message.

"That's my granddaughter," she said as she turned to Tokus. "One of them. Family is about all I have left. But it's all that really matters though. In this world. In this time."

The image of the widow and her children again caused Tokus a nagging discomfort. The vague feeling of having met the son persisted.

"Everybody's looking for a place," Big Ma continued.

"Get out of the way or take his place." The words flashed through his mind and Tokus suddenly remembered the young, black man. Deaugood's son was the crackhead who was with Moose that fateful night of the fight that had ended in death. Deaugood's son had tried to stop Tokus but had failed miserably. If only Tokus had listened.

"So are you," Big Ma said. Tokus turned to her. "You lookin' for a place. And I know where it is."

"You do?" Tokus asked.

"Yes. 'Cause I know who you are."

Tokus smiled grimly. "So do I."

"Do you?" she asked cryptically. "Listen to me, a long time ago the Reverend was a young man runnin' the streets. I knew him all his life. From a little baby to a hard-headed hustler. And he was hard-headed! He wouldn't listen to nobody! Nobody! His mother, his father. Even the police. You know how ya'll young folks get."

Big Ma heaved. "But then Skellum did something that I couldn't forgive. One night he took his girlfriend, his widow now…he took her home and then it was back to the streets, hustling, where he met this other girl. He said he loved her, but the girl wouldn't have him while he had a girlfriend. So Skellum took her. Took her womanhood. It was so evil of him to take a life and change it that way. Forever. I hated him for that. I guess Skellum hated himself, too. His smile, that happy smile, was gone. It went somewhere cold and dark, 'cause he didn't care anymore. Next thing I know… he's in jail. And the girl turned up pregnant. She had the baby while Skellum was in jail. A little boy. I went to her. I tried to talk to her but she was so scared…so different. I couldn't help her hurt…her pain. It was everywhere."

Tokus stared at her. She seemed to be reliving a personal nightmare. Tokus touched her shoulder as his own anger subsided. Big Ma blinked back a tear. "She had a baby boy. She named him Tokus. That ain't a regular name."

She looked Tokus squarely in the eyes. "That's your name."

Tokus returned her stare. "Yes."

"Ma Deaugood," a young man interrupted. "My condolences. Your son was a good man."

"Thank you so much." She looked at Tokus wonderingly. "So…why are you here?"

"I…I…don't know," Tokus stammered.

FISHOUSE FAT

Fishouse Fat was kind of skinny. Tough skinny with a hide of toughened leather from nearly sixty years of suffering the afflictions of blindness and blackness. A nonentity in a painfully physical world. A harsh wisdom had resulted from his journey through the maze of life. And something else. It clung to him while reaching out to anyone around. Fishouse was called a psychic but he, himself, held none of those beliefs. He considered himself a poor man.

But Fishouse Fat smiled. He wore happiness like a coat that should have been bitter to the touch. Instead he exuded an aura of a well-kept man with a soft shoulder, bearing the world. It was a comfortable glow that he welcomed others to share.

Fishouse Fat could usually be found sitting in the park on his favorite bench facing the river. Tokus found the man a joy to talk to, always willing to share his wisdom. He was a source of sound, practical advice. Tokus tiptoed up behind Fishouse, trying to surprise him—something that had never worked on the blind man before. Tokus was barely a step away from him when Fishouse yelled out.

"Don't even try it, young fella!"

"Man!" Tokus exclaimed. "How do you do that every time? I can't ever sneak up on you."

"Tokus, you know you can't...on my worst day. But you won't quit, will ya'?"

Tokus grinned at him.

A smile spread across Fishouse's face. "I like that. You, uhh," Fishouse motioned with his hands. "You, uhh…figure you gonna grow some standin' there?"

Tokus took a seat on the bench next to him. It was a moment before Fishouse spoke.

"You in trouble, ain't ya?"

"Could be," Tokus responded.

Fishouse laughed, a chuckle that rumbled inside him, its echo barely audible. But Tokus knew he was laughing. "You know why you can't sneak up on me?" he asked Tokus. "'Cause of your brow."

"My brow?"

"Yeah. Your brow. Up there above your eye. Your brow. I can feel what's on there. I can feel the pain, the joy, the mean, the worry…all that. So you couldn't sneak up on me 'fore; don't try to sneak up on me now."

Tokus said nothing.

"Yo' call," Fishouse said. "Just don't burn too fast, young fella. Don't burn too fast."

"I ain't tryin' to burn, Fishouse."

"It's more than you though, Tokus," Fishouse argued. "It ain't just one person. It's reform. Reformin' yo' self. Stone gardens is fulla people who fail to recognize."

Fishouse turned and firmly fixed Tokus with an upheld finger.

"Nothing dictates your life. If you take aim at somethin', your life writes itself. But you got to aim at some good shit. Not the shit out here today. Most of the stuff these young boys out here doin' is garbage. Zero, two or three times over. Just bullshit that got thrown at a black wall to see if it would stick. Chillun these days just reach up there and grab whatever's left. But it's all bullshit."

Fishouse counted off with his fingers.

"Drugs! Bullshit!"

"Guns! Bullshit!"

"Jheri curls! Bullshit!"

Fishouse paused, catching himself.

"But I can't say nothing about Jheri curls, though." His hand went to the thin copse of hair that clung stubbornly to his scalp. "'Cause I'm right there on Jheri Curl Street."

"On the corner of Jheri and Curl," Tokus offered.

"On the street," Fishouse finished. "But you see what I mean?"

"On one level, yes, I understand. But on another level, you're looking from the mountaintop while I'm looking up at a monster. You've been to war...you're a warrior. You've been battle-tested while I'm just a soldier going into war."

"But it all boils down to one thing," Fishouse Fat answered. "Fast fuse, young fella. Fast fuse. Kids today live like they ain't 'spectin' to make it past the age of twenny. That's a fast fuse. A short line on a short time. Burnin'. Burnin' quick. And your lives...no sooner'n you started it...it's gone."

Fishouse stared into the darkness through sightless eyes. "Watching thoughts" is what he called it. The gray, dark waters of the Hudson River splashed and twirled as the current whirled the toxic wastes just under the surface. Tokus always imagined that if someone dove into that water he would surface with three green eyes and an extra warped limb. He wondered if the river had ever been a clear, beautiful blue. Over on the opposite shore, Tokus saw two men fishing.

"Tokus," Fishouse began, "it's time for you to make that stand in your life. You only get one chance. You got to know now how you burn. Make the right choice, son. Make the right choice."

Tokus regarded the blind man for a moment. Everything Tokus wanted in life was so close. Graduation. A career with no drugs. Happiness. So close. All he had to do was make the right decision. No easy task.

"Thanks, Fishouse," Tokus said, rising to his feet from the bench. "Much respect. Much love."

"Much love!" Fishouse exclaimed. "Much love for what I said or much love for what you heard?"

"Much love," Tokus responded, "for knowing that I burn."

HEY KILLER!

Tokus had a family, a brother and a sister. A revelation that needed exploring. Developing. He was determined to get to know his newfound siblings, though they were strangers to him. His grandmother, Big Ma, had told him many things about Bug and Doria but she had taught him so much more. About family. He had left Deaugood's funeral with a sense of how beautiful it could be to have a grand relative and the warmth of belonging.

His brother, Bug, lived on Orange Street with his eight-year-old son, Monday.

His sister, Doria, was a junior in high school. A straight "A" student with a good head on her shoulders, according to Big Ma. "That girl got common sense," Big Ma had told him.

Tokus' mind went 'round and 'round with the possibilities of what could be, but after the glow of wonder died to a pulsing ember, there were questions. And no easy answers.

Tokus just wanted to meet them. Doria first. Bug could be a problem but Tokus hoped and wished they could at least talk. About anything. They weren't too old or too grown up that they couldn't become brothers.

The funeral had been days ago yet Tokus couldn't muster the courage to meet his newfound siblings. Rejection would hurt much more than he cared to admit, and he would rather remain silent than face their rejection or cope with their denial.

Tokus meandered down Raymar Avenue amongst the unusual quiet that brushed through the leaves of the trees that lined lawn edges. It was an affluent, quiet section of the city that accommodated rich, white people, tweeting birds and swimming pools. Tokus was headed over to Orange Street. He had been there a few times, standing outside Bug's house, trying to gather up the courage to confront his brother. But he had always ended up just walking away. Issues unresolved; brother unmet.

At the end of Raymar Avenue there was a shortcut, an alleyway, that Tokus usually took. It let out a block away from Bug's house. Actually it was three connecting alleyways, with each corridor equal in length to a city block. It was a strange location for a back way. Dank shadows and dark hideaways contrasted with the security of this prosperous neighborhood. But there was still enough distance to separate the "haves" from the "have nots." Tokus' footsteps echoed in the still, smooth air, crunching gravel from heel to toe as he turned the corner from Raymar into the shadows of the alley. Behind him was the idyllic life that education, perseverance and desire were meant to achieve. And in a world of great and distant dreams, Tokus saw his place at the feast, back there, in that neighborhood, somewhere.

Tokus never heard the dark sedan that pulled into the alley behind him.

Five-O quietly pulled alongside Tokus in an unmarked car. A growl was strewn across his face. The solitude of the back street now took on the makings of a dark trap.

"Hey, killer," Five-O barked at him. Tokus kept walking.

"Hey, killer," Five-O barked louder. "I suggest you stop and get your black ass over here!"

Tokus stopped and turned. Five-O inched the car forward.

"Did you complete the assignment?" he asked.

Tokus shrugged.

Five-O spat. "Just say 'no' because I just saw the old, rubbery bastard an hour ago!"

Five-O beat the steering wheel with his fists and grit his teeth so hard that Tokus thought he heard them cracking. Five-O looked like a madman—stone, cold crazy.

"Now tell me, what the hell is your malfunction, boy? I asked you to do one thing for yourself. One thing! And you want to do it on c.p. time, right? Colored people's time. You want to do everything late, don't you?"

Five-O paused, waiting for a response. Tokus was speechless.

"Well, you don't have late, nigger man," Five-O hissed. "You don't even have now! Come on…"

Five-O sprang out of the car and stomped over to Tokus. His first punch caught Tokus in the stomach, doubling him over, forcing the air from his body in one, shocking instant. His next blow landed squarely on Tokus' jaw, sending him crashing to the ground.

"Oh, yeah!" Five-O growled through clenched teeth as he calmly looked up and down the alley. "I see I have to treat you like the bitch that you are, huh?"

He launched a vicious kick to the ribs that lifted Tokus from his knees over onto his back. Tokus looked up at the cop through a haze of pain. His ribs were on fire and his lungs ached with every breath. He knew that there was much more to come. Blue-clan violence was nothing new; it just had never happened to him before. He could only hope that he wouldn't die in an alley.

"One fucking thing," Five-O ranted. "Just one fucking thing. And you can't do it. Just one fucking thing."

Tokus looked up at him.

"Fuck you!"

Five-O stomped him in the face.

"No, you are the one about to be royally fucked," Five-O roared.

Suddenly, Five-O cried out and began brushing at his neck. A small dart pushed through his skin. It had entered Five-O's flesh with a hard "snick," and he yelled out as he reached for the tiny missile. Five-O plucked at it but it didn't budge. Angrily, he yelled and snatched it from his neck. Small strands of flesh clung to three tiny barbs that protruded along the thin shaft of the needle. Five-O threw it on the ground and stepped forward. His head was on a swivel, searching for the shooter. He felt his neck and his hand come away with a spot of blood as he scanned the alleyway. There was no one.

"Good for your ass." Tokus coughed in pain.

Five-O ignored him, wavering as he bellowed. "Someone's there!" He staggered forward. "You just stay your ass there! Your black ass better not move. I'll be right back."

A man stepped into view from behind a trimmed hedge on the lawn of a large white, two-storied house not twenty feet away on Raymar Avenue.

Five-O laughed with glee when he saw him.

Tokus couldn't believe his eyes.

It was Bug. Half his face was painted in an African mask—red, black and green, primeval, a stark contrast to the pristine surroundings but Tokus recognized him. Bug held a bamboo stick in one hand as he stood defiantly in the open sunlight staring at Tokus. He didn't move a muscle when Five-O yelled, "Freeze," jumped into his car, squealed it into a U-turn and raced up onto the lawn. The wheels of the car spewed up thick slabs of sod. Bug's eyes were locked on Tokus. Five-O braked his car a few feet in front of Bug, jumped out and drew his revolver. "Get those hands up, bitch!"

Bug turned to face the law.

Five-O put his gun back in its holster. "Oh, it's you," he began. "You shot me in the neck! With that! Now I'm gonna stomp a mud hole in your..."

Five-O faltered in mid-stride, grasping at his stomach. Slowly, he fell to the ground in a trembling heap as painful gasps of air escaped from his body. Convulsions wracked him as he simultaneously tried to swallow his tongue and vomit. Deathly grunts emanated from somewhere within the tortured frame of Five-O and in seconds it got worse.

Bug looked down at the fallen figure of authority that had threatened him, at the man who was no longer a maiming insult. When death had finally made its claim, Bug turned and disappeared into the plush foliage of serenity that was God's property.

Tokus watched Bug leave. Escaping a surreal slow-motion nightmare marked by murder. The dart that Five-O had brushed from his neck lay on the ground accusingly. It took Tokus a few minutes to compose himself. There was agonizing pain in his ribs and his jaw, but eventually he was able to rise. He struggled over to where the dart lay, carefully picked it up and staggered down the alley. Tokus threw the poisoned bamboo missile down the sewer somewhere on Orange Street.

His brother would be free.

OVAL TRUST

Somewhere inside his private life, Tokus made the decision that it was time to unite with his brother and sister. To be together, or apart, forever. Inside, Tokus felt enormous, as if he would burst with his secret knowledge, and he wanted to share it. With them.

Gingerly, he touched his jaw. It was still tender from where Five-O had hit him. He thought it might have been broken, but the pain had slowed to a dull ache. He was experiencing a mild discomfort when he took deep breaths, but the kick to his ribs had only bruised them at worst. The anxiety of waiting for the police to come knocking at his door troubled Tokus more than any physical ailment and filled him with a sense of urgency. He had decided to handle his dilemma as he had dealt with any other problem that was beyond his control. He would wait it out. Ignore the problem and it would go away. It had worked before and he could only hope it would net him the same positive results. For the first time in years, Tokus had prayed.

He decided to approach Doria first and let truth step into the light. Tokus just wished that Doria would be able to see beyond the obvious, beyond the harsh negatives and anger, and peep into what he wanted, what he needed.

Plano High School stood three stories tall, in a nondescript fashion, about fifty yards back off Common Street, where Tokus stood waiting for the afternoon bell to ring. He pictured Doria running out with a happy, energetic smile. Like a picture. Oh, yeah, Tokus mused. Right! Kids didn't smile in school nowadays. They mostly ducked and dodged the bullets and the drugs. Thick, plush grass carpeted the ground from the street all the way to the driveway in front of the school, where buses waited to load the raucous teenagers and cart them home. Tokus walked across the lawn to the side of the brick building by the concrete steps, hoping that Doria would use these exits when school was dismissed. He had brought some of his books with him to avoid looking so obviously out of place as he scanned the crowd of crackling, energetic beings known as teenagers, hoping to spy his sister.

There it was. That word. Sister. Tokus liked the sound of it. Its meaning was clear in his mind, even in his heartbeat, as it began to pound loudly—counting off the seconds to the moment that could change his life forever. The school bell went off and Tokus involuntarily tensed as the wait began. Instantly, kids were bursting through the doors in hordes of hustle and noise. They were already late for basketball courts, street corners and home. Tokus remembered the feeling. Three girls pushed out the third exit door. Tokus spied Doria.

She was a beautiful girl. She smiled at one of the other girls and the picture was complete. Her light, slightly burnished skin and pretty, brown eyes seemed uniquely in place. She wore her hair curled down to her shoulders with touches of gold running through it. She probably drove the boys crazy. The three girls were coming straight toward him and Tokus resisted the urge to duck behind the side of the building. Instead, he turned his head in the other direction, away from them, as they neared. They giggled as they passed and when Tokus turned to watch them, he exhaled heavily before he began to follow.

The group of girls walked past the rapidly filling school buses and down the sidewalk to Common Street in a carefree burst of youth and energy, the world passing them by with the promise of a trouble-free tomorrow. Tokus followed at a discreet distance. The moment of truth was upon him and suddenly all his plans seemed faulty. Every reason, every explanation that came to him echoed flatly in his mind. Every word seemed destined to fall on deaf ears, the victim of a sham uncovered. Tokus knew he was running out of room. This was the end of the road...or the beginning. He quickened his pace while his mind raced, closing the gap between himself and the girls while his insides reverberated panic.

"Doria," Tokus called. The three girls turned in unison as Tokus hurriedly caught up to them. Doria watched him with a cautiously questioning eye.

Tokus fidgeted. "You don't know me, but my name is Tokus. Tokus Stone. I need to talk to you about your brother, Bug."

"Tokus!" one of Doria's friends exclaimed. "What kind of name is Tokus? Swahili?"

The other girl said, "No, girl, that's Zulu!" She flirted closer to Tokus. "You look like a Zulu, uh-huh." Both of the girls wore jean overalls with the suspenders hanging down, and Tokus noticed they looked like twins. He looked past them at Doria.

"It's important," he said. "Very important."

"About my brother?" Doria wondered. "Important how?"

Tokus looked at the other girls. "Well, it's important and it's private. It concerns Bug and your father."

"What about my father?" Doria was instantly defensive.

"In private. Please?"

Doria watched Tokus for a minute. She seemed doubtful but curious. The mention of her father had drawn her. She turned to her girls. "Wait for me a minute, okay? I'll be back. Don't go anywhere."

"Are you coming back, too, Zulu?" one of the girls asked.

"It's Swahili!" the other girl squealed. "We'll be right here, Doria."

Tokus and Doria paced a discreet distance and turned to face each other. Doria was very pretty—the beauty of almond smooth skin, shaped gently by an oval trust and kindness that reached up into the corners of her eyes. She was a sister that he would always protect and cherish. Tokus looked her in the eye and began the lie.

"Someone is looking for your brother," he began.

"And?" Doria shrugged.

"Well," Tokus said, "I hate to alarm you…"

Doria was taken aback. "But you are, aren't you?"

Tokus paused. Doria had struck a counterpoint in his plan. Big Ma had told him that Doria was a bright girl who didn't miss much, so he had better be careful with his game of deceit. It was time to improvise.

"Well," Tokus began again, "like I said, this matter concerns you, Bug and your father. The Reverend. And you both need to know. You and Bug."

Doria studied him suspiciously. He could almost hear the gears turning in her pretty little head.

Finally she said, "What is it? What do we need to know? What is so important?"

"I'd rather tell you both together. Then you'll understand."

"Uh-uh," Doria answered. "I don't need my brother with me to hear what you have to say. You might even be the person who is out here looking for him. So tell me."

"Doria, please!" Tokus cried.

"Forget you then." She turned away.

"All right! Okay, then! Damn!" Tokus conceded. His heart beat nervously as he gathered his will to face the moment of truth. Now that it had arrived, Tokus found himself groping for elusive words and meanings that were bound to hammer at his sister's life with the force of a dark unknown... about her father.

"Doria..." Tokus stalled. "Before I tell you anything, I have to ask you to hear me out before you go reacting all over the place. Okay?"

"I can't promise that."

"Promise to try."

"Will you please just spit it out?!"

Tokus did just that. For Doria he used the word "date" and left out the part about rape but everything else was hung out there for her. Considering the severity of the news, Doria handled it relatively well. She stood there, slack-jawed with an incredulous look, rejecting the entire idea immediately.

"I guess you just expect me to believe this?"

"I have no reason to lie," Tokus answered.

"My father would have told us. He didn't keep secrets."

"Everybody has secrets. And you're talking to one now."

Doria had more questions, heavy ones, but she was soon softened by the sincerity of Tokus' entreaties.

"And I just came here to ask you if you would be my sister. If I could be your brother," Tokus finished hopefully.

Doria looked at him numbly. "I guess we had better get over to my brother's house. We were walking past his house on the way home anyway."

She turned toward her friends who were still waiting patiently and said, "Come on, Tokus."

They began walking in silence, the girls quieted by the serious expression on Doria's face. They had never seen her switch moods so suddenly, and all their attempts at conversation were met with curt responses.

After a few blocks had rolled by, Doria looked over at Tokus.

"Oh, yeah," she said. "If you don't know...my brother calls himself T'Challa now."

"T'Challa?" Tokus repeated.

"Now you know," Doria said.

T'CHALLA

The man who stood before Tokus with his arms folded across his chest was not the same man who had run away leaving his friend, fleeing in fear from the screams of pain. More than his name had changed and it showed in his eyes. In his stance. Tokus wondered if T'Challa, his brother, could put that night in its proper perspective. In the past. A forgotten space and time in a life long ago, a dark creature who didn't have to live again.

It had taken a sincere entreaty from Doria before T'Challa would allow Tokus entrance into his home. Tokus took a seat on the beaten, living room couch, as the two men eyed each other warily, each with a brotherly secret of death of which the sister could never be made aware. Doria sat on the arm of the far end of the couch facing T'Challa.

Five-O was gone. Dead. Ghost. T'Challa had taken him out with cold, hard anger, openly defiant in the harsh sunlight. Tokus didn't approve of murder, but he was still breathing a sigh of relief that the threat of the law no longer loomed over him and he could now move forward with his life. Starting here. Starting now.

An awkward, tense silence hung over the room. Doria squirmed in her seat.

"T'Challa," she began. "Tokus gotta tell you something."

"Must be important," T'Challa answered. "You brung him here. All right. What?"

Tokus paused and looked around the room for the first time since he had entered. A woman was sitting at a table in the kitchen. Seated across from her was a small boy. That must be Monday, Tokus reasoned, T'Challa's little boy. Monday was openly curious and Tokus smiled at him. A tiny grin creased his small face and he gave a little wave and chirped, "Hi."

Tokus smiled his "hi" in return.

The apartment was small. It looked like two bedrooms with a closed door just off the kitchen and another one directly behind T'Challa. The kitchen itself was ghetto issue—a room with a sink, refrigerator, stove and brown cabinets.

"I thought we could speak privately," Tokus said. "The three of us."

"What is it?" T'Challa pressed. "What do you want?"

"It's not so important. It's just personal."

"Yeah," Doria piped up. "Very personal. For real, T'Challa. For real."

T'Challa nodded. He called Pharren. "Ya'll go in the bedroom for a minute. Gone."

After the door closed behind them, T'Challa looked at Tokus. "You killed him."

"Who killed who?" Doria jumped up.

"It was an accident," Tokus replied.

"Who did you kill?"

"I didn't murder anybody! I got in a fight. It was an accident."

Doria stepped back, eyes widened in disbelief.

"Look, Doria," Tokus explained. "That guy was trying to kill me. And he had the nerve to kiss me first! On the lips! It was an unprovoked attack. Next thing I know, I hit him and he was on the ground, bleeding. I didn't touch him again after that."

Tokus turned to T'Challa.

"I swear, I never touched him again after he went down. I didn't find out that he died until hours later."

"But why did he jump on you?" Doria asked.

Tokus averted his eyes. He couldn't look at her. "For drugs. I was a drug dealer. It was my last night sellin'. I used to deal up on the Aisle."

"You killed him," T'Challa stated.

"I didn't mean to. But he was trying to rob me. That's not in my best interest. Even if it was in yours!"

T'Challa's eyes darkened. Hard. Tokus wished he could have that last sentiment back. This wasn't going as planned.

"Listen," Tokus said, "I shouldn't have said that. I didn't come here to argue. There's something you need to know."

Tokus proceeded to relate the family secret to a bemused T'Challa. When he finished, T'Challa leaned forward with a thoughtful look.

"That's a good one," he said. "That's a good story."

"He admitted it to me," Tokus said.

T'Challa paused to mull that one over. After a minute Doria's voice came soft and slow. "I believe him, T'Challa."

Tokus looked at Doria gratefully.

"Why?" T'Challa asked.

Doria turned a trusting look at Tokus. In her eyes Tokus saw everything that a sister could be…and he hoped that she saw a brother's reflection. A real brother.

"Who would want to be my brother, unless he was?"

"Or," T'Challa countered. "why would someone want to be my brother… unless he had to be?"

T'Challa was suspicious. The two men knew each other beyond Doria's realm of knowledge. The streets were their common denominator and they both understood that the man on the streets was a menace, not a brother.

"Doria," T'Challa said. "Go in the room with my son. Tokus and me… we gotta talk."

Doria started to object but one look from T'Challa and she pulled up short, rose from her seat and left the room. T'Challa stood and regarded Tokus coolly, then turned and walked across the room. When he was standing in front of the Undamo display he faced Tokus and spoke sternly.

"You left something out," he uttered.

"Left what out of what?" Tokus replied.

"You're older than me," T'Challa answered. "If Deaugood got your mother pregnant, why didn't he marry her?"

"I guess they didn't get along," Tokus answered.

"No," T'Challa replied. "Get along or not get along didn't matter back then. If you got along good enough to do the bump and grind, you were friends enough to take care of your kids. So stop lying."

Tokus hesitated before deciding on the truth.

"Okay," he said. "The good Reverend Minister Deaugood...raped my mother. Bam! There it is. Okay! The cold hard fact. He raped my mother."

T'Challa stared at him stonily.

"So violence begot violence, huh?"

Tokus eyes snapped. "That was low."

"What else did you lie about?" T'Challa snapped.

"Nothing else."

"Now I'm supposed to believe that, right?"

"What did you expect?" Tokus whispered harshly. "You want me to tell Doria that her father raped my mother? Get real, my man. Get real!"

T'Challa walked over and took the seat directly across from Tokus. "You killed Moose."

"It was an accident. Self-defense." Tokus was defensive. "He was trying to rob me and you knew it!"

T'Challa didn't answer. They were quiet for a moment.

"You killed Five-O," Tokus stated.

"I had to. Anyway, it looked like he was trying to kill you."

"Yeah," Tokus replied. "But what about the police? You don't even care if they come for you, do you?"

"Five-O won't," T'Challa replied.

"You left that dart there for the police to find," Tokus said.

"I know," T'Challa admitted.

"No, you don't know. I picked it up and threw it in a sewer about five blocks away. They'll never find it."

T'Challa gave him a searching stare before going over to the bedroom door and calling for Doria. As the door opened T'Challa turned to Tokus and said, "We'll see."

Doria came into the room and then they talked, the three of them. Soon Monday and Pharren joined them. Tokus felt as if they were making progress, even though they really had no starting point and no guidance, no rule or reason. Their journey took place on a narrow path with an unending free fall threatening on each side. The process of getting to know each other was a sometimes awkward, extra sensitive, precarious balance on the precipice of a burgeoning relationship with arms and legs flailing to maintain the perch. Perfect balance was the ultimate goal...the state of "ooommm." The tranquil state of "ooommm" eluded them, but there was a crack of light at the end of the trek.

Tokus also took stock of Pharren. She seemed shy but there was also a quiet strength he sensed there, as if she had brought that quality to T'Challa's life, for Tokus saw it in his brother, too. And Monday was a sheer joy. They connected instantly. He sat next to Tokus on the couch and looked at him happily.

"So you my uncle now?" Monday asked.

Tokus looked at T'Challa before he answered.

"Yes, I am."

"Uncle Tokus?"

"Well, maybe just Tokus, okay?"

"Okay," Monday said and jumped into Tokus' arms. Tokus grinned so hard his face hurt before he released his nephew.

They talked well into the night until, finally, Tokus and Doria had to leave.

"T'Challa," Tokus said as he reached into his pocket. "Doria. I would be so proud if you both would come to my graduation."

He pulled the invitations from his pocket and extended them to the surprised pair.

"I graduate from the university after the final exams," Tokus explained. "Will you be there for me?"

Doria took the invitations. T'Challa nodded in agreement.

BOOK II:

THE ARRIVAL OF THE LIE

ECHO OF HER EYES

He could almost feel it, the echo of her eyes, as they moved closer, consuming him. Red fire burned in their wake. Streaks of white heat danced in the blazing tendrils, and they called him like a bandit to come steal away and take illicit pleasures. John Zabriski hid behind a dark pair of shades from a world that was oblivious to his existence, his eyes warped from the drug that sent his mind on a sinuous journey of heat and love. With a smile, he leaned back in his seat and spoke to the echoes. His words were a whisper against the humming of the plane's engines, but each syllable was clear and precise.

"You are my baby. Absolutely. My baby."

The eyes had him forever. They belonged to him, the eyes were a mere reflection of the feline quality of his own hazy pupils, both elongated and burning. For as long as desire ached in him, for as long as the drug lasted, John Zabriski was in the dubious position of owning and being owned by his new precious creation.

The pills! His hand flew to his breast pocket, anxiously checking for his small bottle of tablets. The label read it contained a prescription for arrhythmia but John's heart was fine. Settling back into the cushioned comfort of his first-class seat aboard the huge airliner, his heart was beating quite lovely at the moment.

"Me and my baby," John sighed.

"And you love your baby, don't you?"

A deep, menacing voice rumbled in John's ear. He had forgotten that his huge, burly companion, Bossman, was seated next to him. Bossman was sinister. John had felt it the moment he had met his new business partner. He was a clothed ape with speaking ability, as far as John was concerned, but he needed Bossman to start the operation in motion, to get the ball rolling. John Zabriski planned on becoming a rich man.

The echo of her eyes caused ripples in his mind, warming John, as they became tides that began lapping and cresting. Bossman faded from his wakefulness as John waited, steadying himself, poised for the perfect wave. And when he caught it, he rode it hard. Blue, translucent eyes hovered in front of him as he rose to the peak of his mind play, his personal ocean where he could frolic barefoot without a surfboard, both balanced and steady as the eyes turned and slowly, slowly melded with his.

He felt a physical blue all over his body. As pure as the clear sky that lingered outside the window of the plane, as blue as fantasy and agony combining to form a hue that was as transparent as lust. John had found her and she pulsated with pleasure. She absolutely resonated a climax that stretched over time and place taking John on a journey that would never end.

Suddenly, he came down. It was a jarring crash that caused him to gasp as he watched the eyes quickly fade from view.

"Hold on," John hissed. "I'm coming."

He pulled the bottle of pills from his pocket, wrestled frantically with the childproof cap and finally, gratefully, popped a white capsule into his mouth. The pill rushed John Zabriski in sparks and flares, bursting into flame halfway down his throat.

The echo of her eyes returned, along with the shifting of his own. He felt his eyes twist and stretch as they went vertical. Feline. Straight up and down. As the tingling glow began spreading through his body, John thought about how much America would love his invention.

"Feenin," he sighed.

That's what he called the white, granular powder he had perfected in the German labs that were now mere images in his rearview mirror. It was just as well that the foreigners were no longer a factor in his plans. "Addictive" and "dangerous" were two words that had been used to describe his product, but they were wrong. After all, he was a scientist.

John had secretly paid a few college students to be his guinea pigs and found positive, stunning results. Physical addictiveness was nil and there was no evidence of any bodily damage that resulted from usage, unlike the poisons that plagued society, tearing at its very fabric. Mental addiction, well, that couldn't be helped. Some people were just born to be addicts of one thing or another. Life is like that sometimes: a trick baby doing what he knows best.

One of the test subjects, a young man, quickly flew out of control with his usage. He had actually come to John's office demanding dose upon dose of the drug as payment for being a lab rat. John had pulled him into his office and given him a few special doses, pure Feenin laced with hydrochloric acid that he kept in his desk for occasions such as this. There couldn't be any wild cards in his deck—the stakes were too high—and after the student swallowed those pills, his brain had done a slow stir-fry. Walking zombies told no tales.

"Aren't you taking too many of those?"

John snapped back into real time when he was interrupted by the gravelly voice of Bossman. John glanced over at the big man, thankful to be wearing the dark, tinted shades, as a strange paranoia crept upon him. He felt Bossman's eyes probing into his thoughts. His pupils felt strange. Bossman's head had taken on a strange shape. It was taller. Straight up and down.

He would be happy to be rid of Bossman, who was looking at him with a severe, studious glare. As soon as the plane landed, when the money started piling up, he planned on never setting eyes on the face of Bossman again.

Feenin would go nationwide. Maybe even worldwide. Everything was in place. Way Jalon would supply the capital to get the venture off the ground, while John provided the product and Bossman set up the mechanics that would ensure the smooth operation of the new machine: the labs, chemicals, distribution and all the other illegalities. John had no intentions of getting his hands dirty or exposing himself to the stains of incrimination.

"Aren't you taking too many of those?" Bossman repeated.

John clutched the bottle of pills to his chest. "No, I'm not. Feenin is not addictive. I've been taking them for over a week...and I'm not hooked. They're just incredibly effective."

Bossman waited as a flight attendant walked past them. There were only a handful of people in the cabin—none close enough to overhear them, but Bossman was nothing if not careful. Brute strength had gained him a fortune, he had told John, but discretion was also golden.

"Listen, Zabriski, there isn't a drug in the world, that when introduced to the human body, doesn't have an adverse effect on the system. The body is, in effect, in an altered state thereafter."

"Let me guess," John said. "You don't drink. You don't smoke. And you probably breathe once every thirty-five minutes to help preserve the ozone layer, right?"

"Oh, don't get me wrong, Zabriski. I have my fun. I do the things I do. I'm just not into denial. I don't delude myself into thinking that if I stuff powder up my nose that I'm in the same state of mind that I was before I snorted."

Bossman grunted as John turned to look out the window of the plane.

"Those little pills that you're popping in your mouth are drugs. They are what they are, so face the reality clearly. Don't wait until you get 'walleyed' and then extol the virtue of drugs to me."

Bossman looked down at his watch.

"You popped two of those pills in less than twenty minutes."

"What are you doing? Writing a book or something?"

"Maybe."

"Well, skip that chapter 'cause it's none of your business," John replied brazenly.

"Really," Bossman replied calmly. "I just like to time things. Minutes. Seconds. Hours. Time is the only constant. It's utterly reliable."

The flight attendant came over to them, smiling. "Can I get you two gentlemen something to drink?"

"Do you have any chocolate chicken?" John asked.

The woman stared. John guffawed and slapped his knee. He cracked himself up. Bossman and the flight attendant waited.

"Can I have a soda?" John exclaimed after his giggles subsided. "Chocolate chicken." John slapped his knee again as the woman turned to Bossman.

"I'd like a beer," Bossman said. John looked at Bossman in feigned shock. "A beer! Are you going to alter your state?"

"Just slightly," Bossman answered.

When the drinks arrived, Bossman looked down at his watch again.

"One minute and sixteen seconds," he told her. "Impressive."

She flashed Bossman a puzzled smile and walked away. John stared wondrously at the drink in front of him, watching the carbonated bubbles rush to the top of the plastic cup. He leaned forward to take a sip and felt the weight of the computer disks in his pocket press against his ribcage. The three disks were his little secret, his life insurance against an untimely death. He had determined to never reveal his formula, but there was just too much data pertaining to the chemical makeup of Feenin for his brain to retain, so he had encoded the information on the disks. If the existence of the disks were ever discovered, John knew he would become expendable.

He needed another pill…but not in front of Bossman.

"Rest room," he said and sprang from his seat. He quickly strode down the aisle and bustled into the small lavatory. After sliding the door shut and locking the "occupied" sign in place, he popped a pill and phased out with the rush for a few minutes, leaning against the wall in the confined space. He splashed purple and blue water from the faucet on his face, looked in the mirror and stared in his eyes, fell in love for a few minutes before he opened the door to go back to his seat.

"I bet you feel better now, Zabriski," Bossman growled. John took his seat and picked up his soda. Now wasn't the time for words…it was drinking time. One long, lovely swallow of all that color, the oranges and the reds, and those briskly moving bubbles.

"Shut up," John said and raised the beverage to his lips. Gently, he put the drink on the small shelf in front of him. It was half-empty. Or half-full.

"I'll do you one better," Bossman said. "I'll shut up forever."

Bossman reached inside his breast pocket and pulled out a vial that had traces of a white powder clinging to the bottom.

"See this?" Bossman began. "This stuff seriously alters your state of mind. It's unusually fast acting…takes about one minute to do you in. When ingested it makes its way directly to the heart, tightens it with every beat but never lets it expand again. You just drank a good quantity of it about—" Bossman consulted his watch. "—forty-five seconds ago. So now...I'm shutting up."

Zabriski started to reply when he felt a tension in his lungs. He clawed at his chest as he felt the clamping of his heart. The slowed beating was beginning to echo louder in his mind. He pursed his lips as he tried to yell out, but a hiss was all he managed. Fifteen seconds later, Zabriski's body bucked a few times before he left the world on a jet plane, following the eyes that still beckoned to him, even in death, with a quiet twinkle and burning tendrils.

"Foolish man," Bossman muttered as he searched the dead man for the Feenin and the three disks. He put them in his pocket and arranged Zabriski in his seat and fastened the seat belt around his waist. He wedged a pillow under Zabriski's dead head and turned it toward the window, making him appear to be asleep. The plane would be landing soon and Bossman planned on being the first man to depart before the body was discovered. It really didn't matter in the end because it would take quite some time before the cause of death was discovered. If it was discovered at all.

Bossman leaned back in his seat and relaxed, the dead man next to him now a forgotten casualty of the high stake game of monopoly. Now only two players remained: him and Way Jalon. Bossman liked the new odds and could only see success for himself in the future. Losing was not on his agenda.

He thought back to the look on Zabriski's face as he had popped those pills. The Feenin was what he had called it, and Bossman wondered about the high. He pulled the bottle out of his pocket as the pilot announced that the plane was beginning its descent into JFK Airport. He had a connecting shuttle directly from the city to Albany where Way Jalon was waiting for him.

Before the wheels of the aircraft touched down, Bossman felt the warmth of her touch. And felt her breath rush down his ear. A blue wind that carried her voice with the softest, electric touch. The azure zephyr brushed a wing gently against his brain...and he saw them. He couldn't help but stare. He was lost as he gazed deeply into the echo of her eyes.

PAUSE AWAKENS

Pause always awoke from the recurring dream in a start, surprised by the intensity of its grip. A subtle tinge of animosity trembled through her at the callousness of her life, at what she would never be in an existence that was dictated by what she had become: death.

Yet she dreamed.

Little Eva hid from her father in her sister's closet, between a box of folded clothes and one filled with dirty laundry. His temper rampaged around the household on a daily basis, differing only in severity and form. Abuse wasn't a syndrome back then. It was only a formality, a consequence of being born female in a masculine world. It had been hours since her father had stomped around the house searching for her, angrily calling her name. Little Eva had prayed in her silence. Begged her higher power to stop him from finding her. Hitting her. Touching her.

She thought she heard the loud click of the front door downstairs, that maybe her father had left but she was afraid to leave her hiding place. She had made that mistake once before. Her father had gone to the front door and slammed it as if leaving. When she emerged from her hiding place, he was standing there, waiting. He strapped her to the bed, naked, and beat her until angry, red welts covered her bare behind. Then he touched her and stroked her while she cried, violating her while he told her what a bad girl she had been.

One by one, her illusions of happiness had been shattered by the truth of her father's brutality, by the pain of his voice and the fear of his footsteps.

Now she found comfort in the darkness of her sister's closet, safety in the quiet, and soon she was lulled to sleep.

She awoke to the sounds of creaking bedsprings and synchronized grunts. She froze. Listening. She couldn't identify the sounds. Or the voices.

She listened harder.

"Gentle at first. Mmmm!"

That voice registered. It was her sister.

"I know what I'm doing, baby...right there. Right?"

Who was that?! Little Eva inched the door open a crack. She could just see the bottom edge of the bed. The mattress was rocking, doing a strange dance to the sounds of moans and groans that seemed to crowd the room, getting louder and longer. But Little Eva couldn't see into the bed, couldn't see who was in the bed making those sounds. Doing whatever he was doing to her sister. All she saw was feet. Four feet. Twenty toes. Pointed downward. They stuck out over the edge of the bed and from her vantage-point, Little Eva noticed a big toe that was black and germy. It was nasty. It looked as if a coat of dark smut had plastered itself to the nail and stayed there. Little Eva eyed it, fascinated, as she slowly rose to her feet. Careful to be quiet, Little Eva stood with her eyes opened wide in wondrous expectation, her senses sharpened. She felt the grooves in the wood as her fingers trailed up the wall. Her pupils widened and from darkness there came vision. The pants and groans grew in proportions and fell into the rhythm of time and place.

Little Eva saw.

She didn't know what it was, but she saw.

Kelly, her sister, was on the bed, naked, with a naked man. Kelly was on her hands and knees with the naked man kneeling behind her. With one hand, Kelly reached back and pulled the man closer. The man thrust harder and Kelly tilted her head back and groaned. The man leaned forward and kissed her neck, licked her ear. From the closet, Little Eva could see their tongues wrestling like pale snakes, and soon the two bodies found a new rhythm. Little Eva covered her eyes with her fingers, as her mind screamed, No! No! No!

"Fuck me, baby!"

Little Eva's eyes popped open and she looked again.

"Come on," she heard her sister cry. "Fuck me! A…little…harder."

So now it had a name. Fuck. That was a bad word. Well, not baaad, bad. It was sometimes bad. Little Eva couldn't help but think of all the times that she wanted to call her father that word. He used it so often, Little Eva considered it generic. It just seemed to fit him most of the time. Like a snakeskin.

Suddenly the room grew quiet, causing Little Eva to focus on the silence, straining, trying to see what her sister was doing in the bed. Then she heard a scratching sound. A flame flickered to life in the man's hand. He put the fire to the tip of a funny, twisted looking cigarette. He put the cigarette to his lips, inhaled and pushed his hips forward as he exhaled. Kelly looked back over her shoulder and pursed her lips. The man held the cigarette to her lips. She inhaled, then smiled and ground her hips back into him as the smoke escaped from her nose in small, billowing wisps.

The acrid smell of marijuana soon filled the room, catching Little Eva by surprise. It was an odor she had smelled before, at school in the dark corners of the playground. In secret. Her best friend, Susie, called it "mind benders" because some of the kids who did it sometimes came back from recess, bent. All silly and giggling with eyes as red as fire.

But why would her sister want to be bent? Little Eva had long ago given up trying to understand her sister. It wasn't that she and Kelly shared any real sisterly closeness; in fact, Kelly considered her more of a nuisance than anything. Kelly was a wild child, rebellious. She defied their father, even though the consequences could be painful, and dared to be free from his iron rule. Little Eva envied her sister's bravery.

"You know what to do, baby," she heard her sister moan.

The cigarette was gone but they hadn't changed their position. Kelly was still kneeling with the man behind her. She rocked gently as she spoke.

"You're good! But you're wild. C'mon. Give it to me." The man responded with a grunt and a thrust, meeting Kelly in the middle. Little Eva noticed the heaving of the man's chest, the rise and fall of it, as he rubbed his hand over her sister's body. He seemed to be trying to touch everything!

"You high?" he asked Kelly.

"Yes," she replied and the man suddenly picked up the pace. He bucked faster and faster. The bed squeaked frantically, trying to keep up with the staccato slapping of flesh against flesh. Little Eva watched as Kelly gritted her teeth and then traced her tongue over her lips. She closed her eyes and reached back for the man again.

"All of it! All of it! Mm, mm, mm," she groaned. Kelly put one hand against the headboard of the bed and pushed back frantically, meeting the man's thrusts. Her head was bowed with her long hair dangling down, obscuring her face.

A flash of silver danced in a sliver of moonlight that shone through the bedroom window, reflecting directly into Little Eva's eyes. Her mind pitched in panic when she saw the serrated edge of a knife in the man's hand. It was raised high over his head, and he brought it down in a vicious arc toward her sister's neck. Little Eva felt herself falling away in shock but her legs were wooden and her body was firmly frozen in place as her eyes remained riveted on the sight that her young mind told her was not happening.

The knife came down on the back of Kelly's neck and the point came out the other side. Eva heard a surprised gurgle escape from her sister's body even as the blade was savagely ripped from her throat. Kelly fell face-first on the bed, her naked body obscene from the intimate violence. Blood flowed in a thick stream through her clasping fingers, spreading dark stains over the sheets.

"Yeah, bitch!" the man yelled as he turned her body over. His eyes were big and mad. Little Eva's were, too.

"Never again," he cried and brought the knife down again, driving it into her chest over and over in a fanatical fit. It seemed like ages had passed before the man calmed himself enough to notice the splattered blood coating his naked body.

Kelly's chest was split wide open. The opening grew in proportion until it was a fissure, a chasm that glowed a hellish pink-blue. The man stepped away from the bed, taken aback at the strange cold that emanated from his victim. An eerie frost filled the room as Little Eva, more curious now than frightened, stared at the unreal drama that she witnessed. A chilling noise emitted from the hole in her dead sister's chest and Little Eva saw a slight movement. Suddenly, a frozen tiny hand reached out of the hole. Something quickly climbed out. It was a golem, a doll-sized man. He was very small but Little Eva saw his face in close-up. The miniature black man limped forward and looked Little Eva in the face. His eyes were slightly twisted and Little Eva noticed that his entire stomach was missing. She saw completely through him. A tiny white man was next out of the hole. He had garotte marks around his neck and jelly for a right eye. After him came a dark-haired lady, but she looked perfectly fine. No bruises or cuts were visible on her body.

She had been poisoned. There was a toxic substance inside the woman that had eaten its way into her stomach, lungs and heart and burned them into death.

Little Eva didn't know this fact.

Adult Eva did.

A dove flew out of the glowing opening of her sister's chest. It was a frozen blue-black color with a white face. It turned to look at Eva...and she felt her soul harden. On the dove's face...was a single, blue tear that froze midway down its face.

Pause always awoke from this night terror with a shout, sweat covering her body and soaking the sheets. It was a recurring dream that always seemed to shake her to the core. But once awake it meant nothing to her, its meaning a drowsy backwash. It could be overcome, just as any other obstacle that threatened her path. She found joy in repetition.

Little Eva, even Adult Eva, only existed at the periphery of her memory now. They died a lifetime ago along with her father, her sister and her hopes for love. Everything is nothing and now there is only Pause. And a Pause would kill.

SLIPPING INTO DARKNESS

When Pause opened the door, she was struck blind by the darkness. Kelly kept the curtains drawn tight to the windows, shutting out the light. She would occasionally slip from room to room, removing the light bulbs in the hallways, bedrooms, bathroom, and even the kitchen. Pause had confronted Kelly on many occasions regarding this penchant for darkness, so Kelly simply steered clear of Pause's bedroom whenever she was on a mission to plunge the house into inky blackness.

"Kelly!" Pause called out while she stood in the doorway and waited for her eyes to adjust before moving into the living room. The two-story townhouse had four bedrooms—two upstairs that they never used, and two downstairs. Pause remembered the first time that she saw the townhouse. She had been struck by the openness of the front room and the modern appliances in the kitchen, the glass surfaces and wooden countertops, especially the thick carpet that ran throughout the house. The bedrooms downstairs sat directly across from each other along the short hallway that led to the small, fenced-in backyard. She knew instantly that the house was perfect for her, and she quickly signed the lease.

She hadn't been prepared to deal with Kelly, though. Her sister was an emotionally scarred woman who had been hardened by life on the streets. The years since their separation had turned Kelly into a distrusting person, concerned only with self-preservation, but Pause was working to chip away at the stony distance that had grown between them. Since they had been apart, they had become strangers, yet Pause was determined to hang onto the memory of the person she had once known. Back in the day, before she became Pause, when she was Eva, Kelly's adoring, innocent little sister.

Burn in Hell! Pause cursed their father for his abuse and, as she moved through the darkened house, she laid her sister's current malady at his feet. Kelly's eyes were hard and lifeless. Her spirit had been taken away and there seemed to be no return in sight.

They had both suffered from his hellish lusts even though Kelly had managed to flee their home years ago, escaping the pain of his regular visits to her room late at night. In her dreams, Pause could still hear the sounds that would emanate from Kelly's room late at night; her father's groans and her sister's screams, intermingling, pulsing, growing louder and louder until she would wake up in a cold sweat, her heart thundering madly. Kelly had escaped, leaving Pause alone to fend for herself against a man that she feared more than death itself. She cried until there were no more tears and as the days and nights of suffering from the abuse of her father continued, sorrow and pain were replaced by the appeal of death and blackness. The abrupt ending of compassion signaled a strange feeling of freedom from her father's iron rule and fear was replaced with brazen indifference. The breaking point came on her fifteenth birthday—Eva's spirit broke free and she became Pause.

That night, Eva woke her dad from his sleep with a kitchen knife to his neck. It was a small knife; the blade itself was only a few inches long but its surface was wide and the edge was very, very sharp. It wasn't a killer knife. She doubted the knife would be able to cut bone but she was sure it would tear right through his flesh. She pressed down and the tip sunk into the soft meat of his neck. When the point of the blade pierced his skin, his eyes flew wide open. Dazed confusion was quickly replaced by anger but his reaction was tempered by the insanely calm expression on the face of his youngest daughter. She had the tip of the knife digging firmly into the soft flesh of his neck and he could feel the blood well up and spill in a slow trickle down his skin. He found his breaths coming in quick, frenzied gasps, his body tensed in nervous response, panicking until his eyes adjusted to the darkness and then he wished that they hadn't.

Eva's hair hung forward, casting a menacing shadow across her features, stunning him momentarily when he couldn't see her eyes. He could see her lips, though, pressed into a thin, angry line, creased in concentration—but her breathing was calm, unhurried. An angry glint appeared in her father's eyes. Instinctively, he moved, trying to push himself away from the knife that pressed urgently into his throat but Eva moved with him.

"I can die." Her voice was dead, monotone. "I can die now."

"What?" her father blubbered and tried to move again.

Once more, Eva moved with him. "I'm ready. I can die." She exerted more pressure on the knife. "But you go, too."

Her father's hands balled into fists as he came to grips with the situation. One slip and his throat would be sliced open. He looked at her face and his heart sped up with a twinge of fear when he noticed one teardrop slide from the darkness and down her cheek.

"You can't keep on touching me." Her voice rose slightly. "It ain't right. It ain't!"

"Eva," he said. "You need to think about what you're doing. Think!"

"It! Ain't! Right!"

"I'm bleeding, Eva. Think!"

Eva's mind went elsewhere; to the feel of her daddy on top of her. Touching her. Kissing her while telling her that she had been bad and to be better next time. Except there was no 'better'—even though there was always a next time. Anger rose inside of her. She pushed forward with the knife.

"I know what I'm doing!" she screamed. "I know! But you don't think about the things that you do to me. That's why Kelly is gone. That's why I'm all by myself now. Because of you."

When she looked down into her father's eyes, she saw his fear, she saw his eyes begging her to stop the madness. They looked, eye to eye, for what seemed like an eternity but in reality was just a millisecond. Her father began to gather his wits and slowly his lips curled up into a smirk and a steely hardness replaced the shocked disbelief that accompanied his initial reaction. She had seen that calculating look before and had never seen anything good come from it so she braced herself for whatever would happen next.

"You ain't gonna do nothing, girl." The menacing growl was back. "What you gonna do, is put that damn knife down…away from my neck…and then go lay down. If you're lucky, I'll forget that this shit happened! Now move that knife away from me, girl." He stopped and gave her a hard glare. "Before I have to punish you again. Because this time you've been bad. Real, real bad!"

"I told you." Eva felt a calm wash over her. The painful existence that she had endured in her short life—the anger, the abuse, the defiant look in her father's eyes—all served to temper her anger while providing a clarity that helped her see things clearly for the first time in her life. In that moment, she felt power…she felt control. "I don't care anymore. I don't have to live. I can die…And so can you."

Her father reached for the knife. Eva pushed down as hard as she could and gazed in fascination as blood started pouring out of the wound in his neck, quickly soaking the bed sheets around his head. *She had sliced his neck good!*

It wasn't a deadly cut but it was deep enough where she could see the flesh folded up like half-turned pages of a book while her father thrashed about on the bed, screaming in pain. She purposefully strode out of the room and away from his sexual abuse.

Eva was placed in a group home—a dark, menacing place where she discovered, among the rough and tough females that she was forced to live with, that she had a penchant for violence. Stabbing her father in the throat had somehow liberated her; her only regret was that she hadn't killed him.

Over the years, Eva often received word of Kelly's whereabouts. Once she heard that Kelly was working a corner in South Albany. Another time she heard that Kelly was working the stroll over in Schenectady, which was way too far for Eva to travel. Once she had even heard news of her sister from Angela Fell, the school gossip and busybody. With that special glee that gossips enjoy, Angela related a story that she heard from her sister's girlfriend's brother—so it had to be true. Kelly was in a relationship with a drug dealer who passed her around from man to man, engaging in abusive sexual relationships until she was returned to the crack dealer who would then beat her for being unfaithful.

"If you're lying," Eva told her, "I'm going to come back here and hurt you really, really bad! Okay!"

Angela Fell was a gossip, not a fighter, and she quickly admitted that it was all a story that she'd heard. That was the last that Eva ever heard from Angela Fell. Despite all the talk, Eva kept the childlike hope that one day she would find her older sister and they would be together.

Her years in the group home awakened a bloodlust in Eva that she found many of the girls there shared. The female residents often told their stories of the path that had led them to the group home, tales of pain and retribution, wrongs and revenges, punctuated by well-thought-out madness. And Eva learned. She learned of the unconscious, lust-driven hearts of men and their weakness for pretty, young flesh. She also learned that she was more than pretty. And once, after getting into a fight with a much bigger girl who bloodied her lip, she sat in the nurse's office, sucking the blood from the cut in her mouth and smiling. Eva learned that she liked the pain; it made her feel alive.

When she was finally released from the group home, Eva decided to embark upon a new career. She decided to get paid for human disposal. She wanted to live a killer's life. A killer for hire. She easily slipped into the underworld and lost herself there. She learned more about her beauty and how to use it to deadly measure. She learned how to "ugly" herself down, make herself inconspicuous, a small figure easily forgotten. For the first time, Eva felt herself wondrously alive and empowered, liberated from the past and reinvented for the future.

Eva decided to become a new person, develop a persona that would enhance the legacy that she planned to leave. She became Pause, cold-blooded stealth and female death. Pause would blaze a new, brighter path. And a Pause would kill.

It wasn't long before Pause found herself on her first hit. Her first mission was to take out an executive of Key Loans and Savings Bank. He was an older, distinguished bank executive by day—a decrepit pervert by night—and he had landed on the wrong side of someone very powerful. Someone who wanted him face-down dead!

His name was Erroll White and after following him for a few weeks, Pause discovered that he was a closet pervert, a pedophile in denial. His public persona was that of a philanthropist, giving to the less fortunate while mindful of the cameras and the publicity shot, while his alter ego was a man who found strange vices to be the crux of his hunger.

Pause watched him. She followed him for two weeks, from his work to his home, taking note of his habits and trying to determine the perfect opportunity to take him. Sitting across the street from his house, Pause watched Erroll White step through the door to the sounds of squeals of joy, as his two children, a boy and a girl, raced across the floor and jumped into his open, welcoming arms. Pause saw them through the kitchen window as Erroll White tipped up behind his wife, who was at work preparing a meal, and surprised her with a bear hug and a long kiss on her lips. She returned his embrace and they held each other for a moment before she turned back to the stove. The rest of the evening proved uneventful as the Whites settled into their evening routines and daylight faded into dark night.

The alter ego of Erroll White appeared in the front doorway hours later, emerging from the shadows and stepping into the moonlight. He was a "downtown" creature, cautious by nature but a predator nonetheless, who had long ago given in to his carnal lusts. Yet he still maintained enough control to take his dirty business to Schenectady. There the flesh trade was much more of an open market, which reduced the chances of him being recognized by an acquaintance. In the short time that Pause had been shadowing Erroll White, she had uncovered his routine. He would get a motel room, change from a business suit into sweats and sneakers, and then head out on the prowl in an old Ford van that had seen much better days. He drove up State Street, hooked a right and then a sharp left up Georgia Avenue through the hustle and bustle of streetcorner dealing. The van pulled up to a porn shop called Triple X, which sat next to a strip club on the corner of Baron Cameron Avenue. The red light district was dotted with strip clubs, whorehouses, and various peep-show houses, but Errol White was partial to Triple X for his forays into the night because they sold the best sex toys and he could get in and get out quickly. He was sticking to his routine and Pause knew where his next stop would be so when he went inside the store, she raced ahead of him to set the trap that would be the end of Erroll White.

She pulled into a vacant parking lot around the corner from Baron Cameron Avenue, killed the engine, and climbed into the back seat. Warren Street was the next street over and down one block, where it intersected with Union Street; it was the out-of-the-way corner that Erroll White chose to do his business with his night toy girls. Pause reached for her makeup bag and felt the first rush of anxiety flood through her body. There would be no turning back once the act was completed. A twinge of apprehension passed over her—maybe she didn't need to do this thing, to kill this man— but her thoughts were lifted and a smile spread across her face when she envisioned what the future held for her. No turning back.

First Pause donned the long, auburn wig she pulled from her bag and she became a redhead with soft curls that hung down around her shoulders, giving her a bouncy, cheery effect when she tossed her head. She pulled out a large compact and checked out her reflection. *I'm going to be damn hard to resist*, she mused. *Just have to lure in the beast.* Pause was perfect... and she knew it. The fates had determined that she make her mark in the underworld of murder. She would not fail.

Memories returned and invaded the moment. This was her turning point, the purpose that she would serve. The soulful pain and the hopeless rage. The glorious screams when the knife plunged into her father's neck. Then the nightmares. Golems climbing from corpses. Bloody tears. Doves. Screams. The nightmares that plagued her, paradoxically, drove her—somehow the night horrors set her free.

Pushing those thoughts from her mind, she fluffed her hair, pulling a thick strand so that it hung in front of her face, she affected a schoolgirl persona that she knew would attract Erroll White. Next out of her handbag came a miniskirt, along with a matching top, which together resembled a cheer- leading outfit. Taking a quick peek around the parking lot, Pause changed clothes in the back seat, quickly slipping on the skirt and top before taking a moment to inspect her special pair of stilettos. The long, slim heel on her right shoe was actually a real stiletto; a long, sharp dagger that left deadly puncture wounds when used correctly. The real beauty that the knife held for Pause was that the stiletto stabs didn't bleed heavily and sometimes not at all. The man who had hired her had made the shoes that she wore, exactly to her specifications. She had simply told him what she wanted and the next day a shoebox was hand-delivered to a hotel room that she had paid for with a fake credit card. The heel of the shoe, which could be detached with a quick twist, also had a pressure-sensitive button that would instantly extend the blade an additional three inches. Pause was quick and deadly with the stiletto, well-versed with the knowledge of the vital points of the human body and skilled with the ability to hit them. She took comfort in her gifts, confident that physically she could hold her own in any situation. A final check in the mirror was met with an approving nod before she climbed out of her car and hurried toward the corner to wait for Erroll White.

When Pause arrived on the corner, two girls were already on the stroll, scantily clad in the most revealing outfits imaginable. As the women shouted propositions to any car that slowed in passing, Pause took a moment to mentally get in touch with her own inner ho. Before stepping from the shadows, she got her stroll together; hips loose and swaying, her stance open and inviting and an indifferent expression on her face. Wordlessly, she positioned herself on the corner, a few feet away from the other working girls and waited for Erroll White to drive up.

The Black woman paced the sidewalk, a flesh-peddling professional with a micro-miniskirt that barely concealed the mound between her legs, clinging to her ass so tightly that Pause saw the distinct curves of each cheek. A car horn blew a long, deliberate honk, which she responded to by turning her ass to the street, tilting her hips forward to give the cars a full view of her shaved pussy. "Come get some!" She shook her moneymaker. "Ha! Ha!" Even her laugh had a nasty, sexy tone. She wore her hair straight down to the middle of her back, and she moved with the assurance of a woman who knew that she looked good enough for men, or women, to pay for the pleasure of touching her. The small amount of material she wore hugged a figure that was full and thick with promises that were issued by her every movement, which in turn invited lust...and hers was for sale. When she turned from the street, Pause was struck by her beauty and felt an odd kinship with her. Expressive eyes reflected none of the hard knocks that living a whore's life entailed. Indeed, the flash of sexiness exuded from her lent an adventurous vibe to her lure. Her face was gently curved, not delicate— strong—with lips that held the hint of a sexual purse, full and ready. Her stare was smoldering yet hard, a spirited woman who seemed at ease with any sexual possibility.

The other woman stood on the far side of the corner, occasionally shifting her hips in a practiced pose of exhibitionism with a cigarette dangling between her fingers. When she brought the cigarette to her mouth, Pause noticed her long, slender fingers and her surprisingly pale skin. There was a feline quality about her; the way that she moved suggested a cat-like sensuality. Painted, thin lips and a narrow nose completed the image with dark hair that cascaded around her face, lending her an exotic look. She wore a thong and a plastic, see-through miniskirt accompanied by a black, pushup bra. She pledged a big bang for the buck.

Pause watched them both...and made a promise that a street corner would never be her fate.

Time to get with the program. Erroll White will be coming to the corner and I need to be ready. The short, cheerleading outfit that she wore was riding high up her hips, the flimsy material barely covering the soft swell of her ass when Pause struck her provocative pose, discreetly checking the street for a sign of the van.

"Who you with?" The Black woman stepped to Pause.

"I'm with me," Pause answered. A cloud of anger began to form on the woman's face and Pause stepped to her before the storm could gather wind. "And I'm the 'me' that you don't want to fuck with." Her voice was a harsh whisper, yet clear and distinct. The woman was taken aback at the aggressive tone and she hesitated. "I'm minding my own business, hooker." Pause looked at her. "I suggest you mind your own."

The woman stood over Pause. She was territorial about her corner and the other hooker joined her as they glared at Pause. Pause stood her ground.

"You just a trick out here, baby," the Black woman finally spoke. "Don't let me have to trick you!"

Pause let the threat pass. She had a purpose for being on the corner, none of which included getting involved in hooker etiquette. She could give a damn about the whores or the corner if she tried. But she wouldn't. This was her very first hit and she would let nothing distract her. She looked up the street. Still no van. Erroll White was running late. In the weeks that she had been following him, Erroll White had never deviated from his routine. Something was wrong.

Stay calm, Pause reasoned. *I have the ability to adjust when things happen. Think on the fly.* In order to be effective in her chosen profession, she knew she would have to develop the skills of the chameleon, be as ever changing as the situation warranted. Every situation would be a new test.

She decided to wait.

In the intervening moments, Pause was subjected to the stark realities of the lustful nature of men, the desires that drive them and the intimacy between them and the degradation of their lost souls. Johns came from all directions, in all shapes and sizes, on foot and in cars with their hunger pulsing and pounding, desperation driving their requests for sex. Each appeal was made with trembling, outstretched hands. There was no short-age of Black men approaching Pause, eager to sample her young, white flesh. It seemed that the darker the john, the deeper the craving. She turned them all away. Whatever price a john offered, she would double or triple the asking price and they would take their money to the next girl. Pause looked up the street. *Where the hell was Erroll White?*

Business was brisk on the corner, however. Both of the hookers had caught two johns, disappeared into the night, only to return a short time later and resume their hustle on the corner. Pause was about to abandon her mission for the night when she spied Erroll White's van coming down the street. When he neared the corner, Pause made eye contact with him and smiled. He slowed down and pulled over to the curb in front of her. Pause sauntered over to his car and leaned into the open window.

Erroll White's eyes bulged when he took in the gentle swell of her breasts poking out of her cheerleading outfit. "Hi," he said.

"Hi!" Pause forced perkiness into her voice. "You looking for a date, daddy?"

Erroll White felt his manhood stiffen. "Why don't you step back from the car? I want to see you."

Pause stepped back and slowly turned, giving the man an eyeful of her slender legs and short miniskirt. She bent slightly at the waist, giving Erroll White a good look at her ass before she came back to the car window and smiled. "You looking for a date, daddy?" she repeated.

The eager, schoolgirl expression stirred Erroll White's loins and the decision was made. "Get in," he commanded.

Pause swung the door open and climbed inside.

"I got fifty dollars," Erroll White said as he swung the car away from the sidewalk.

"That means you've got a hundred!" After a second of silence. "What's on your mind, daddy?" Pause continued with her masquerade.

"Well..." He grinned at her. "I need special treatment."

Pause didn't miss a beat. "One-fifty."

"Done." Erroll White slapped the dashboard, sealing the deal. "I have a motel room that we can use. I don't take my pleasures in the street. In a car? Hell no!" He took one hand off the wheel and ran his fingers down Pause's thigh.

"You're looking at two hundred now, big daddy," she said in a lilting voice.

"I like it when you call me that." Erroll White stared through the windshield. "I like that. I am your 'big daddy' tonight."

Pause regarded him for a second before she spoke. "What kind of special treatment are we doing, daddy? What do you like?"

"Fantasy. Fantasy with a strong mix of role-playing."

"Role playing, huh? I might need a chaser for that." She pointed at a liquor store they were approaching.

Erroll White looked at her and grunted. "Get liquor on your own time." He sped through the traffic light. "I don't need you all liquored up."

Pause cursed under her breath when she realized her error. She had planned on talking Erroll White into getting out of the car and into the liquor store by telling him that she was not old enough to buy it. While he was inside, Pause had planned on getting her stiletto ready and making her move. Her miscalculation was one of inexperience. Erroll White may have sex with prostitutes but he didn't trust one enough to leave her unattended in his car. *Damn!*

She fell back into her cheerleader persona. "What kind of fantasy kick are we on tonight, daddy?"

"There's no drinking involved." He glanced at her.

Pause watched him a moment before a smile spread across her face. She was still in control.

Erroll White nodded approvingly before he continued, "I want a spanking. I want my schoolgirl to give daddy a schoolgirl spanking while I'm doing the do...and then...and then..."

"What, big daddy?"

"I'll...I'll tell you the rest in a minute." He swung the van into the motel parking lot and stopped the car directly in front of his room for the night. The place was a dump...exactly the type of place where Pause knew he would take her. Erroll White sat in the car for a few moments, looking carefully around the parking lot, checking in every direction to be sure that he would not be seen. Pause sat next to him thinking that she couldn't have done a better job of scouting the area herself.

When Erroll White was satisfied that the parking lot was totally deserted, he jumped out of the van. "Let's go."

He quickly walked to the red door with no number on it and slid his key into the lock. Pause followed him inside and stood right inside the doorway, taking in the surroundings. The cheap room had a single bed jutting out from the wall into the center of the room facing a television set that sat on an elevated shelf above an old, raggedy air conditioner. She noticed that there were brown and black stains on the pocked surface of the unit, and tiny pools of moisture had accumulated there also. She looked on as a cockroach climbed from its hiding place and crawled toward the wetness. The curtains in front of the window were pulled tight. A dim, translucent flash of light could be seen through the material, pulsing on and off, and the only sound heard was the faint flow of night traffic. Erroll White snatched a remote control off the bed and pointed it at the television and a porno movie blazed to life. A shapely, young blonde in a nurse's uniform sashayed into a hospital room and announced to an older man in the bed that she was his *head nurse*. She then began unbuttoning her blouse.

Pause took a moment to survey the rest of the motel room. An open bathroom door faced the bed and she heard water running. And then it stopped. This could be trouble.

"Is there someone else here?" she asked.

Erroll White stood in front of the television, enraptured by the scene playing out before him. Another young nurse entered the room and with a flourish, disrobed. The camera zoomed in on her crotch, revealing a penis and vagina between her legs before she climbed into the bed with the anxiously waiting couple. Erroll White turned to Pause, his eyes roaming over every inch of her body with undisguised lust before moving over toward the bed.

"Are you ready to get started?" he said.

"Well..."

"Let's get it on!"

"Let me use the bathroom first." Pause stepped toward the door.

"Well, see..." Erroll White stopped her. "That's the other part of my fantasy deal." He walked over and stuck his head in the bathroom door. "Come on out! We're ready."

A woman stepped into the doorway.

Pause felt her heart stop.

FIRST BLOOD

Kelly stood in the doorway butt-naked with a pom-pom in each hand. A smile was plastered across her face, as if this sexual situation was an everyday occurrence. Pause was stunned to see her sister—her sister who she had spent years searching for, only to find her naked and in the midst of selling her body to a man who was marked for murder. *Kelly!* Her jaws went slack. *Oh my God! Kelly? What are you doing? You have to sell yourself? I've been searching for you! And you never came back for me!* Pause's mind raced and she hesitated. Her uncertainty gave her a moment to think twice about impulsively running over and taking her sister in her arms. After all, she did have a job to do and she was determined to make it happen despite the shock of her sister's presence. She decided to play it cool. It would all work out. She would simply have to adapt to the circumstances. Her sister's presence explained Erroll White's earlier delay. Apparently, he had made a side trip to pick up Kelly who seemed to have played this game before and was accustomed to the nuances of Erroll's fantasies.

Kelly had grown into a beautiful woman. She had their mother's face; those same startling green eyes, elegant cheekbones, and thin lips that framed the same dazzling smile that Pause had seen in their family photos. Pause looked at her and was momentarily taken back to her childhood, to the secret admiration that she once had for her sister but was too timid to openly confess. Pause had emulated her sister's mannerisms and always held out the hope that one day she would grow up to be like her. Those days were gone. Things had changed.

Kelly had been the only constant source of love in her life. More times than she could count, the difference between despair and hope had been shared moments of quiet understanding between Pause and her sister. When they were together, Kelly's steely exterior had been pulled away to reveal a caring soul who helped share the pain that only they two could share, displaying a love that had no place in their home. Pause looked at her sister and realized that the hurt was still ravaging her mind. Life had changed them. But they could still make things right. Together.

"Hi!" Kelly greeted her enthusiastically. Pause searched her face, looked deeply into her eyes and realized that Kelly did not recognize her. They hadn't seen each other since Pause was in junior high school and, though she was wearing makeup and a wig, Pause was still inexplicably hurt that her sister could look her in the eye and not *see* her. With an effort, Pause pushed all thoughts of her sister from her mind and concentrated on her mission. First things first, she mused as she turned her animosity toward Erroll White.

He stood between them, looking from Pause to Kelly, taking extra time to stare at Kelly's naked body before nodding at her, apparently a signal for her to commence with the fantasy. Kelly grinned even wider, put her hands on her hips and began a cracked-out version of a high school cheer. Her arms and legs flailed. Her perky breasts shook. Erroll White took a seat on the bed and began massaging himself through his pants.

"He's okay! He's all right!" Kelly cheered. "He's gonna hit this thing tonight!" She stomped her feet to the rhythm of the cadence.

"Come on!" Erroll White urged. "I want some enthusiasm! Some school spirit! Show me what my money can buy!" He massaged his hardness again. "I paid for this!"

Kelly sang again. "He's okay! He's all right! He's gonna hit this thing tonight!" She stomped again. This time harder and louder.

"Let me see you dance," he commanded. Kelly dropped her pom-poms and dropped to her hands and knees, making her ass undulate, mimicking a sexual act while looking back over her shoulder at Erroll White with a smile plastered across her face. He turned to Pause. "Now it's your turn."

Pause's steady gaze held him. "Not yet. You forgot something."

Erroll White's eyes widened in question.

"No money. No honey," Pause said.

"You're spoiling the mood for me." Erroll White frowned at her. "I've got my cheers going…"

"He's okay! He's all right," Kelly chimed in from the floor. "He's gonna hit this thing tonight!" This time she shook her body to the cadence.

"I've got my visual stimulation." He indicated the porno playing on the television. "All is right with the world."

"Don't know about your world," Pause replied. "Money is what makes my world go 'round. Everything else is pure enjoyment."

Erroll White spread his legs apart when Pause moved closer to him; her breasts and slim, curvy waist captured his attention. She had that pretty, freshly scrubbed teenage look that really turned him on.

"You're just paying for the limo ride." She posed for him. "You do want to ride. Don't you?" When her tongue darted out, tracing the outline of her lips, he quickly reached for his wallet.

Erroll White began his slide into the fantasy. "I didn't go to my prom."

Pause noticed the huskiness in his voice. "Well, here's your chance."

"So what are you charging?"

Pause slanted her eyes at him. "Two."

"Two what?"

"Two bills."

"Two hundred dollars!"

Pause teased him by inching her skirt down past her youthful hips. "That's the price for your fantasy. And I told you…my limo rides."

"Oh. Yes. Yes. Yes." Erroll White snatched his wallet from his pocket. Pause discreetly eased her skirt back up. Erroll White looked from Pause to Kelly and back again. "This is going to be the one!"

Erroll shook with excitement, trembling with the anticipation of a fantasy about to be fulfilled. He handed the money to Pause and began to undress while she counted it. Climbing into the bed, he motioned to Kelly and patted a spot near the headboard. She stood but remained rooted to the spot, watching him. She was silent, all of the pretentious school cheer gone, as she extended her arm, palm turned up in request for payment. Erroll White took in the slim, petite figure standing in front of his face, poised and ready to do his will. Her breasts jutted up into the air at a gravity defying angle, her stomach was flat and smooth, her body was tight from daily street exercising—hustling and hoeing—and her slender, shapely legs had that smooth, unblemished sheen that was granted by youth. Kelly was a beautiful, young girl who had a streetwise sensuality that sparkled with a smoldering promise of sexual fire. Erroll White paid her.

Kelly snatched the money from his hand and glanced quickly at Pause. Moving back toward the doorway, she stepped into the bathroom to put the cash away. She pranced back into the bedroom with a smile on her face, looking as if she were ready for the action to begin.

Pause watched her sister climb into the bed and assume the position, on hands and knees in front of Erroll White. A pang of regret thumped inside of Pause. What she had promised herself she would never become, her sister seemed to embody. The regret that she felt at finding Kelly living a life of degradation was replaced by the strength of a new purpose. She would help her sister find her way out of this broken existence, but first things first. Erroll White had to be put down. She sat on the edge of the bed and began to take off her shoes.

"Now let's get started." He pointed at Kelly. "I want you to be my school-girl crush. I'll call you Tiffany. My Tiff." He moved behind Kelly and ran his hands over the soft swells of her flesh. "And you." He turned his head to Pause. "I want you to be Joannie. My sister. And every ten strokes, I want you to spank me. Hard!"

Pause grabbed her shoe with the stiletto in the heel. "Okay, daddy."

Erroll White smiled. "I like you, girl!" He turned back to Kelly, running his fingers over her rump, which she was wiggling back and forth like a stripper. Erroll White plunged his fingers inside of her. "Yessssss…" The word escaped his lips in a heavy hiss. "You have the makings of a sweetness, Tiff. Remember?"

"Yes!" Kelly squealed and leaned back into the stroking hands that kneaded her rounded flesh. Her pubis protruded like a dense thicket and Erroll White grunted when he stuck his fingers back inside of her.

Pause twisted the heel of her shoe and pulled the stiletto free.

"My little sister, Joannie," Erroll White spoke to Pause while he slipped his fingers in and out of Kelly. "She likes to walk around like those promiscuous girls." He pulled his fingers out of Kelly and held his hand out in front of his face. He smelled his fingers and closed his eyes in ecstasy.

Pause pressed down on the button and the stiletto grew three inches longer.

"Ahh. So young." Erroll White's tongue flicked out and darted across his fingers. "And so sweet."

Pause jumped him. She swung her arm in a precise, powerful motion, plunging the stiletto into the back of his neck. She felt the friction of the blade scraping his vertebrae before she quickly pulled it out and jabbed him again. *Again!* A red-hot voice of panic screamed inside her head, reverberating insanely. *Again! Again!* She stabbed him in his neck numerous times before Erroll White realized what was happening. She was plunging and scraping now, sticking him wherever she could make contact; his arms, his ribs, his chest, and Erroll White cried out with each wound. As Erroll and Pause fought, Kelly was knocked off the bed and went crashing to the floor in a heap. Kelly crab-crawled away until her back hit the wall where she watched in horror as the battle unfolded. Pause moved in frenzy, seemingly possessed, inflicting serious damage to Erroll White's body but he kept grabbing at her. Pause struck again and again, each strike eliciting a pained curse but within seconds, he had wounds all over his body. He responded in desperation. Reaching out he snatched Pause in a bear hug and squeezed. Pause was surprised at the strength of Erroll White as the air was suddenly forced from her body. They were chest to chest when Pause twisted her upper body, which created enough space for her to reach over his shoulder and plunge the stiletto so deeply into his back that she lost her grip when Erroll White flung her to the floor. He collapsed facefirst on the bed, screaming in pain with the handle of the weapon sticking out of his back. Pause jumped back off the bed, her chest heaving from the fight. She looked on in disbelief when Erroll White reached back and grasped the handle of the knife. He screamed in pain as he slowly pulled, and the thin blade of the stiletto came out inch by inch. Erroll White flung the dagger away and flipped over onto his back. Puncture wounds speckled his chest, arms, and neck where Pause had hit him with quick, deep strikes yet, strangely, there was no blood pouring from the wounds. He pulled himself to an upright position, each movement rocked his body with pain, and his chest heaved with each ragged breath he took. But when he looked at Pause, his eyes widened in anger. He swung his feet over the side of the bed to the floor. "You bitch!" He roared and lunged toward her.

A sinister smile crossed her face as Pause took a step back, waiting, as Erroll White staggered toward her; she was ready for him. When he stumbled within range, Pause executed a perfect sidekick, her heel catching him squarely between his legs. The color drained from Erroll White's face as he sunk to his knees, frozen in pain, when suddenly blood began to ooze out of the many holes that Pause had inflicted upon him with the stiletto. His dark, red, life fluid began to stream from his body as if it were a tube of toothpaste that had been punctured in a hundred different places and then squeezed by a giant hand. Finally, his body trembled and he collapsed to the floor; his last breath was a watery gasp.

Kelly sat with her back against the wall, watching the horrific scene unfold in front of her. A thin wail escaped her lips as she sat there shaking her head and looking fearfully at Pause. She opened her mouth to scream but when their eyes met, the protest died in her throat. Pause moved closer to her.

"Kelly." Pause reached her hand out to her sister. "It's me."

Kelly's eyes darted wildly around the room, from Pause to the dead man to the carnage that was evident in the cheap motel room. When Pause called her name, Kelly's head snapped around in response, but she quickly looked down at the floor and began mumbling. "Oh god! I promise! Promise! Promise!"

"Kelly," Pause repeated softly. "It's me. Eva." Pause moved forward, taking special care to avoid leaving footprints in Erroll White's blood. She stepped over his body to her sister who was still huddled in fear with tears now streaming down her face. "It's me, Kelly. Eva. Look at me."

Pause slowly knelt down in front of Kelly, drawing her eyes from the dead body lying in the middle of the room. She took her wig off and threw it on the floor so that Kelly could see her face. This was a crucial moment for Pause, a risky situation, because she didn't know what Kelly's reaction would be to what she had just witnessed.

"I've been looking for you for so long," Pause said. "I knew we would find each other! I knew it! And we have, Kelly. We have. You went away. I know why you had to go away but I missed you so much. One day, I came home and my big sister was gone and I was all alone. All by myself. I'm sorry that you had to leave, Kelly. So sorry."

Confusion seemed to wage a war inside of Kelly as her eyes darted from Pause to the body sprawled across the floor with blood spreading in a pool around him. Her mouth worked spasmodically before she finally let loose with a terrified scream.

Pause jumped to her feet and swung her fist, punching Kelly and smashing her head against the wall, effectively knocking her out. Her body slumped to the floor and was still.

YOU SWEAT, YOU LIVE

He was going to have to be careful with that stuff, that Feenin. Having a modicum of control was of the utmost importance to Bossman, and he would never let any drug overcome his drive or threaten his well being. Harmful urges, the lusts of life, had been purged from his mind since the day he had become bull-headed and tightened his sphincter to the point where only air threatened to escape. No drug could change that.

But the Feenin was a strangely beautiful lady crying out in the night. She had beckoned him to the skies as the plane touched down, and he had risen from his seat and raised his arms to the heavens—he could fly! The flight attendant had brought him back down, breaking the siren-call of the beautiful lady, when she had said in a strange voice, "Are you okay, Sir?"

"Just stretching," he had answered without turning to face her.

Bossman walked down State Street among the tall, government buildings that seemed to have been designed with squares and transparency in mind. He turned south on Madison Avenue. The twin towers of the plaza loomed before him. They were big, blue structures of glass and steel that stretched across a four-lane street, connected by an overhead tunnel that funneled the privileged to and fro, eliminating the need to mingle with regular folk. A testament to money and the ego it sometimes bred.

Soon, Bossman contemplated, he would get himself an office on one of the higher floors—a huge one with a bathroom and a bedroom. A nice little spot to entertain women. Perhaps help enhance their performance. The thought excited him. He decided to go downtown and get himself a hooker after the meeting. The sixteenth floor would be an ideal location to live that life. Bossman knew, his instincts screamed, that the Feenin would explode. The same way that it exploded inside his brain when he had tried it. All of his blood had rushed out of him and into some secret place and in its stead, his heart had pumped pleasure, physical euphoria all over his body. Of course, his mind had to shift to an altered reality to handle such bliss and, amazingly, it landed on a spiritual plane that was parallel with his vibrating self. Bossman shook his head in wonder at the memory and thought, *it's a good thing I'm not hooked on that shit.*

On the fifteenth floor of the Plaza was the office of Way Jalon, the man who waited for Bossman to deliver the disks with the formula encoded on them. Way Jalon was money, old money, untouchable and defined by the power that went along with that stature. The Jalon fortune reached back in time to the Schuylers and Cornings—wealth that spanned generations and became imbedded by history into the very soil of Albany, New York. The Jalon family made its fortune in everything from shipping—hauling slave cargo—and moving forward into the prosperous heyday of the city's industrial revolution to its modern-day ownership of a multitude of companies. There were stories of the founding father, William Jalon, that told of a ruthless and devious man who eschewed honor for money. It seemed to be a trait that was passed down through generations to Way Jalon.

Bossman knew the old badger was up there now, staring out of that glass wall of his. Every time that Bossman had been to Way Jalon's office, the self-proclaimed King of the City was always standing in front of that glass, staring out. Bossman imagined pulling him back to earth and then taking his place on the pedestal reserved for the powerful.

Rows of people crowded the street leading up to the huge, glass doors that accessed the concourse of the Plaza. Bossman plowed along with them down under the archway and on through the wall of glass doors that led into the Plaza concourse. He strode directly to the elevators and waited, looking up at the glowing numbers as the elevators went from floor to floor, all four of them avoiding the bottom landing.

The plane ride coasted into his thoughts.

Bossman had left John Zabriski dead in first class, with his seat belt securely buckled. He had made his getaway, leisurely checked through Customs and escaped to his waiting car. Zabriski had been a foolish man. He actually had believed that Bossman wasn't aware of the existence of the disks or the information encoded upon them. To add insult to injury, the poor man had the audacity to keep the disks in his possession. On him! Sometimes the smartest people—the brainiacs—could do the dumbest things. Zabriski had downloaded the information onto disks three days ago. Bossman had had him under surveillance for the previous five days. It had been too easy to take everything from him...his disks and his life.

Feenin had that effect. Feenin, that's what Zabriski had called it. It made the mind lazy. It was very disconcerting. One dose and there was a hot, sexy flash followed by an agitating hunger that would explode into tiny, bursting emotions. And it was all good. Bossman had caught sensitivity by the tail, saddled it and went splattering in every direction.

Yes. Bossman knew.

Ten minutes after Zabriski had gasped into death, curiosity had toyed with Bossman, challenged him into a gray zone, a no-man's land, a "sometimes" place where some people sometimes went and sometimes never returned. Bossman had popped one of the pills and took a trip without the luggage. His first journey sent him soaring to the north and he went for miles and miles before he returned, regretfully, to his body. Another pill...and Bossman raced west. He went east. South. Southeast. Northsouth. Westsouth. Bossman went every which way before the plane touched down. But when they landed, he didn't take another. There were still a few pills left in the bottle in his pocket.

The elevator arrived and when the door slid open, Bossman piled in with the crush of people who jammed themselves inside. He wouldn't touch the Feenin again, he resolved, because he could control his primal urges. Those destructive whims that tended to deprive the sane of what should be theirs. His iron will, his drive, was the reason he was Bossman.

The car stopped at the fifteenth floor and Bossman wedged his wide body toward the door. He occupied looming space as he moved forward. His presence preceded his mass as the other passengers turned and twisted to give him room to exit. A determined demeanor furrowed his brow, a single-mindedness that hid his intellectual capability. He stepped from the elevator and turned to his right, passing the doorways of buzzing secretaries and vain, male drones.

Bossman snorted. They were nothing to him. College-educated and alumni-appointed with no real purpose in life. They were plodders, trudging from day to day, watching the grand picture of life on a two inch screen. They had no power. Power was the thing buried deep in Bossman's pocket. Computer disks with numbers and symbols, inscribed with a formula that might soon change the world.

He stopped at beveled glass doors that announced that these were the offices of Way Jalon, president of Jalon Holdings. Bossman stepped into a large room. A secretary sat behind a small desk at the farthest point from the door. She looked up at Bossman and reached for the phone. She mouthed a few words into the receiver, hung up and spoke to Bossman.

"Mr. Jalon will see you now." She indicated the huge wooden doors behind her. Bossman passed her without a glance and went inside.

Way Jalon stood in a far corner of his office, looking out of a huge wall of glass that overlooked the city, his back to Bossman. The office was rich. There was a wet bar to the left of Way Jalon, fully stocked, Bossman noted, which stood facing a set of futons that looked like a year's salary. The futons were plush, with big, stuffed cushions surrounded by leather. They each sat across from a lavish, high-backed, wooden chair that was obviously reserved for the great Way Jalon, a simple reminder of exactly who ran the ship, an unspoken confirmation of who held the reins of power. There were also two huge doors on that side of the room. Bossman had never seen them open nor had he ever seen anyone allowed past them. He wondered what secrets those rooms held.

When Way Jalon turned to face Bossman, a hint of a smile tugged at the corners of his mouth.

"How was your flight?" he asked.

"Successful," Bossman said simply.

"So," Way Jalon motioned to a chair facing the desk in the center of the room while he took his seat behind it, "can we proceed with the operation?"

"Absolutely," Bossman said as he settled into the hard, wooden chair.

Way Jalon was old money, what Bossman considered unearned income, accompanied by unearned respect. Way rose from his chair and strode over to the wet bar while Bossman took a moment to consider his new partner. Bossman saw an Armani suit, tailored to fit a forty-something-year-old back. A businessman with a cloying ability to smell where the money was to be made and a ruthless demeanor that would serve them both well. Here was a man who had transcended mere money and taken the giant step to magnate.

They had reached an agreement of mistrust immediately.

"Drink?" Way Jalon offered.

"No thanks."

Way Jalon came back with a Scotch in a fluted snifter and took his seat.

"So," he began, "where are we now?"

"I have the disks," Bossman replied. "That's my end of it. From this point forward there are only two players. You and I. There will never be a third party present whenever we meet. Acceptable?"

"Absolutely."

"Good. Is distribution in place?"

"On request. All that remains is the manufacture of the product." Way took a sip of his drink and waited.

Bossman paused but finally reached inside his pocket and produced the disks.

"Everything you need is on here." Bossman passed the disks across the desk. "I think we have a winner here. The profit will surpass your wildest dreams. That is, if this endeavor is handled correctly."

Way Jalon held the disks with the reverence of gold.

"There are two things that I never do," he said. "One is dream; the other is fail. That's where you come in. I need you to spearhead the day-to-day operations."

Bossman shot forward in his seat. This wasn't part of the deal, but Way Jalon stopped him with a raised finger.

"Don't worry. You will not have any official capacity. Your name will never appear on any books, anywhere. I want to minimize mistakes and maximize profits both quickly and quietly. You have a vested interest in this venture which should ensure your motivation and provide me with a degree of insurance also."

Bossman regarded Way Jalon with the suspicious eye of a trapped rat who suddenly realizes that there is no way out of a gilded snare.

"Is that really necessary?" Bossman asked.

"It's imperative."

"Well, I don't think it is."

"It's really quite simple," Way began. "You see, I don't trust people who have nothing to lose. Someone who has no reason to sweat will never be cognizant of the real value of water. No water, no life."

Way Jalon paused to look Bossman in the eye. "You sweat, you live."

"That's all well and good, philosophically," Bossman replied. "But in realistic terms, I don't know if you've ever experienced a sweaty emotion in your entire lifetime, so I question your method."

Bossman looked around the lavish office at the expensive frills and perks and privileges before he spoke.

"But I don't question your abilities. Or the results you achieve. Let's make progress."

"You'll find that 'progress' is a pseudonym for success," Way Jalon said. "At least in my realm of expertise. My expertise...my knowledge...is what you need. It's what my fifty percent of this arrangement is costing you. So let me inform you of what you are paying for. Our success is dependent upon blind obedience. Specifically, your blind obedience, your ability to carry out any objective that I issue. No questions asked. Secondly, and this is of major importance, is that you must never let yourself become vulnerable to anyone or anything."

Way Jalon drained the remainder of his drink and walked over to the bar to pour another. He half-turned to speak to Bossman.

"Obviously, if a situation develops where you become a pawn to another, then you become my albatross and I simply cannot allow that."

Bossman watched intently as Way returned to his seat with his drink.

"If that happens, rest assured, you will go down in flames," Way Jalon finished, leaving no doubt about his warning. Bossman leaned back in his chair with unworried ease.

"But you know," he began, "anyone can catch fire and burn. Even you."

Way Jalon leaned forward. "So we have an agreement?"

"Agreed."

"Then let's move forward," Way replied. "This is how we move into the rarefied air of tax-free millions…"

Approximately one hour later Bossman made his way out of the Plaza with a grudging respect for Way Jalon's business acumen and a gnawing suspicion that he had just jumped from the frying pan headlong into the fire.

TEN LETTERS

Way Jalon stood by the window, looking out over his city. The window ran the entire length of one wall of his office on the fifteenth floor of the Plaza. The glass, clear and thick, was tinted blue by its width. Strong and safe, it would almost hold up to the force of a bullet. This was just one of the perks granted to him as one of the most powerful men in the city. There had been problems with the construction. The glass wasn't up to code—it wasn't nearly thick enough, but Way Jalon could change codes. ZIP codes, if necessary. So he had his wall.

Way Jalon was a man of success, a descendant of wealth. The first Jalon touched the shores of New York along with the Schuylers and Livingstons and Van Rensselaers. William Jalon came up the Hudson River by boat and straggled off the pier into the woods. He walked up to the biggest tree he could find and flung his arms as far around the thick trunk as he could. He looked skyward and proclaimed, "You are all mine!"

Way Jalon paused to reflect on his family's history, a city's history for all intents and purposes. He looked through the glass to the south. Downtown, past North Pearl Street, exit ramps looped up into the sky over the Hudson River and came down in East Greenbush and Rensselaer. The long and winding river snaked narrowly between Albany and the eastern side of the state at this juncture before it wiggled and twisted its way down to New York City.

Way could almost see William Jalon embracing a huge birch tree while anointing himself king. That birch tree would become part of the first ship

William Jalon put underway. William Jalon amassed a fortune in a hurry, beginning with shipping, transporting anything that fit on board. He built whaling ships that operated out of Hudson, a small town that thrived from the fishing industry.

From there, William Jalon prospered. As his fortune grew he began to hunger for something more. Power. He wanted a city. He wanted his name stamped on a map. He spent the rest of his life gobbling up anything money could buy and destroying what it couldn't in his drive to rule over all.

William Jalon bestowed his dream upon his two sons, Seth and Blaize, who carried it on wholeheartedly. The two brothers stepped their father's goals up to a new level. They dreamed bigger. They were industrious and greedy—an effective combination—and together they reached into the guts of the workingman's life, via politics and pocketbooks. They bought mayors, they shaped laws and enforced their bottom line. Their whims became facts—laws that had force every day on every street in Albany.

They had what they wanted but they still yearned for more.

The Jalon brothers kissed fate when they stumbled into the slave trade. They had an abundant fleet that could move the human cargo quickly and efficiently, which led them to open offices in every state on the East Coast.

The Jalon brothers raked the money in by the shipload, and the legacy grew as it was passed from generation to generation, down to the present Jalon: Way.

Way Jalon wanted to add his own chapter to the story.

The glass wall was indicative of his stature, as was his office. It was huge. Bigger than some homes, and at times Way had spent weeks on end there. There was a bed in a comfortable-sized room through a set of double oak doors adjacent to a fully-stocked wet bar in the far corner. An assemblage of two futons and a high-backed wooden chair sat directly across from the bar, which was where Way Jalon negotiated his most important business matters. Over drinks, drugs, women...whatever it took, terms were set and agreements were made there. In front of the window-wall sat a huge desk. A small, uncomfortable chair faced the desk, a seat for his subjects as they came begging favors. The entrance to his office stood some fifteen feet away over a solitary expanse of carpet. It was a horribly long and lonely distance to cover, a walk which gave Way a chance to intimidate the peasants by staring intently at them as they approached his kingly throne. He usually had a plan in mind before they reached him, and as he extended his hand to greet them, he had already decided their fate.

The window-wall afforded Way Jalon the chance to oversee what he owned, his land, his empire. Way saw the big picture, which was why he needed a big window. His vision was wide, panoramic, encompassing large pieces of the puzzle that smaller-minded people failed to grasp, even if he glued it to their fingers. But the pieces always fit. His many businesses spread over the city like a suffocating blanket, but Way knew that he alone was the only man who could make it breathe. With but a touch and a command.

But Way felt the urge to go higher. Scale bigger mountains. So naturally he couldn't let this opportunity slip by. Not on his life. This was going to be pure, worldwide power. Feenin. A drug so new it wasn't illegal yet, and by the time it became a crime to use it, its destructive effects would be evident and its momentum too strong to stop. And Feenin didn't cost much to manufacture. The expense had been cut down to almost fifty-five cents per pound! Way Jalon introduced the Feenin to the world, well, not the world, but to a test market of drug users, at fifteen dollars a pop, thereby undercutting the twenty-dollar cost of crack, and the fiends came running. And it was surprising to identify some of the worst fiends. The affluent were expected. The poor, again, were expected. But the middle ground was terrible. Terrible eyes. Terrible needs. Wonderful money.

Feenin was hot. It had spread beyond the sample users like wildfire and now Way Jalon had to adjust and move his plan slightly ahead of schedule. Positive adjustments were easy for him to accommodate and a joy to implement. He sometimes whistled while he did this work.

Way Jalon smiled out the window-wall and thought, *I have their lives!* He turned from the wall of glass and looked down at the sheet of paper on his desk. A name was scribbled on it that represented the first squashed bug that he would step on as he climbed to the top. His mind pointed and counter-pointed any difficulties that might arise from that hastily scrawled name. He had left nothing to chance. Everything and everyone connected to that name was a bit in the data banks of Way's brain. The name was a man, and the man is an animal. The male animal was the most difficult to predict when no rules and regulations existed. When the male animal sensed the absence of protocol, his whim became law and the consequence became survival of the fittest. His very ferocity toward life made him the most unpredictable and wildest in his own jungle.

While Way Jalon had a grudging respect for the man behind the name— those people surely had courage—it was a respect tinged with animosity. Way glanced at the huge oak doors next to the wet bar. He kept his anger there, behind closed doors where his expression could be free. A forbidden room that housed a haunting portion of his legacy, handed down through generation in hushed tones and kept alive by its legitimacy. Way shared his secret with no one and guarded it with fervency. Entrance through those doors was prohibited and no mistakes of entry were tolerated.

Way thought about the man who would become a part of the legacy. The ten letters. Yet there was no room in his regard for any type of under-estimation. Herbert Mulne had held the man in low esteem, and had paid with his life. Not that Way attached any significance to the intellect of Herbert Mulne, known as Five-O to the criminal element that he moved amongst. He was a greedy, unimaginative little man whom Way had known since his college days. Herbert's pathetic, little intellect had ended up on a cop's payroll, stealing and swiping when he could, while Way had gone on to amass a fortune. Herbert had thought he was untouchable, because he was a cop, but he had paid the devil's fortune. Years of payoffs; taking drug dealers' money before sending them to jail; physically abusing the defenseless; just to let off steam, had all come back to visit him and left him lifeless. He had been found dead beside his car on someone's lawn. How appropriate.

Way hadn't really liked Herbert but he didn't need to. They conducted business with a mutual disrespect and a harsh dislike for one another, yet they got things done. Herbert had come through again with the delivery of this man, the ten letters that were spelled out across the paper on Way's desk. Way looked down again. This guy was perfect. He would take a big fall and be speechless, defenseless and completely dumbfounded when he heard the giant splat.

Way had a plan. First, Way intended to remove the man from his habitat, his element, get him away from the ghetto. Take him, body and soul, from his lifestyle of bleakness and hopelessness to a morning of roses and fresh pussy and watch his instincts fall away with the finality of a warm death. Way would attack the animal at the base of his confidence, at his very existence. His strength.

Way stared at the name. It was an important component of the plan.

Phase One included appointing this man as the head of operations and distribution of Stoneway Incorporated, unaware that he would be a high-tech drug dealer with all the trimmings...and all of the accountability.

Phase Two involved preparing the Feenin for nationwide distribution. Way had converted two warehouses into labs in order to manufacture the drug in massive quantities if needed and they were up and running. Since only two labs were in production, distribution was an integral component of the operation, a vital part, and there was no room for miscalculations.

Way had decided to go all out. He would move the product in massive quantities by every available means—trucks, planes, couriers—and he would even do a few special deliveries. At the moment Feenin had a not-illegal status, no laws were being broken. But that loophole wouldn't stay open long and Way Jalon had to be prepared for the sly manipulation of the law. Authority didn't really apply to him. No court could hold him, but it could be so predictable that it could often create surprise out of the mundane. Ask O.J. He had escaped the monotonous long arm of the law with a painful backhand to the face of America, with a force that stung, aimed at its unjust justice system.

Way Jalon read the name again. Ten letters. He counted his at worse; he only had eight letters. Maybe, Way figured, he should use someone else. Someone like Chris Rock, or maybe Clarence Thomas...Nooo! That would be too easy. These ten letters had heart. His story was one of sheer determination. His man had started selling drugs at the age of seventeen, in the streets all hours of the night, and yet he had still managed to graduate near the top of his class in high school. His parents were nowhere to be found but he survived, utterly alone, as he moved with direction into college. What Way Jalon found amazing was that the young man had never been caught. He had absolutely no criminal record, not even a misdemeanor charge. At the university, the young man seemed to surge even higher. He went through college as if he had caught the tail of a tiger, tearing through four years at one of the best universities in the state. His nightlife remained the same, however; he sold drugs to the drugged.

That was where Herbert had found him. On a street corner selling drugs. Herbert had done a background check and brought him to Way Jalon's attention. Now that Herbert Mulne was dead, Way had to carry out the remainder of his plan himself. He would have to meet the target and offer him the biggest break of his life, a chance to move into a higher tax bracket. Way hated to get personally involved but this time it was unavoidable. The fewer people involved, the better.

Way Jalon would take this man.

Studies proved that he couldn't stand. For anything! The numbers were there and statistics are the basis of reality. A professional baseball player who can hit three out of every ten pitches is hitting three hundred percent. Miss seven out of ten balls and make millions. It's all basis.

Numbers don't lie.

There are more African-American men in America's prisons than there are in America's colleges.

They wear numbers.

In this great country of his, a Negro has never been counted among the fifty richest people in the nation.

Not one.

Most black people wore handcuffs on the evening news.

Nightly.

Way Jalon would take this man.

When he had briefed Bossman on the architecture of the operation, its two levels— legal and illegal—he hadn't told him about this man. He saw no reason to mention it. Strike one on Bossman.

Way Jalon would use one business to power the other. Nationwide, if necessary.

Stoneway Incorporated would have its hand in everything. From stationery—letters packed with Feenin—to grain—trucks designed to carry flour would instead be loaded with white pills. The culprit of Stoneway Incorporated had already been hand picked and investigated. He was perfect. A former drug dealer with a college education. Someone who could always be pointed at with an accusing finger. Way picked the piece of paper off the desk and smiled at the name, scrawled there, like fate. Ten letters.

The first five read, T-O-K-U-S.

SNAPSHOT

The blinking light of his private line caught Way's eye. He reached for the phone expecting to hear a familiar voice. "Way," he said into the mouthpiece.

"Pause," a female voice answered.

Pause was a sexy, sick woman. Her beauty, the deep blue eyes that held men stiff, the sensual figure that moved with the promise of a pleasure pulled slowly from deep within and the powerful air of femininity that she wore like expensive perfume, was truly beguiling. She wore her long, blond hair in a variety of styles, each appealing and complementing a face that held the eye just a fraction of a second longer than the libido needed. What she was blessed with on the outside only hid the curse that bred inside of her. She was a cold-hearted, twisted killer behind a stiffened, skin-toned mask. She was the perfect assassin...with a deadly smile. Way thought it best to keep her at a distance. That was why she was one of the few people allowed to use his private line. Pause affected him. She disrupted his mind with lust. It was a craving Way recognized and knew there was no controlling, so he dealt with her over the phone as much as possible.

"What have you found?" Way asked. Sounds of street traffic droned in the background so he knew she was at a pay phone. Pause preferred public phones. She felt she could speak freely in the open spaces they provided.

Way Jalon had assigned Pause to watch Bossman. Way was suspicious by nature, but in Bossman he saw an especially evil intent which always led to downfall. Besides, anyone who dared to attempt to play on an even field with Way became a target of ill will. Way considered himself a polished professional and Bossman a complete brute. An animal. And like any beast, Way figured, he would be intoxicated by physical sensations—be it booze, drugs, skydiving, fire-walking…whatever. Bossman would live through the rush, the glow of feeling, the joy of pleasure and plunge headlong into the next kaleidoscope of tingles, flushed with excitement and looking for more. Now Way's intuition was proving true.

She had been watching him for the past two days and this was her first report. Pause was a heavy hitter. Insidiously psychotic, she loved to hit things and make them die. He had hired her many times.

"You and Bossman must have a really sweet deal," she said. Way heard the loud squeal of a big vehicle braking to a stop.

"And that concerns you?" Way demanded. She was overstepping.

"It's just that Bossman has been on a drugging and whoring binge since I got on him," Pause answered. "I figured you sent him to drugs and whores, whores and drugs until he dropped."

"Did he drop?" Way asked hopefully.

"No," Pause answered. "But he does talk quite a bit. Hold on." Way listened as Pause growled at someone.

"No!"

"I can tell! I see you!" Way heard a feminine voice exclaim.

"I said, 'no'!" Pause repeated.

"I just wanted to meet you. We can do it," the voice pled.

"If you don't get the fuck away from me, I'll hurt you! Now fuck off!" Pause returned, "Okay."

Here it comes, Way thought. The real reason Pause had buzzed him on his urgent private line, the real situation that would probably result in the setting free of someone's soul. Strike two, Bossman.

"What is he talking about?" Way asked.

"I caught up to the hooker Bossman had last night and I paid her to do me. Afterwards, I asked her about Bossman. She said he liked to get high. She said he had some different kind of drug…not cocaine. It looked like cocaine but she knew a coke high and this wasn't it. It felt different, tasted different when it drained back down her nostrils into her mouth. But when Bossman snorted it, he got freaky deaky on her. She said they were rutting like animals. He put her on top and grabbed her by the ass and just started poking up in her and grunting and friction and she thought he started barking, so she started barking and…"

"Get to the point, will you!" Psychotic bitch, Way thought.

"Well, *I* enjoyed the moment," Pause said. "Anyway, she said that right in the middle of the rutting, Bossman would stop bucking and start talking. He told her about this new drug called Feenin and about how it was coming soon to a theater near you. And if she had a snapper, if her sex was good enough, she could clamp it onto his rod and ride to the top with him."

Way didn't even think about it.

"Take him," he ordered.

Pause gasped with joy.

"But I don't want a mess on this one," he amended. Pause could sometimes get carried away with her work. "Don't let it come back on us. And make sure the police never find a trace of the Feenin. The product isn't ready for public exposure. Clear?"

Pause hesitated. Way waited patiently, listening to the street sounds that seeped from the city into the phone to his ear. He knew Pause had trouble with orders that required restraint.

"Clear?" Way repeated.

"Clear," she sighed.

"And Pause? Try to be gentle," Way added oddly.

"Like a snapshot," came the reply.

"While you're at it, take out the whore, too."

"Already did," Pause answered before she hung up.

SIMPLETON BRICK

Way strode confidently through the halls of the university up to Convention Hall in time to watch the newest crop of graduates cross the stage. He had a singular purpose for being there, a grand design that had caused him to leave his office and ride the long stretch of Washington Avenue to the university—to observe Tokus Stone. Tokus Stone needed to be handled personally and delicately, gently steered and manipulated. Way Jalon left nothing to chance.

As diplomas were being handed out, Way came through the huge double doors and stood off to the side, watching and listening, amused as the gaiety of the event hovered thickly in the air. A celebration bubbled slightly under the surface of the moment, waiting for a signal to vent itself late into the night. The smiles of happiness would fade into oblivion if those young people knew of the harsh jungle they were entering. A wilderness with teeth, for some, while others would ascend mountains, but each would come at a cost that would leave deep, serpentine marks. After all, a diploma was just a piece of paper that hung unread on the office wall.

"Tokus Stone," an amplified voice announced.

Out stepped the object of Way's desire. Way put Tokus at about six feet, two inches tall, approximately two hundred pounds. Two-ten maybe. His face held a rugged determination that suggested graduation was only the beginning, that the stage he walked across was the starting line, not the finish. There was no hint of the foolish joy that was usually exhibited at a moment like this. None of the dancing and yelling that the other graduates saved for center stage. This was just a secondary triumph. He knows, Way mused. He knows that society is out there, waiting for him with a blindfold in one hand and a dagger in the other, smiling.

Soon, they would meet face-to-face.

After the caps were tossed into the air and the crowd had settled into a reasonable hubbub of excited activity, Way Jalon searched the throng for his quarry. He spotted Tokus standing alone in a far corner of the auditorium and began nudging people aside as he made a beeline in that direction.

Way cornered Tokus and greeted him with congratulations.

"Mr. Stone, may I be the first to add my 'well done' to your list of accomplishments." He offered his hand.

Tokus looked at him, surprised, recovered and shook his hand firmly. "Thank you."

"Mr. Stone," Way continued. "My name is Way Jalon, president of Jalon Holdings…I'm sure you've heard the name before. I'm here to make you an offer."

Tokus turned his full gaze upon the distinguished-looking man who stood before him. An air of money and power clung to him, those things no longer a privilege but a birthright.

"My company, Jalon Holdings, has been watching your progress at the University for the past two years, and we were impressed with your tenacity and decision-making. Your degree is well-earned. Your grades are excellent, and you have the presence of leadership that, combined with a thinking man's ability, impressed us greatly."

"Well…" Tokus seemed at a loss. "Thank you."

"Combine those talents with another factor that we require and you are, by far, our best candidate."

"What factor is that?"

"You are a black man."

Tokus rocked back, his eyes narrowed. He looked Way Jalon in the eye before he answered.

"The blackness is a plus, huh?"

"Yes." Way looked at Tokus. "I'm sure you have some idea of the complex world of high finance, it's high pressure, high income, and immensely diverse. Indeed, it is mostly a separate entity from the rest of the world. It's also very, very exclusive."

Way paused importantly, measuring his words with a casualty that belied his purpose.

"You see, Tokus, even in the rarefied air of the 'haves,' we are still subject to the whims of public opinion, the 'have nots.' Affirmative action is one of those flights of fancy. So we comply. In our concession, however, we have only one certainty that allows us to proceed with surety. That certainty is ability. Your ability, Tokus. As I said, we've been watching you and we are quite sure that you have what it takes to get the job done."

Tokus was silent.

"Listen," Way continued. "Tonight is your night to celebrate and I've taken up enough of your time, so here's my card. I'll be expecting to hear from you soon. You come to my office and we'll talk more."

Tokus took the business card and put it in his pocket.

Way extended his hand to Tokus. "Once again, congratulations."

Tokus shook his hand firmly and looked him in the eye. "I appreciate your candor. And I'll give this a lot of thought."

"That's all I can ask." Way smiled, turned and walked away.

T'Challa and Doria, with Monday in tow, passed Way as they approached Tokus.

T'Challa looked into Way's eyes and felt the frost of privileged insensitivity bred by voluntary isolation from a warm, passionate world. Instinctively, he reached for Monday as they walked toward Tokus. Doria rushed into Tokus' arms with a big hug. "You did it," she cried. "You made it."

"Was that the man?" T'Challa asked, indicating the retreating figure of Way Jalon.

"He offered me a job," Tokus replied.

"You da man!" Monday squealed. Tokus squatted so that he was eye level with his nephew.

"No, you da man!"

"You da man!"

"No, you da man!"

"UH-UH. You. Da. Man!"

Tokus extended his fist toward the little boy.

"Slap my hand, black soul man," he said. They tapped fists and Monday rushed into his arms. T'Challa detected a tear in his brother's eye before Tokus released his son. T'Challa was surprised at how quickly Doria and Monday had accepted Tokus as part of the family. Tokus seemed so genuine in his feelings toward them with his yearning for a family, that when the affection was returned, it all seemed like a natural fit.

"You gonna take the job?" T'Challa asked.

"Maybe."

"The man."

"Yeah. You felt it, too?"

"What kinda job did he offer?" T'Challa asked.

"We didn't get into specifics," Tokus said. "It wasn't an official interview."

"The man," T'Challa repeated.

"Yeah," Tokus agreed. "But he was kinda straight with me. He needs a token black to balance his ledger."

T'Challa mulled that one over for a minute.

"Just don't let him hit you in the head with a simpleton brick," he advised.

"That's not possible," Tokus replied.

"Remember, they don't have to play you," T'Challa said. "But they can play everybody around you like a Milli Vanilli song and then drop you like a bad bag of dope."

"True that," Tokus replied. "True that."

A PAUSE CAN KILL

Bossman was high. High on life. Greed. Pleasure. And Feenin.

Every time he used Feenin he discovered new attributes that elated him with wonder. Dollar signs floated past his twisted, bloodshot eyes—so many that he had stopped counting hours ago.

Bossman had a bag of powdered Feenin on the nightstand next to the bed. He had gotten it from a warehouse that had been converted for the production of Feenin. It was coming out of there by the pound. Any day now they would be going into full distribution and the windfall would be large. He was sampling large amounts of the drug on a daily basis; an ounce here, an ounce there. He didn't have to answer to anyone and his jaded eyes could spy success, looming on the horizon.

Way Jalon had chosen well when he decided to manufacture Feenin in a row of warehouses that moved product constantly. Every day, all day, huge trucks would leave the many buildings carrying all manner of Feenin-packed merchandise. The shipments took place on a fairly, normal business day, on a fairly normal schedule.

He felt a movement next to him in the huge, canopied bed that was part of the honeymoon suite he had reserved. The room was huge and elegant. Bossman wondered what the rest of the suite looked like. He had taken the woman from the door directly to the bed without a glance in either direction and taken her warm body until it glowed as red hot as he was.

He felt the girl next to him stir. Bossman stirred, too, when his mind replayed the things this girl—what is her name?—had done to him last night.

"Mmmm," she purred as she reached for Bossman. He smiled at her and reached over to the nightstand for the bag of granulated Feenin and scooped some up his nose. Two sniffs sped to his brain and everything opened. He had an idea.

The girl was sitting up now, her eyes aglitter and focused on the freakish substance.

"Let's do what we did," she pouted, "last night."

"No," Bossman said. "Let's go a little higher." His pupils were turning strangely vertical, straight up and down, as he eyed the girl anew, wondering where he had gotten her but ecstatic that he had her. She was thick, like a black woman—breasts standing proud, hips, waist, ass, all pliable and plush.

"Are you sure you don't have any nigger in you, girl?" He reached under the covers and cupped her ass.

"No," she answered. She looked at Bossman, then at the bag in his hand and back at him again.

"So what do you think about my product?" Bossman asked the girl. "How do you like it?"

"What is it?"

"I call it Feenin. It's synthetic. I made it myself. It's fucking great, isn't it? I even like it myself. But unlike the junk that's out there now, this substance doesn't damage your body. There are no side effects."

He paused to scoop a tiny spoonful out of the bag, and waited with his hand in midair.

"It comes in powdered form, liquid or 'rocked' into pill form. But for you…" Bossman put the spoon over his pubic hair and tapped the powder out. He continued, "It can be ingested, smoked or sniffed." The spoon came out of the bag again as the girl went into action, her tongue eagerly darting here and there in his hair, then on him. Bossman sniffed the powder and relaxed as he watched her work. Inch by inch, warm friction enveloped him and from there she worked by feel and instinct. She moved slowly, carefully and smoothly, pausing to get every speck of the soft, white powder. Finally, she seemed satisfied that it was all gone, and with a sensuous stare, she began a touching crawl up to his chest. The feel of her skin on his bare flesh pulsed wherever she touched and when she kissed him, her tongue demanded submission. She traced her tongue over his lips.

"Bitchin,'" Bossman whispered, smiling at the girl who sat astride him. "You will be gentle with me, right?"

"If you are," she replied.

"I'll hold you to that."

Bossman dipped the spoon again and brought it to her nose. She took the hit. Bossman snorted the rest in one shot. She paused a moment, waiting for her brain to ignite, and when it did, she smiled and reached back to guide Bossman inside her. Once inside, Bossman went deep, but only once as he grabbed her around the waist and held her there. She groaned and bit his shoulder, leaving a mark. She started sucking the mark. Then they rocked. Slowly. Gently. Bossman felt her sheer walls come tumbling down like Jericho and the speed of her hips start moving much faster than "gentle." He had to slow her down. He grabbed her by both ass cheeks and held her motionless. His fingers sank into the firm, round lobes, and he couldn't help but linger there a moment. The urge for a nipple crept upon him and soon his lips found one. He kneaded and nibbled. Sucked and licked. He looked up at her and said, "Now this is foreplay," before returning to his milking post. She placed her hand on the back of his head and guided him with squeezes and taps and rubs. Bossman leaned back and peered between their bodies and watched, enraptured by the clash of the sexes. A hard, moist, warm exchange that brought an inkling. The inkling tripped an alarm inside him. She swayed and plunged on top of him; she was on fire. Inside. A fire that twisted in a circular urgency. Her muscles gripped him with a lustful, hot crush.

Suddenly, Bossman felt red, hot flame rushing from his stomach back up his throat. He coughed and felt the burn whistling in his nasal cavity, past his eardrums and straight to his brain. The girl began to gag. Her lustful cries became agonizing fits of convulsions as she sat atop Bossman and dug her fingernails into his neck. Bossman mouthed a "What the…" But the words came out in a fetid rush of dead air. His heart began beating in jackhammer sequence and his body tightened. Immobility seized him, except for the staccato tics of a retarded spasm, and bile rushed to the back of his mouth with every burst of his speeding heart. His bowels released. His last thought before dying was of what he had lost. His money, not his life.

vvv

A dark, slim figure darted into Bossman's hotel room, quietly closing the door behind her, listening for any sounds, and watching for any movement. When satisfied that nothing was stirring, the figure moved softly to the nightstand at the side of the bed. A shaft of light peeked into the room and illuminated her darkened face. She seemed unfazed by the horrid surroundings. The bed was full of squalor. It smelled of the chaos of vomit, blood, sex and seared guts, all straining to stain the satin sheets in a deathly art motif. A bloody tear ran from the corner of the girl's eyes. Murder was strange art. Calmly, she surveyed the filth and naked death sprawled before her. The dead no longer held surprise.

Now she worked quickly. She replaced the tainted bag of Feenin with a large bag of pure cocaine. She had poisoned the Feenin with an exotic, rare, crystalline substance that was virtually undetectable and mimicked the symptoms of a heart attack. Tenderly, she lifted Bossman's dead hand and forced the bag into it, effectively fingerprinting the bag and placing it on the table. She stopped to look down at the bloody tear on the girl's face and smiled. Not everyone appreciated art, its powerful emotion, with the proper respect. But Pause did. The Feenin, she put in her pocket. Visually, she checked for any spots where the Feenin might have fallen but she saw none. The silver spoon lay on the bed near Bossman. That also went into her pocket. Done, she thought and headed for the door. She eased into the hallway, checking in both directions and sauntered next door to her room.

Once inside, she picked up the phone and punched in seven digits. It was picked up on the second ring.

"Way," the voice said.

"Pause," she answered.

The phone went dead in her hand.

STONEWAY

Way Jalon stood looking out the window of his office as the sun shone down with favor on his property, the entire city of Albany, New York. He had a drink in his hand, a victory splash in the morning to celebrate the winning of the day. In a few moments, Mr. Tokus Stone would come walking into his office and become the biggest pawn that Way had ever played in his economic game of rape and plunder.

Tokus Stone of Stoneway, Inc.

That had a melodic ring to it and Way was sure that Tokus would hear the musical notes in the title. Blacks are creative that way.

Stoneway, Inc. would be a commercial hub, moving product from here to there with Tokus Stone at the helm. All types of product, from high-tech components to potato chips, would move with a Tokus Stone thought.

But the Feenin belonged to Way, the synthetic substance was the wave of the future and he owned the entire beach, from sea to shining sea. Nothing illegal about it…yet! Therein lay the reason for the need of a Tokus Stone, a nigger, a jigaboo with high-falutin' ideas. Basic in his existence and necessary only by some big mistake.

Feenin was an unknown quantity that would soon be renowned for its smell, taste, feel and name. When it became a physical entity—a bad habit with a name—someone would have to take the fall for the phenomenon that would sweep the streets of the nation. It would be Tokus Stone of Stoneway, Inc.

Had a nice ring to it, actually.

The phone on his desk beeped. His secretary's voice came through the box. "Mr. Jalon, your nine o'clock is here."

Way pressed the button. "Give me a moment."

He strode over and put his drink on the wet bar, gave his city one last look over, went back to the desk and pressed the button.

"Okay, Connie," Way Jalon said. "Caveat Emptor."

The secretary turned to Tokus Stone, who was looking around the room. "Mr. Jalon will see you now."

"Thanks," Tokus said and pushed through the office door.

Way Jalon watched the young man as he approached, noting a determined stride and the set of the bright eye that had been turned on, machinelike. The eye that saw and heard everything. Way was sure he had made the correct choice in Tokus Stone.

They shook hands and exchanged amenities before getting down to business.

"Do you remember our first meeting, Mr. Stone?"

"Explicitly," Tokus replied.

"And you can see the advantages of joining our corporation as an executive of Stoneway? This would be your baby, from birth to infinity, with all the controls in place."

"Sounds like a perfect setup," Tokus said. "As long as it's not a setup to fail."

"Mr. Stone. Tokus. I don't, I repeat, do not want you to fail. Success is imperative. I'm not in the business of losing money. When I spoke to you of our needs for a black man for this position, I did not mean to imply that a black man would just 'have' this position. Tokenism is, after all, just a word. Not a faith. Not a belief. Not some anonymous creed to live by. It's just a word. Business comes in one hue, one color. Not black, not white. Just good old-fashioned green. Green moves obstacles and constructs mountains out of molehills—thousands of them. The question is: Can you build a mountain of your own?"

"I've been climbing them all my life," Tokus answered coldly. "The biggest obstacle I've ever encountered have been the sub-humans."

Way arched an eyebrow in question.

Tokus continued. "Ahh...I see you aren't familiar with that particular race of people. Let me enlighten you. The sub-humans are a race of people with concept problems. Their vision is skewered. They can't see. When they look at a man, any man that is different from them, they see something evil...something inferior. They see something other than what is so painfully obvious. They don't see a man. They see the skin he's in."

Tokus leaned forward and looked Way Jalon in the eye. "I need to meet every key man that you have on staff. If you've hired any sub-humans, I want to shake them loose. Is that acceptable to you?"

Way paused only for a fraction of a second before answering. "It's your show, Tokus. Whatever you want. Whatever you feel is necessary."

Now Way leaned forward behind his huge desk and gave Tokus the hard eye. "Just don't waste my money."

They had reached an agreement.

Way went on to give Tokus the lay of the land, bare bones information about structure and personnel, procedure and company policies, projections and profits. Way was grudgingly impressed with Tokus' intellect. He had an astutely curious mind that soaked in knowledge and logically placed it into its proper context. Tokus had a competent hand.

Way was determined to see if he could shake it.

They had been talking for hours and lunch was fast approaching. Way leaned back in his chair with his fingers steepled under his chin.

"Tell me something, Tokus," he began. "When I find something fascinating, I have to ask questions and this is something only you can answer. Enlighten me. Exactly how does it feel to be a black man in America?"

Tokus waited.

Way raised a hand in supplication. "Don't misinterpret my question. I ask it with honest curiosity and no evil intentions ...I'm not being deceptive. But African-Americans are really in the most unique position of any race in this country."

Tokus waited quietly.

Way continued. "I must admit, though, you are the first black man I've ever spoken more than two words with. I see them on the news and they don't look hospitable. Sometimes they even have cuffs on…negative images abound! But I'm a logical man and I know this can't be factual, so I wonder. Again, enlighten me."

A moment passed between the two men before Tokus spoke.

"Mr. Jalon," Tokus replied. "I'd best describe being a black man in America as being an apple hanging on a tree. It's a big orchard, so basically it's just a matter of hanging out with all the other apples waiting for the man to come and pluck you. When that doesn't happen, if that doesn't happen, you just hold on, hanging there until you rot off. If you drop…you're apple cider. The tragedy occurs to you right before the inevitable 'splat.' It comes in a flash. This had to happen."

"Well, that's a pretty dire existence," Way responded.

Tokus chuckled. "No, Mr. Jalon. What's dire is the idea that someone could explain their existence in a few sentences. Explain their life and ideals and their sense of right and wrong in five minutes or less. Me? I'm strictly new generation, Mr. Jalon. Bred on mind power and strength of heart—I don't just hold on. And tragedy! Tragedy is a story told by the victorious."

Tokus paused to fix Way Jalon in his stare.

"I'm sure you could tell your share of tragedies, Mr. Jalon. And I'm also sure that you have no shortage of apple cider."

VERTICAL EYES

Tokus looked down at the mark on the floor. It read: "The bull starts here." And he toed the line and threw a dart. He didn't care what he scored; he just felt happy and prosperous. Stoneway, Inc. had been under his guidance for a scant three months and Tokus felt fully in control. The only fly in his ointment had been Way Jalon, the man himself. In a few instances, he had found himself being second-guessed and his orders overridden by Way Jalon. That in itself wasn't that bothersome—he supposed that the man with the most to lose would be the one with the most nits to pick—but the very nature of Way's demands were contradictory and seemed counterproductive to what needed to be done.

On occasion, Tokus felt that he had come close to stepping over the line with Way Jalon. Way wanted to send out forty-eight of the fifty trucks from the warehouse in Industrial Park on one of his "private deals," their destination unknown. Way had done the same on a few separate runs, each time setting Tokus further and further behind schedule. But this deal would cost Tokus dearly and he refused to allow it. He stormed into Way's office and made demands.

"Either one of two things will happen: I succeed, or you fire me. But I won't lose because you won't let me do my job. I need those trucks. They're mine."

Way was furious but in the end he relented.

For the most part, however, Way Jalon had remained true to his word and let Tokus deal with a free hand.

Success had finally found him and Tokus intended to hold on to it for dear life.

He felt that a celebration was in order, a kiss to the fulfillment of optimistic dreams, to the fruition of hope. Tokus ended up at a corner bar, playing darts and drinking beer, enjoying himself in silent triumph…and a second beer buzz.

"You can't beat me." A sultry voice, one that demanded attention, pulled Tokus in its direction and his eyes feasted while his heart raced to keep pace. She was a picture. The kind of woman that was a figment of the imagination and had to be sketched on paper before the illusion slipped away. She wore a black miniskirt that fit her snugly, not too revealing, and a beige top with a plunging neckline that held a promise that begged to be whispered. Her eyes were wonderful; sexy and deep and Tokus found himself at a loss, speechless for the first time in recent memory.

"Holy smokes and gees, girl," he stammered.

She laughed.

"Did I say that out loud?" Tokus asked her.

She smiled and nodded her head. She was one beautiful black woman. Chocolate. Her hair hung in curls almost down to her shoulders, framing her face, eyes and full, lush lips. He imagined she could drain a man of pain and anger and then fill him with the pleasure of having her. Especially if she was touched in the most intimate way.

"What's your name?" Tokus asked.

"Parise," she answered sweetly.

"Can I buy you a drink? Maybe engage you in some thrilling conversation?"

"Got one already, see?"

"Okay." Tokus smiled. "Then I guess you won't take this ass whuppin' personally, right?"

Parise laughed and gestured for Tokus to go right ahead and take his turn. She sat at a nearby table and watched as he threw three darts that netted him eight points. Tokus walked to the dartboard, pulled the darts out, walked back to Parise and said, "So…so…so there! See if you can beat that!"

She gave him a ridiculous look and stepped to the line. Tokus was more than happy for the view as she stood there. He would give anything just to be able to touch her. She turned to him and closed her eyes before she released a dart and scored twenty. She smiled at him. He appreciated it.

"What's your name?" she asked him.

"Tokus," he responded.

"Well, Tokus," Parise began. "Where did you learn how to play darts?"

Tokus took a swallow of his beer before answering. "Never did. I just need activity. A happy mind is a terrible thing to waste."

"Happy?" she asked.

"Ecstatic," Tokus replied and tipped his beer up for another swallow.

"That's good," she said.

Tokus nodded his head and they were silent for a moment. Something about this woman pulled at him, drawing him toward a silken trap that he would clamp around himself with no desire to escape. Suddenly, Parise stepped closer and looked him in the eye.

"Tokus," she said. "You're looking at me like you don't have a woman."

"No woman, no cry," Tokus replied.

"No cry?" she said.

"No cry, bumba clot, Rasta," Tokus sang.

She laughed. And Tokus fell for her smile. He knew he shouldn't. Now was not the right time. It was Parise's fault for looking at him that way, with an invitation.

The hint of high times pinched the outer edges of the smoke-filled bar, its few patrons capturing the rhythm of the music from the jukebox in toe taps and head nods. Tables lined the wall from the doorway to the dance floor, which was a tiny, twenty-foot square of hardwood that was dimly lit. The long L-shaped bar faced the wall and formed a corridor guarded by an old, drunk, white man who wore a dirty tank-top tee shirt. His exposed skin was covered with tattoos—his arms, shoulders and even his bald head. He lingered over his drink, looked into the top of the glass and broke out into a huge grin before picking it up and tossing it down in one long gulp. He waved impatiently at the bartender for another.

Tokus rolled the three darts in his palm as he watched Parise. She was much better at this than he was.

"You know something?" Tokus said. Parise looked at him. "I've never lost. At anything."

"Oh, yeah?"

"Oh, yeah. So let's make a bet."

The tattooed drunk rose from his stool and staggered toward them.

"Hey, young people," he said in a voice gruff with alcohol. "You know, you two make a nice lookin' couple. I mean that. I do." To Tokus he said, "If I was your age, let me tell you…"

Parise cut him off. "That sure is a lot of 'skin art' you've got goin' on. Even on your skull."

The old man said, "Yeah. Yeah. Look, I got a lot of them, all over. I even got one on my pecker." They looked at the boozer, mildly taken aback. He rambled on, "Know what it says? It says 'Ti.' But when it gets hard, it says 'Ticonderoga'!"

Laughter exploded spontaneously. The drunk wobbled over to the table next to them and, still laughing at his own joke, put his drink down and took a seat. Parise turned back to Tokus.

"What kind of bet?" she asked.

"If I win this game," Tokus said. "And I will win! You go out with me. Deal?"

"But you're not going to win." Parise laughed.

"I never lose. Bet me."

"Okay. Bet." Parise agreed.

Tokus took a drink of his beer while Parise prepared the game. He noticed the drunk sitting at the table with his back to the bar, a dollar bill folded lengthwise in his hand. Tokus didn't need to look to know that the old man was getting ready to sniff cocaine out of it. Parise had the game ready and Tokus turned and picked his darts up from the table, giving her a confident look before he took his turn.

Halfway into the game, Tokus was being crushed. Parise had tripled his score with a giggle and a well-curved figure.

"You know," Tokus cried. "You really should have some mercy. The gloating and giggling and stuff…well, that is not attractive, girl."

Parise sauntered over to him. "So, I'm not attractive?"

"Yeah, you're attract...I didn't mean..."

Parise watched him wriggle.

"Listen," Tokus took a deep breath. "You are a beautiful woman. Beyond attractive. I see you as a 'Soul Kiss.'"

Parise looked at him skeptically. "A 'soul kiss'?"

"Yeah, a 'Soul Kiss.'"

"You mean that I could kiss your soul?"

Tokus looked deeply into her eyes.

"I'm a man on a mission,
in search of a Soul Kiss.
To find that special someone,
Who knows that emotion is this.
Satisfaction is forever a moment,
Your toes will never uncurl.
Touching deep inside the woman,
And from there, comes the girl."

Parise and Tokus looked into each other's eyes. In silence they almost touched and in that moment they had each other, inside where feelings were real.

"That was beautiful." Parise touched his hand.

Tokus held her hand and said nothing, not trusting his voice at the moment.

The tattooed drunk rose from his chair and began shimmying from side to side, doing a trembling dance. He threw his head back and yelled, "OOOO, OWWW," and began doing a spastic catwalk-waddle toward them. The old man stopped in front of Tokus with another yell and stared drunkenly. His red eyes were oddly shifting and Tokus noticed a strange dilation of the pupils. Tokus felt as if he were looking into the eyes of a cat. Feline eyes glowed at him from a bald-headed mask of tattoos, wide, open and green. Haunting in a strange, alien way...unless cats with huge, bloodshot eyeballs were common. There wasn't the laser beam dot of cocaine high in his eyes, nor was there the soft fuzziness of a marijuana excursion.

The pupils seemed to glow, grow and warp. They were vertical eyes. Straight up and down.

Just as suddenly as it began, the old man seemed to shut down and a smile creased his face. He sang, "Hi, neighbor," turned and danced his way back to his table. Tokus wondered what kind of drug was inside that old man!

"What in the hell is his problem?" Tokus said aloud.

Parise shrugged. "I wonder my mys—"

A chair came flying through the air, crashing into the wall directly behind Tokus. He spun around and saw the old man standing there with that stupid grin on his face.

"Hi, neighbor," he sang. Tokus calmed himself and reached for his beer. The bottle lay broken on the floor. Tokus growled and stepped toward the old man. Parise stopped him with a restraining hand on his arm.

"He's just an old drunk," she reasoned. "The bartender will take care of him." The bartender, a large, stonefaced woman, came around the counter to Tokus. "You all right, man?"

Tokus nodded curtly.

"All right, Bernie," the bartender yelled. "You ain't gots to go home but you will get the hell up outta here!"

The drunk started singing a protest. "We shall overdriiink. We shall overdriiiink."

"Go! Now!" commanded the barkeep. The drunk muttered his way out the door.

"Let me get you another beer," the bartender told Tokus. "On the house."

Tokus and Parise sat at another table and talked well into the night. But Tokus was distracted. Something about the old drunk had unnerved him. What could make an old drunk behave so badly…so totally out of control? A man who had at least twenty years of drug use on his resume. He had probably tried everything from corn liquor to cocaine without the effects that Tokus had witnessed. The thought nagged at him.

Parise sensed his distraction. She gently touched his cheek and said softly, "Tokus, it was just an old drunk."

That was when Tokus realized it was his eyes. His vertical eyes.

DEAD 'EM

Way Jalon stood looking out at the city from his fifteenth-floor office, drawing the lines that divided his sphere of influence. Albany was nearly all his now and soon, with the launching of his newest product, there would be a new order. A new city: Way, New York.

Pause watched Way intently while she waited patiently. She knew that conceit was the result of success and she sensed in Way Jalon the ultimate pride. He would be God…if he could. But even Way had his limitations. Pause found him intriguing physically— he was a richly handsome man— and psychologically. As far as men went, Pause had a talent for being able to identify their deepest drive—that one peccadillo, that one destructive urge, and tease it with a magical touch that would help her "dead 'em."

But Way was different.

He didn't vary much from mortal man. Her talent had proven itself again. She had found his inner love, but his was a vainglorious obsession that was beyond even her ability to manipulate. Way Jalon loved his children. There were two, both of them male: Money and Power. They were adopted, of course, born and bred by men long dead, but they belonged to Way now and he huddled them against his bosom and reveled in their scent. Openly.

Though Pause had completed many assignments for Way Jalon, this was just her third time in his office. They usually handled business over the phone or via a pager, but this time she was being given the privilege of waiting, while he looked out of that egotistical wall of glass. From the street one would look up to see Way, standing there, keeping watch over his children. Men! They deserved labor pains twice a day.

Way turned from the window to face Pause.

"I have an important assignment for you." He walked over to his chair behind his desk. He sat while Pause took the chair that faced him across the expanse of polished desk. Way opened a drawer, moved his gun aside, a pistol he always kept loaded, and pulled out a large, glossy photo that he pushed across the desk to Pause. It was a picture of Tokus Stone.

"Watch him," Way said.

"That's easy," Pause replied, looking at the picture. "He's handsome."

Way smiled at her. "I want him controlled. I don't want any wild cards in my deck or wild hairs up my ass. Understood?"

"This guy is a wild hair?" Pause asked doubtfully. "I mean, just looking at him I could tell you some things about him. Most of which, I bet, are probably true."

"Like what?" Way wondered.

"For one, I would say that he is a hard worker with a lot of brains. 'Smooth' is a word that comes to mind. Secondly, I'd say he is probably happier than a faggot in boys town just to have a job working for you and making the big bucks."

"Very good," Way said. "Yes, he is very intelligent. I've seen that first-hand, but he's bucking up against me now. I've given him the impression that he matters. I want you to keep that illusion alive but with a little twist."

"Well," Pause replied, her interest piqued. "How do you want him?"

"Compliant. Submissive. The only word he should utter is 'yes.' To whatever I say. The fool nearly cost me a good deal of money recently and that is simply not allowed. I only need him for a little while."

Way saw no need to tell Pause about the incident that had taken place between Tokus and him. Tokus would have quit on him if he hadn't given in on the trucking shipment issue. Way was sure of it. Tokus definitely would have quit. Way had needed those trucks badly. He had scheduled the forty-eight trailers to be packed with full loads of Feenin and shipped to destinations in fifteen different cities. He had wanted to hit America with a bang.

But Way needed Tokus more than any grand plans.

Way would work around him…for now.

"So he lives," Pause stated.

"Yes," Way replied. "He lives."

"No dead 'em," Pause prodded.

"No dead 'em," Way repeated.

Pause regarded Way thoughtfully. She wondered if he ever imagined a hint of her motivation, of the urge she had to bend him, break him and watch him grovel, subservient at her feet with the fear of death trembling his knees. The things she would do to him. The very thought of it made her center heat up as she crossed one leg over the other and squeezed. She looked at the picture of Tokus Stone again.

Way regarded her critically. "Now listen, Tokus Stone was once a drug dealer and one night he encountered a man called Moose…"

Way Jalon related every detail he knew about the night of Moose's murder, everything that was in the file kept by Herbert Mulne, the rogue cop know as Five-O. When he finished, Pause looked down at the picture again.

"I've got it," she said. "The means and the method."

"Do it." Way rose from his desk and walked over to the wall to look over his real estate. Pause had been dismissed.

She stared at Way Jalon. She didn't like being treated as if she were an under-thought, an insignificant, pesky insect. She wanted to rattle his cage.

"Way Jalon," she called in a sweet voice. "How come you never let any-body into that room back there?" She indicated the two oak doors over by the bar. Way Jalon didn't turn around.

"None of your business," he hissed.

"What's back there? Some freaky shit, I bet!"

"You have your assignment," Way growled. "Now get to it. Because I promise you, you don't want to find out."

Pause glared angrily at his back…and she thought of Delton. She had seduced Delton and drugged him. When he awoke he was hog-tied with a piano wire looped around his neck. The other end of the wire was tied to a wooden curl bar about three feet long. Curling that bar, with a foot squarely planted between the man's shoulder blades, was Pause, straining with effort as she pulled.

As the wire began cutting into Delton's neck he tried to scream around the gag crammed in his mouth as his body bucked violently. Pause eased up on the wire and walked around to face the bleeding man. She knelt down close to his face.

"You're crying," she said softly. "Ohhhh, baby. Poor baby." Pause made kissing noises, smacking her lips loudly, soothing him. The man whimpered through the gag. Pause rose to her feet.

"Bitch!" she yelled, before she gave the wire one last powerful pull.

Pause threw the photograph on the desk and got up to leave. She had a burning desire to see a man in pain, and Tokus Stone would wear napalm burns on his back.

IMANDÉ

A silent warmth had developed between Tokus and T'Challa over the course of the past few months, a bond that was strengthened by a mutual respect and understanding. Without knowing it, they had become brothers, rooted in the same earth, branches on the same tree.

It had taken Tokus a little while to adjust to T'Challa, to reconcile the fact that his brother was a different man than the cowardly crackhead who had fled down Heath Street one dark night. T'Challa was a strong man, small in size but giant in presence, who would give rugged affection, and then, only to a select few. He spoke his few words carefully but he usually said volumes; his actions a strong reflection of the man he had become.

T'Challa had filed "fear" somewhere distant, banished it forevermore from his being. There was nothing or no one that he wouldn't stand up to. It was now only a matter of how much he wanted to fight. Tokus saw it in T'Challa's eyes whenever the hint of an insult came near.

Tokus turned the corner from Lark Street onto Orange Street and headed toward his brother's house. He was going to offer T'Challa a job at Stoneway. A better paying job than the gigs T'Challa had been getting recently. It was tough surviving on a janitor's pay, and flipping burgers didn't leave much room for a budget. Neither job turned out to be steady, permanent work. Tokus understood his brother's need to be his own man, to stand on his own two feet to support Pharren and Monday, but he hoped that T'Challa would relent on this one. It wasn't that T'Challa would be indebted or anything, but what good was success if it couldn't be shared with family?

Tokus offered T'Challa a job at Stoneway once before and had been flatly refused.

"No," T'Challa had answered.

"Why not?" Tokus asked.

"I ain't qualified. I don't fit."

"You don't have to fit."

"Yes, I do."

Tokus hadn't asked again. T'Challa would fit. Tokus knew it. His brother had instinct, raw intellect and savvy—all assets that could drive any career upward. T'Challa had just lost a job that he badly needed, so Tokus figured that the time was right to renew the offer.

T'Challa lived on the first floor of an old, blue, two-story house with a cinderblock porch composed of three steps and a rickety handrail that threatened to fall off at any given moment. It was one in a block of identical houses, the only variation being the color. People were sitting out on their porches—ghetto patios—just lounging, enjoying a seasonably warm day.

Tokus mounted the steps and knocked. Pharren opened the door with a worried look on her face.

"Tokus," she said loudly. "Come in." She closed the door behind him and hurried off to the bedroom, mumbling something Tokus couldn't understand. Tokus walked over to the mantel where the Undamo Assassins were on display. One of them looked familiar. Tokus looked closer. Its face was painted red, black and green with intricate designs on the right side. In his mind's eye, Tokus saw that same design on his brother's face as he stood on a lawn on Raymar Avenue with Five-O lying at his feet.

"Tokus," T'Challa called to him. He stood in the bedroom doorway with his arms folded across his chest.

"What's up, my brother?" Tokus greeted him.

"Nothin'," T'Challa replied. "I got Monday in the bed, though. He's sick."

"What's wrong with him?" Tokus came alert.

"Don't know. I might have to take him to the hospital if he don't get any better, though."

"Can I see him?"

"Yeah. Come on."

Monday was lying on the bed with his head in Pharren's lap. She was brushing his forehead with a damp cloth and holding him tightly. The boy shook violently and mumbled incoherently with his eyes wide open. Tokus watched him closely. His pupils were swollen and vibrating vertically. Tokus recoiled, alarmed. He had seen those eyes before. Those vertical eyes. Feline eyes. Long and hazy. They were the eyes of a blathering drunk on a rampage fueled by a chemical reaction in a chemist's lab—the man's brain. This drug was something foreign to Tokus, something new, and he knew it was something that shouldn't be ravaging the body of an eight-year-old.

Concern etched deeply into T'Challa's face as he watched his son thrash and fight against the sickness that punished his young body. He turned to Tokus with a bewildered expression before he made a decision. "Let's take him to the emergency room."

"T'Challa," Tokus rasped. "No."

T'Challa spoke to Pharren. "Where are his shoes?"

She pointed to the floor at T'Challa's feet.

"We got to take him to the hospital." T'Challa worried as he picked up the child's shoes. "Find out what's wrong with him."

"T'Challa," Tokus said louder. "You can't take him to the hospital."

T'Challa sat down on the bed and grabbed Monday's foot, trying to put on the shoe. He reached for the right one.

"Yes, I am. He's hurtin'."

"You can't," Tokus pleaded.

T'Challa paused with the shoe in midair. "Are you blind to all this or can't you see! My boy is hurtin'."

"I know, T'Challa," Tokus cried. "I know…"

Suddenly, Monday began tossing wildly in Pharren's arms, bucking her back against the headboard of the bed. "Imandé! Imandé!" Monday chanted as Pharren wrestled with him.

T'Challa stared openmouthed at his son until the fits began to subside and Monday's body calmed to a low moan. Pharren looked worn and ragged.

"We better go," she said.

"T'Challa," Tokus said. "You can't take Monday to the hospital."

"Why you keep sayin' that?" T'Challa demanded.

"Because there would be too many questions."

"They had better ask questions," T'Challa growled.

"They'd ask questions because…"

"Can't you see I don't give a fat, rat ass right about now?"

"Because I think Monday has some drugs in him!" Tokus exclaimed. "Some new shit. Some new kind of drug. I saw this same type of reaction a couple of days ago. The same eyes. It's some new shit … I just don't know what it is, though."

T'Challa dropped Monday's shoe and stood facing Tokus.

"Drugs?" he whispered harshly.

"Yes, drugs," Tokus said carefully. "If I'm right, we just need to wait this out. Maybe an hour or two."

"Drugs?" T'Challa didn't want to believe it.

"Yeah," Tokus responded gently. "I saw this old drunk the other night, you know, one of those fifty-year users, and he was buggin' out. Really trippin'. His eyes…his pupils…they were long. Vertical. Just like Monday's eyes. It made me wonder, so I asked around…trying to find out what's up. There's a new drug out there. They call it Feenin but that was about all I could find out. A name. It seems like it will take addiction to a new level."

T'Challa looked at his son, tossing and turning in Pharren's arms. "We gonna find out who gave this stuff to my son, yo! And when I do! I got something for that ass…whoever it was!"

Monday began to chant anew, "Imandé! Imandé!"

"Let's wait this out," Tokus said. "Give it an hour. If we take him to the hospital, there would be too many questions to answer. The authorities are trouble. You know that as well as I do."

T'Challa looked from Tokus to Monday before making his decision. A thin sheen of sweat had broken across the child's forehead and he seemed to be calming down, coming out of it.

"Imandé!" The voice came again. "Imandé!"

T'Challa turned to Tokus. "Imandé is an Undamo word."

"What does it mean?"

"It means 'avenge,'" T'Challa replied.

PASSION'S TURN

Pause decided to make him burn—to light him and watch as he melted into a mound of chocolate, spiral-shaped shit. Her game had changed from one of physical terror to one of mental intimidation, but manipulation had its own joyful quirks and kinks. And Pause felt real kinky.

She had spotted Tokus coming out of his brother's house on Orange Street. She sat behind the wheel of a jet-black Chevy Blazer with tinted windows, watching, as he emerged with a solemn expression on his face. He had been inside the house for hours but Pause was on assignment, so patience was mandatory. She looked at her watch. It was nearing midnight.

She followed Tokus to a bar called The Branch, a local club where college kids partied. She pulled into a far corner of the parking lot and reached into the back seat for a large handbag. Inside was a makeup kit. Pause could be many a woman due to the contents of her kit. She could be a beautiful mermaid or a snarling harpy. All her parts were parts.

Tonight, she decided, she would use her sexy, come-bed-me persona. She brushed her long, blond hair straight back, letting it fall in a cascade over her shoulders, framing her face. She wouldn't need much makeup, just lipstick, because Pause was a natural beauty. Her looks were a key component of what made her the best at what she did.

Pause checked herself one last time in the rearview mirror—everything about her said "come-on." Perfect, she thought, before she got out and walked inside the club. Sounds of drunken revelry shook the building, music blared and people bounced, rocking and rolling. Groups of people stood by the bar. Others edged the dance floor, screaming independent yells of triumph and guzzling alcohol in mass amounts that went down like happy juice, instantly obliterating inhibitions.

Pause waited for her eyes to adjust to the darkness and the strobing lights. She scanned the room, searching the dance floor and the booths that lined the far wall for her target. She spotted him sitting alone at the bar, tossing down a drink.

"Hey, let's dance." A young man hopped up to her, moving up and down in a pale imitation of a dance he had seen on *Soul Train*. Pause gave him a frosty glare and walked away. She slid onto the stool next to her victim. The bartender hustled right over. She ordered a drink and observed Tokus discreetly in the mirrored wall that ran the length of the bar while she waited. He wore a faraway expression, his mind in other places. One corner of his mouth was slightly down, curled in a sneer, the product of angry thoughts. He had both hands clamped tightly around his drink. Tokus Stone looked like he could use a friend. Problem was, he wasn't giving Pause a glance. That was highly unusual in itself. She had presence.

"Hi." A dark-haired man sidled up to her. "Care to dance a little?"

"No," Pause replied curtly. He started to rephrase his question when Pause turned on him with a scowl that looked like spit in his eyes. He walked away. Her drink arrived and she tossed her head back and downed it in one gulp. The swift motion caught her target's eye as she watched him observe her in the mirror. She saw a glint of interest flicker in his eyes. Their mirrored eyes met.

"Another," Tokus motioned to the bartender. Pause repeated the motion. The bartender brought two glasses and placed one in front of each of them. Vodka on the rocks. Tokus lifted his glass in the air in a toast and waited for Pause to join him. She did.

"And I wanna taste her, straight, no chaser," he sang and tossed his drink down his gullet in one swift motion. Pause smiled at him, looking deep into his eyes before she tilted her glass and quickly drained hers, too. They watched each other intently for a second while the alcohol burned its way down to their bellies. They motioned to the bartender and two more drinks appeared.

Pause picked up her drink and looked over at Tokus.

"Are you drinking happy or drinking sad?"

"I'm drinking pissed!" Tokus replied.

"Well, I'm drinking drunk," Pause said. "What are you pissed about?"

"My nephew's sick, is all." Tokus sipped his drink.

"Oh. Listen. Tonight, drink drunk with me."

Tokus bit his upper lip as he watched her. Pause knew what response was coming. A smile slowly spread across Tokus' face.

"Tonight?" he grinned.

She playfully pushed his arm. "You know what I mean. Come on."

"How about if I drink 'don't care.' Cool?" Tokus asked.

"That's cool."

Tokus raised his drink. "Salud."

They chugged down the drinks. Pause fought the irritating burn that charged down her throat and slammed the glass down on the bar.

"Enough!" she announced.

"They ran out of liquor?" Tokus stammered.

"Let's ask," Pause gasped. They signaled the bartender who looked at them warily before coming over. The alcohol had taken full effect then, as they both began talking to the bartender in languages that were somewhat based in English, with drunken dialect slurring all over the vowels. After two minutes of that, the bartender held up one finger, silencing them.

"We got no more. Fuckin'. Liquor," he pronounced.

They exchanged looks and burst out laughing.

"A beer then," Tokus ordered.

"Me, too," Pause echoed.

After the beers arrived, Tokus and Pause looked at each other.

Pause sipped her beer. "Is that a myth about black men?"

Tokus burped. "Excuse me. Which one?"

"About sex."

"What about sex?"

"About the black male size."

"What about the size?"

"You know," Pause said, exasperated. "You're going to make me say it, huh?"

"No. You don't have to say it." He took a sip of his beer. "You know what? That is one myth I would never shatter. Yes, it's true. It's even strapped to my ankle as we speak." He smiled drunkenly at her. "At least, I think that's my ankle."

Pause returned his smile. "All right," she said. "Tell me this. Do you date white women?"

"I'm not dating anyone."

"But do you like white women?"

"Depends."

"On what?"

"If she can forgive herself for loving a black man."

They watched each other for a moment before returning to their beers. After the tension drained, Pause built some more.

"My name's Eva," she said.

"Tokus," he said, offering his hand. She took it.

"Forgiveness isn't on my agenda," Pause said with a gleam in her eye. "Just pure, physical fun. Sex." She inched closer to Tokus and whispered, "With you."

Tokus didn't answer. Instead, he turned the glass up and gulped the rest of his beer. He looked over at Pause, whose eyes scorched him with hot promises and passion's turn. He nodded his head "yes" and ordered another beer.

Pause smiled.

FULL FIRE

Tokus awoke with nylon ropes tied to his wrists and ankles as he attempted to filter sunlight through his pained eyelids. Eva sat at the foot of the bed, naked, watching him. The strange sensation of waking up in an unknown bed disoriented him, causing him to flinch as he replayed the past twenty-four hours trying to locate himself. He saw Eva through the strange shadows of his hangover.

"It's good to see that some myths are true." She looked down at him.

The woman from last night was gone. Tokus shook his head, trying to clear it, but that only made him wince in pain as his alcohol-swollen brain banged against his skull. He narrowed his eyes and focused. Eva sat on the bed with her legs crossed under her. Her hair was pulled back in a tight, severe bun. She had an officious look in her eye. She was still a beautiful woman but her pale skin, which had been soft to look at, was now legally tight. Tokus was groggy, his head hurt and a raw soreness was pushing its way into his consciousness; but he still registered her eyes.

"Yo." Tokus' throat was raw. "Yo. What did we do last night? Ropes!"

He held his arms in the air, looking at the loose ends of the ropes dangling in front of his bloodshot eyes.

"Ropes? Damn, woman!" He smiled at her. "I was all right...right?"

"Very," Pause answered shortly.

"Hope so. All this and I didn't come off correctly...my head is killing me. I'll never drink again."

"You were so good last night that I want you to do something for me," Pause said. "We are going to have sex."

"We are?" Tokus slowly sat up in the bed, ignoring his nakedness.

"Yes. Whenever I want it and however I want it."

"Listen, Eva…" Tokus began untying the rope around his wrist. "Listen, Eva…"

"Leave that!" Pause commanded.

"I really would like to, but I need the bathroom. My stomach is boiling. I hate alcohol." He had one wrist untied before Pause spoke.

"Read this." She handed him a card. Tokus squinted at the card. It seemed to be moving and fading, but after the initial struggle, he read it. He cast a puzzled eye at her. She definitely had a plan.

"You're a lawyer?" he asked.

"Yes, I'm a lawyer. An attorney with a firm downtown. In that office, we have a file on a Mr. Tokus Stone. The long and the short of it is we know what you did. It wouldn't take much to put you down and away for quite some time."

Tokus regarded her carefully. She still hadn't said anything specific. His gut instinct told him she was bluffing. That voice might have just been the alcohol talking.

Pause leaned forward. Her breasts, which had seemed perfect in the moonlight, swung ominously toward him.

"I know all about you," she whispered.

"So what?" Tokus replied. "I know all about me, too. So what?"

"I know that you are a once-upon-a-time drug dealer with blood on his hands. 'Moose' blood, if I recall correctly."

Tokus nodded and focused on her face. So, this is the thing called "life," what everyone had warned him about. The fate of the fearless and the reckless running in circles and circumstance, never free to rest. He knew this was just the beginning.

"So, is this the new wave of rehabilitation?" Tokus snorted. "Instead of jail, I get a good roll in the sack with a white woman?"

"Not exactly," Pause said.

"Well, what, exactly, do you want Eva? Damn!"

"Two things," she began. "First, I want information on your boss, Way Jalon.

Whatever moves he makes, we want to know about them. He's making moves and we want specifics."

"Who is this 'we' you keep referring to?"

"Don't ask questions. Secondly, I want that," she said, prodding his penis. "And I want it when I want it, how I want it."

"I'm not a slab of meat, Eva," Tokus replied, untying the rope from his other wrist.

"Yes, you are."

"No, I'm not. So let's be real. What is this all about? Money? Control? Is this the way it is up here? On the hill where the power brokers play? We had a night together. That's all. Now we have complications. Why? Why are you so suddenly in my life?"

Pause looked stonily at Tokus before she spoke. "Doesn't matter in the end, does it? Your fate is always just a phone call away. Three digits. Nine. One. One."

Tokus stared at her in disbelief. Pause reached up to the back of her head and her hair cascaded down around her face. She shook it into place and her beauty returned.

"Now this is how I want you…"

Later that night, Tokus lay in Pause's bed with his hands chained to the bedposts and his feet shackled. She stood over him, enjoying his naked helplessness. She wore a judge's robe with nothing underneath it. He wore an old pair of tattered pants that reached only to his knees with the crotch cut out. He was flaccid.

"Get it up, boy!" she thundered.

"I can't, Your Honor." Tokus spoke his line.

"Then the judge will have to get you up." She pounced on the bed. "I'll get him up." She took him in her mouth. Tokus felt himself responding as the blood began rushing to engorge him. He succumbed to his rage as she engulfed him with warmth. Inch by inch, friction slid down the length of his shaft and, inch by inch, his body was unable to deny his base instincts. His mind to told him "no" while his body reacted with a thoughtless "yes." His wrath would bend her, twist her to the tune of the pain she was inflicting on him. Red rage. He focused on that. The anger.

She climbed atop him and mounted his manhood. She began violently bucking and grunting. Her face was grim as she leaned forward and raked her fingers across his chest, upward until her hand gripped his throat. She began to tighten her fingers around his windpipe.

"Don't stop, Mandingo," she growled between bucks. "Don't! You! Dare! Stop!"

Pause groaned and went off somewhere by herself, faster and faster. She twisted her pelvis and Tokus felt small tears rip across the flesh of his shaft. It hurt. She was oblivious to the anger that spewed out of Tokus' eyes, a full fire of hate and venom. He watched her as she raped him and his fingers felt his chains. Slowly, he began to pull.

BLIND TRUTH

While they were out on their first real date, Tokus came to the realization that Parise was "the one." She awakened an "aliveness" within him with her smile, with a subtle glance, a look that spoke of desire and fueled an attraction that startled him. But he was determined to explore the endless possibilities of her sensuality. The relationship game was not his forte, so there were no guidelines for him when it came to dating—but he truly believed that upon meeting the woman of his dreams, there would be no doubt. Parise was exceeding his expectations.

She was *fine!* No doubt about that! But she was sexy, too. A woman qualified as *fine* if her body was bangin' the way he liked them; thick, shapely and bad as hell from three angles—front, back, and sideways. A curvaceous ass that holds its form and elicits a hard stare, nice, firm, heaping cups of titties, pretty brown skin, soulful eyes...*fine!*

Parise was fine but Tokus also found himself ignited by the sexiness she exuded. He had learned that there is a distinct difference between fine and sexy. A sexy woman has all the attributes of finery and knows how to wear them. She knows how to get into a man's mind before he can get into her pants. She has that sexiness. A groove that entices a man, luring him deep into that furrow with an essence that has soul power, a sensuality that sustains the imagination and fuels the fire of the afterglow. Parise had all of that... and he sensed there was much, much more.

Tokus stole a glance at her as they made their way down Madison Avenue toward the Italian restaurant where he was taking her to dinner. *Parise has that sexiness*, he thought as he looked at her. *And she knows it, too!*

Parise caught him looking at her and a slow smile spread across her face. "What?" She nudged him with her shoulder. Tokus put on his most innocent expression and shrugged.

"What's on your mind?" Parise inquired. "You've got things on your mind."

Tokus smiled and shook his head.

"You were thinking about me, right?"

She knows it, too! Tokus mused. To Parise, he said, "I'm just diggin' on you, gurl."

Without giving it a second thought, Tokus reached out and took Parise by the waist, pulling her body to him. The contact between them was hot and sensuous...and right!

"I have something that I have to admit to you. It's going to sound like I'm crazy but...I ain't totally insane. Okay? Listen." He looked into her eyes before telling her, "I don't really know how to date."

When she leaned away and looked at him to see if he was serious, Tokus rushed on. "For real! I'm dead serious. Dating and going out and stuff... that's never really been my thing." He paused to relish the feel of her in his hands. Her body was soft, with curves that were firm and enticing. He even imagined that he could feel her heat on his fingertips. "I had to be really lucky to meet you, though. The fates have smiled."

With an impish grin, Parise gingerly stepped from his embrace. "You don't know how to date, huh?" He could hear the skepticism in her voice. "So you know nothing about chemistry? Or what it would feel like to just...connect? To just..." Her hands fluttered in the air as she searched for the appropriate word. "Just 'click' with someone?"

"Click," Tokus said. "I guess 'click' is close enough."

Parise smirked.

Tokus reached out and touched her hand. He knew exactly what she meant. It was the love fallacy. An intangible concept built by romantic dreamers. Love at first sight! Right! Lust at first sight was much more common in his experience. The lust of the eyes. Tokus was a man of the flesh; his eyes, more times than not, had ruled his days. The female form had tempted him on many occasions, and eventually he had given in to his urges, not with any conscience thought but merely by the temperature of the blood that was ignited inside of him.

This was Tokus' ghetto version of the truth—a truth so prevalent in his life that it took the shape of reality and echoed the nuances of realism. He had assumed the standard masculine stance needed to survive the hardcore existence that he was forced to confront on a daily basis. Yet reality was on the other side of that truth now; a naked truth that he wanted to share with Parise despite his fear of the consequences of baring his soul. It would be foolish of him to try to keep the facts from her. As the saying goes, what is done in the dark will play out in the light. But then again, he reasoned, what she didn't know wouldn't hurt her.

They reached the end of Madison Avenue and turned down Lark Street past the assortment of shops, delis, pizzerias, and clothing stores that lined the block. Lark Street itself had been paved with a pink, rustic cobblestone in an effort to recapture the look of a bygone era. Albany's history reached back to when the first settlers set foot in America and the city's leaders clung to its lineage as one of the oldest cities established in New York.

"I think that I want to be honest with you," Tokus said as they walked. Parise glanced at him but remained silent. They turned the corner from Lark Street onto Central Avenue, which bustled with activity. Antique streetlamps were posted on each corner, reaching high into the night; lights flickered inside of their metal housings, lending a carnival atmosphere to the hum of the crowd. "Is that a part of that connecting 'click'?" Tokus asked.

"Depends," Parise said. "So, why haven't you had a girlfriend before?"

"What?"

"You said that you've never been on a date before, so I'm asking. Why isn't there an ex-girlfriend lurking around somewhere in your life?"

"I've had a girlfriend before," Tokus said. "It's just that I've never been on a date before."

Parise looked at him. "Really?"

"Yeah. Really." They stopped in front of Fragnoli's, an Italian spot that served the best linguini in the city. "You like Italian?"

"Love it," Parise replied.

"But, are you feeling Italian?"

"Well…"

Tokus began reading from a menu that was taped to the front door of the restaurant. "Look at this. They've got linguini, fettuccini, lasagna, ravioli…"

"All right." Parise started laughing. "You win!"

Tokus was on a roll. "And they even have tortellini!"

"You win." Parise took his arm and pulled him toward the door. "Come on."

"Is that chemistry?" Tokus smiled at her. "When we like the same things? When I like the fact that we like the same things?" They looked at each other for a moment before Tokus opened the door to the restaurant and ushered Parise inside.

Fragnoli's was a small eatery that was packed with evening diners, which meant that they had to wait nearly half an hour before they could be seated. They spent that time across the street, sitting on a bench in front of the public library, talking and people-watching as they learned the little things, the subtle details about each other. Tokus found Parise to be an enigmatic wonder. Her opinions were strong; even though they swung wildly from subject to subject, but she held firmly to what she believed. He had judged her to be the projects version of a porcelain princess but then he chided himself. The old adage "don't judge a book by its cover" came to mind, and he realized he should have known better.

He came to the realization that, as a woman, her trials and tribulations required physical and emotional strength beyond his awareness, yet she managed to maintain her femininity. She was determined to succeed and decided that nothing would stand in her way. "'There is no substitute for hard work.' That was my daddy's mantra," she told him. "And there is no reason in the world that I shouldn't succeed." Tokus didn't know if he totally agreed with that edict because he had discovered firsthand that sometimes there was much more required than hard work. But he found comfort in her strong will, simply because he could relate to that inner drive, the same intestinal fortitude that had helped him fight his way through college.

When they were finally seated in the restaurant, they chatted easily as they perused the menu, discussing each item before deciding on their orders.

Tokus ordered a plate of linguini with an Alfredo sauce and spiced shrimp, while Parise settled on a vegetarian ravioli dish smothered in a light, red sauce with seasoned, Parmesan bread sticks on the side. The waiter handed Tokus a wine list from which he selected a bottle of Chardonnay and after their glasses were filled, they sipped their drinks and relaxed.

"Parise," Tokus said, "do you want to get married?"

After a shocked breath, Parise answered, "To who?"

"Whoa! Whoa! Whoa!" He had to laugh. "Pull your radar down, Miss Lady!" He smiled at her. "What I mean is, will you consciously decide on a life partner? Do you plan on being married with children?"

"Am I mistaken, or did I hear a bit of attitude in your tone?" she replied with an arched eyebrow.

"Not really. I've just always wondered how anybody could possibly plan on marriage. And kids."

"That's not something you want?" Parise watched him intently.

Tokus wanted nothing more. To Parise, he said, "What about you? Tell me about you?"

Parise took a sip of her drink and leaned back in her chair, watching him over the rim of her wine glass. "I've been off the dating scene myself for a few years now. I was in a serious relationship for a while but that didn't work out."

Tokus cut her off. "Parise, I'm really not interested in your past relationships. I hope that doesn't sound too rude, but I've discovered that the only relevance of the past is how it has molded and shaped the person sitting in front of me right now."

Parise watched him for a moment. "Spoken like a person with secrets."

"We all have them. And there's usually a reason why they're secrets."

They lapsed into silence when the waiter came with their dinners.

Images of Eva flashed across his mind, accompanied by a chill at the memory of their encounter. She was an evil bitch who had invaded his life with the ease and agility of a big game cat—one with poison dripping from its fangs. He understood and fully accepted his role in the events of that fateful night, but Eva had an agenda—and he was the focal point. Tokus discovered later on that he had been a target, the victim of a greater hustle, and his fate had been predetermined. After all of the years of tears and fears, all of his hustling at night while struggling through four years of college—those efforts had been reduced to nothing. He felt an unfamiliar twinge of rage at the very thought that his untamed lust had ruined his life.

"Is something wrong?" Parise was watching him intently and he realized that his expression must have reflected the anger he was feeling.

Tokus took a moment to study this woman whom he found himself drawn to; attracted to with an undeniable force. He had never been one to let his emotions influence his actions but Parise was the exception to his rule. He planned on fully surrendering to his weakness.

"No." Tokus flashed a smile. "I had a work-related flashback. I'm fine. Besides…" He gave her a meaningful stare. "…I wouldn't let anything interfere with my evening with you."

"Good," Parise said, visibly relaxed. "I'm enjoying myself, too."

"I'm glad for that."

Parise was a beautiful woman. Her dark brown eyes sparkled when she laughed and he noticed a slight crinkling at the corners of her mouth when she smiled. Her chocolate skin was smooth and without blemish, which he loved, and her body stirred him. Tokus imagined what she looked like naked, imagined what promise her body held for him and felt his desire surge in response. He never considered himself to be a man easily swayed by the wiles of women—especially the sexy ones with curves of appeal. Of course, he had experienced his share of women who flirted with his fancy and led him into their intimacies, but they only appealed to him on a physical level. Parise brought much more to the table.

He remembered the night he met Parise. He had gone out to a local bar to celebrate his new position at Stoneway when he had noticed her sitting at the bar. Tokus found himself staring at her and when she turned and looked into his eyes, he sensed that she was feeling the same connection that he felt. Her presence invaded his mind and drew him to her before he had a chance to formulate any other thought. They had ended up talking until they were the only two people left in the bar.

It was Parise's calming influence that helped diffuse the situation earlier that night when the wild, old man with the crazy eyes had gotten violent and thrown a chair that nearly hit Tokus in the head. Tokus sprang from the table, preparing to charge straight toward the old man, when Parise's gentle touch stopped him cold with the unspoken voice of restraint. They watched as the drunk staggered out of the bar.

Turns out that Parise was having her own celebration. She had recently completed her second year at Hudson Valley Community College and had been accepted at State University to pursue a degree in Criminal Law.

She was a hometown girl, born and raised in South Albany and she admitted to him that she was a driven, goal-oriented person with her mind set on obtaining her degree. Passion flared in her eyes when she spoke of her place in the world and the balance that she could help restore through education and social involvement. Tokus was impressed with her dreams, altruistic as they were, because those ideals had never entered his mind. He had spent his life trying to get his; to take care of himself. Perhaps he could help others by becoming so wealthy that money would drip off him and shower the less fortunate around him. Tokus found himself drawn even more to her.

Who was he kidding? He had been mesmerized by Parise from the start; even the rough edges that occasionally flashed to the surface only served to heighten his desire to have her. By the time the night was over, Tokus was anxiously anticipating the next time that he would see her.

But that was before the incident with Eva—a regrettable night of drunken sex with a beautiful stranger that now threatened his freedom. The events of that night forced him to reevaluate the depth of his own personal demons. Time for him to man-up! Time to face a part of himself that he hadn't been willing to admit even existed.

"Parise," he said. She had been enjoying a bite of her ravioli, the round pasta was piled on her plate, topped by a red tomato sauce, and she regarded him while she daintily munched. "Do you believe in blind truth?"

She didn't respond—only watched him expectantly.

"Blind truth," Tokus went on. "The truth as the ultimate liberation. The bare facts with no expectations or judgments. Whatever it is…it is what it is."

"The truth," Parise answered slowly, "delivered like a punch in the mouth? Is that it?" There was a glint of challenge in her eyes, as if his answer would contain some great revelation, some intricate insight into his emotional being.

This was *his* moment of truth. This was his chance. He wanted to tell her about Eva. He wanted to share his burden, his shame, more importantly, share a part of himself with her. He wanted to break down, kick himself, curse himself until there was nothing left but the truth, in all of its ugliness; and he wanted to do it with Parise, knowing from that ugly truth, she would see the ugly beauty and help lift him up anyway.

He had made a mistake with Eva. A monumental error that had placed his livelihood at risk and Tokus was determined not to make another foolish mistake with Parise. She needed to know.

"The truth," Tokus said, "sees you in your Wednesday worst, even when you wear your Sunday best." She tilted her head at him. Intrigued. He answered her look. "A poem I heard."

Her beauty was suggestive to him; suggesting heated embraces and an intimate closeness that he would wrap himself in like a blanket that was both warm and comfortable. The realization struck him that he would be taking a great risk with Parise by sharing the darker portions of his life.

Time to make a choice: Blind truth or Parise.

The terror of Eva and the control she held over him or the pleasure of Parise and the vibe that they shared from the moment they looked in each other's eyes. Eva had been an intense clash of lust and physical sensation that quickly cooled and then hardened into a cruel reality that could cost his freedom. Parise was the key to growing possibilities and he saw nothing but joy with her in his life. His decision was made.

"Parise," Tokus began. "Have you ever lived in circumstance?"

"Circumstance?" Parise sat up straight and brushed a strand of hair from her forehead. Tokus found the gesture appealing, like pulling back a curtain and revealing a prize. "Everybody does." She paused to give him a meaningful look. "That's the point, isn't it? Life is about fighting circumstances. Endlessly sometimes."

"Yeah, I know," Tokus said. "Projects. Remember?"

The waiter came with the check.

They left Fragnoli's and decided to walk back to Washington Park. He told Parise about his childhood and his trials and tribulations in getting through it alive. She listened without comment as he took her through his early years. He noticed a hint of tears when he told her about the incident with his mother and stepfather. She nodded occasionally as he took her through his nights on Addict Aisle and the struggle to achieve his goals. Strolling through Washington Park, she leaned into him and his arm encircled her waist, pulling her close. Tokus had never felt such intimacy with another person. Even though they were each alone with their thoughts, he felt that they were joined emotionally and he decided that he would try to make it real—this feeling that he had with Parise.

He learned that Parise had been born to a middle-class family; her father was a construction worker while her mother was a nurse at St. Peters Hospital. They had taken great pains to ensure that she would have equal opportunities and the work ethic to take advantage of those opportunities. She lived with her parents and two brothers in a two-story house in Colonie, a suburb of Albany, where she was exposed to a culturally diverse upbringing but still felt the sting of social inequalities that came along with the color of her skin. But she was determined to never give any person with a racial agenda power over her spirit; be the racism spoken or implied. As a result she developed an openness that was instantly inviting and refreshing. *Perhaps it is our differences,* Tokus mused, *that add so much spice to our mutual attraction.*

"I always knew that I would get out," Tokus said.

"No, you didn't." Parise gently nudged him.

"Well, no. I didn't," he conceded. "But I always felt it. Escape, for me, was a goal I wasn't even thinking about. It was a given." He paused, warming to his subject. "It was like when I played football…the first guy that came at me, I never thought that he would be able to tackle me. I would actually be looking at the second guy, the guy right behind him. That was the way things happened for me."

"So you were able to sidestep them both." Parise went along with the analogy.

"More like I juked him. Just straight dipped on him." Tokus dropped a shoulder to emphasize his point.

Parise smiled at his enthusiasm. "I think you should be proud of what you've done with your life. It's important to give yourself a pat on the back for making it. You've done well."

"Yeah," Tokus said.

"Do you?" Parise looked at him. "Do you pat yourself on the back every once in a while? You know, occasionally you have to cater to your soul. You have to find out what it needs and then nourish it so that you grow."

Tokus pulled Parise into his embrace and they looked into each other's eyes, their faces inches apart. Slowly, Tokus brought his head down until their lips met in a soft, probing kiss that turned into something much deeper.

Tokus decided to keep his secret to himself.

WATCHING THOUGHTS

Tokus and T'Challa saw Feenin up close. From green vertical eyes to brown feline eyes to red burning slits that ran straight up and down. It was a twisting, vibrating path that the addicts were dancing upon, all to their own rhythm of life. Tokus and T'Challa had spent the better part of the day scouring the city, seeking answers, but a definitive solution had eluded them. The two brothers were no more informed than when they had set out that morning to find out about the newest drug to hit the streets. A drug that had left T'Challa's son worn and frightened after a bad trip down an acid highway.

Night fell quietly on Tokus and T'Challa as they combed the neighborhood, watching and prowling, searching for the one bit of evidence that would lead them to the person responsible for giving Monday a dose of poison. Tokus saw a raw determination in T'Challa that was frightening and driven by the anger of watching his child do the junkie jig, a dance that T'Challa had banished from his life by changing the music. He was seething with anger and the intent of finding the person who had introduced Monday to this new drug and its deadly, musical stylings.

But they had come up empty. Feenin was quickly becoming the high of choice, but its origins were still a mystery. No one was talking and Tokus was sure someone knew where the drug was coming from, but since the addicts were tripping, he couldn't push the issue. As far as they were concerned, they had found a new gravy train and if you weren't on board, you would have to find your ticket elsewhere. A junkie's secret. Who would've ever believed that could happen? It was scary.

Tokus had one last straw to grasp. They were going to see Fishouse Fat. His ears were always open to the sounds of the street that floated his way and he usually heard more than what was said. All was quiet as they walked the long, winding pavement through the park around a sloping, grass hill, toward the monument of the Buffalo Soldiers.

Fishouse Fat was sitting on his bench facing the river, "watching thoughts" through sightless eyes that were hidden behind his blind man's shades, seemingly frozen in time. When they drew near, Fishouse Fat turned to them and smiled.

"Tokus!" he greeted. Tokus had been trying to sneak up on the sightless, old man for years, but Fishouse always knew who he was.

"Fishouse. Fishouse, my brother is with me. This is T'Challa."

Fishouse turned his head toward T'Challa—as if seeing him—with a look of surprise and excitement.

"Whoa, boy!" he exclaimed. "Undamo! You Undamo!"

T'Challa looked on, openmouthed.

"I can see it," Fishouse continued. "They came to you at night. They changed you. Inside."

"Yeah!" T'Challa wondered aloud. "But how you know all that?" T'Challa looked from Tokus to Fishouse back to Tokus with an incredulous question.

Fishouse said, "I can see it! Tokus, I think I can see! I think I got vision! I mean, I ain't never seen befo' so I ain't 'xactly sure, but I see shapes and lightness. And it's deep. Real deep."

He turned to T'Challa. "Imandé."

T'Challa fell silent. Something inside him seemed to grow. Fishouse's words appeared to be a confirmation, a sign, something foretold of life, of his life and what he needed to do with it.

T'Challa breathed his reply. "Imandé."

Fishouse looked out into the silence. Watching thoughts. Waiting for sights. After a moment, Tokus spoke.

"Fishouse. Look, I need to ask you about something. And it's really important."

"Feenin," Fishouse said. "It's new junk. A high that's brand-new and hard to duplicate. Stuff that's mixed up in a lab-a-tory. It makes things open up. Like my eyes."

"Where's it coming from? Who makes it?"

"Your eye," Fishouse said. "Tokus, watch out for your eye."

"Okay, Fishouse," Tokus replied. "I'll watch out for my eye. But we need to know…where are the drugs coming from?"

"They got a little 'ping' to ' em. Feenin. It does! It goes 'ping.' Ping hurts." Fishouse sang, "It's a thin liiiine…"

"Fishouse," Tokus interrupted.

"Between love and pain…my cryin' blues."

"Fishouse!" Tokus cried.

"Boy…" Fishouse smiled. "Ain't many songs I can sang, but…" He sang again, "It's a thin liiiine…between love and pain." He shook his head, chuckling to himself.

"I don't know where they comin' from, Tokus. But I know some come from that big buildin' over on Industrial Park. They ain't been open long but they ship candy and tayta chips and soda and stuff out to the stores. They ship Feenin, too. On the down-low, you know."

Tokus' face darkened as he listened. "Are you sure about this, Fishouse?"

"Yeah. Real sure. Sure as sure can be."

"Son-of-a-fuckin' bitch!" Tokus exploded. He marched backed and forth in front of the park bench ranting. "Damn! Damn! Damn!"

"What's wrong?" T'Challa watched him. "What's up?"

"Fuck! Fuck! Fuck!" Tokus yelled. He spun on his heel and cursed the sky. His fists were clenched so tightly that cords stood out thick and ropy on his forearms.

T'Challa waited patiently. When the stream of curses dried up, Tokus turned back to the stunned pair with a drained look on his face.

He spoke softly, "Thanks, Fishouse." He motioned to T'Challa. "Come on."

Tokus was steamed. Anger slipped from beneath the mask of control he had pulled over his face. His shoulders were squared in a hulking mode.

Fishouse called out, "Tokus! Watch ya' eye! Watch ya' eye! Hell, you can even watch mine." With that, Fishouse took his shades off and for the first time ever, Tokus saw his eyes. The pupils were vertical. Feline. Straight up and down.

"I think I see," Fishouse said. "But it hurts."

Tokus wanted to reproach him for using Feenin, but he couldn't. Drugs happened to people, anyone could succumb, as he and T'Challa had seen.

"You can see, Fishouse," Tokus replied. "Better than most people can. I'll get with you later, okay? T'Challa, let's roll."

Tokus strode from the park without another word, anger etched deeply into his face. When they turned onto Central Avenue, T'Challa tapped him on the arm.

"What's up?" he said. "Somethin's on your mind. What?"

"I'll show you," Tokus answered shortly.

They crossed the street and went downtown. Bistros and restaurants lined the street in this section of the city. Establishments of fine dining with entrees, minus the prices and definitely no cheeseburgers or French fries on the menu.

"Tell me," T'Challa said. "Now!"

Tokus stopped to look at his brother. So many things had changed about him. Once he had run away; now he was making demands. Tokus felt a surge of pride.

"You know that building that Fishouse was talking about?" Tokus said. "The one that the Feenin is coming from? That's a Stoneway building. My building. That's where we're going now."

Tokus reminded himself to inform Eva about these developments when they met for her slave sex game. The demented bitch. If something illegal was happening, Tokus wanted to implicate her with the knowledge of wrongdoing. He had to play her game but he could make up his own rules. Tokus had never felt such hatred for another human being as he did for Eva. She raped him while she despised him. Well, if the law came knocking, she was going down with him because Tokus knew she would never work within the framework of the law. Her brain was illegal. Sick woman.

A noisy crowd of people were gathered across the street in front of an eatery that advertised "high dining in French cuisine." The front of the building was constructed entirely of tall, black glass embroidered with intricate gold designs. An old, dark Mexican man stood facing the glass with a brick in each hand.

"Here come the cops!" someone yelled.

"I don't care," the Mexican yelled back. "Look in my eyes. You don't see no fuck in there. I don't give a fuck." His eyes were feline and hazy. "They took my job. They took my 'partment. I got nowhere to live. I wanna go to jail." He reared back and threw the brick at the dark glass. It shattered the storefront explosively. The entire wall came crashing noisily to the ground. And in that instant, that heartbeat, Tokus himself, was watching thoughts. He saw snatches of his life through the falling shards of glass that dropped in tingling, dark raindrops in the background of his memories.

The image of Five-O in a church popped into his mind. His eyes were exorcist marbles that glinted as he barked into a cell phone.

"What are you doing? Watching me through your precious glass wall?"

He saw the mental image of Way Jalon standing in front of the window-wall in his office. That thought was stamped onto Tokus' brain, but the picture faded away only to be replaced by a glimpse of Eva's face through the falling glass. His mind raced back to a hotel room. Eva sat on the edge of the bed, looking down on his naked body.

"Moose blood, if I recall correctly," Eva whispered through a foggy haze. How did she know Moose? In Arbor Hill, he was Moose; in society he would be Billy Badass or some such shit. But "Moose!" No. But she knew him as "Moose."

These thoughts were a glimpse, a solid imprint in Tokus' mind when the old Mexican man shattered the dark glass of the restaurant, explosively bringing the entire wall tumbling down.

These thoughts were inspired by the slingshot of fate that flung a rock at a glass house and shattered a secret. Way Jalon was sitting at what had been a private table a second earlier. He wore a stoic look of a man whose evening had been interrupted by a fly in his soup. Across from him sat his dinner companion, Eva, a flirtatious smile adorning her face.

As the cops came and dragged the Mexican away, Way Jalon looked up and saw Tokus. Their eyes locked. Everything clicked into place for Tokus Stone in that brief moment of contact. It all made sense. Way Jalon was setting him up. No one else could move Feenin through Stoneway without Tokus' knowledge.

Five-O had been working for Way Jalon! But why?

And Eva, if that was her real name, was extra flavoring, the proof in the pudding, probably one of Way's checks and balances for which he was infamous. That was how she knew about Moose. Way had told her. He truly left nothing to chance.

Five-O's manipulations had been the result of Way's commands.

Eva's demented sex games were one of Way's countermeasures.

Feenin.

But Way Jalon had made two miscalculations. Selecting Tokus for the fall guy was one. The next would be his arrogance.

Tokus turned to T'Challa. When he spoke, his voice was tight with the slightest hint of anger coiled in his throat. "Come on. Let's bounce."

They walked away. Tokus had a meeting to attend. In the office of Way Jalon.

I HATE THE MOOR

The Plaza loomed before them and Tokus peered at the light from the single window on the fifteenth floor, the office of Way Jalon. He imagined he saw the silhouette of the great overseer as he stood there, looking out. Watching. Waiting. The tall, modernistic structure stood fifty stories high, reflecting images of a dark city back into nowhere, the lone light shining like a beacon.

Tokus glanced at T'Challa before they went through the double glass doors. They hopped down a few steps to the marble landing, walked down the escalator over to a bank of elevators and waited.

T'Challa turned to Tokus. "What floor is his office on?"

T'Challa wore a pair of dark, baggy pants and a slightly darker shirt with an African flag emblazoned on the right shoulder. He stood with his feet slightly spread, his eyes focused, determined. He was definitely hyped, fully prepared, and almost overeager, yet he still seemed tightly controlled.

"Fifteen," Tokus answered. He was dressed in a severe casual suit, no tie with a high collar that fit comfortably. His freedom hung in the balance, on the fifteenth floor, with a man who had made all of his goals attainable only as part of an elaborate scheme that would lead to ruin. It was a face that Tokus had seen before, but it still hurt whenever it smiled.

"Okay," T'Challa said. "I got it." He paused and stepped closer to his brother. "Look, I got your back. Just remember that. I got your back." Slowly, he extended a clenched fist toward Tokus.

"No doubt." Tokus returned and tapped the hand with a clenched fist of his own. T'Challa turned for a door that led to the stairs. Tokus called out to him.

"T'Challa, be careful, yo!"

T'Challa shrugged. He had a small, bamboo stick in one hand; two poison tipped darts in the other. Tokus had seen those little missiles before and he remembered their deadly impact. His brother pushed through the door and was gone. Tokus waited a few minutes before he pushed the button to signal the elevator.

Way Jalon had played him. The very thought of it pissed Tokus off. All his life, he had worked and worked hard with a goal in mind: prosperous freedom. From the abuse of his stepfather to his mother leaving him to the drug-dealing nights and tough school days, he had fought each battle and been thrilled with each victory. He had found a new family. A brother, a sister, and even a precious nephew who had put a little color back into the picture of his life. The bad things—the drugs, the fight, Five-O—they had been filed away in a gray area, no longer a part of what counted. The here and now. The living.

But Way Jalon would destroy all that. Way Jalon would count Tokus' life as a mere plaything, a toy to be discarded when the batteries wore out. It was all so obvious now.

Way Jalon had hired him to smuggle Feenin because Tokus had a past history of drug involvement. He would be the perfect victim to a perfect setup, and he would fall forever into the pit of a cage that spoke in steel "clangs" and hollow "snicks." Cells that don't multiply; they just retreat into solitude. Alone forever.

The elevator arrived and Tokus stepped inside. He pushed the button for the fifteenth floor, the home office of Way Jalon Holdings. Tokus knew he was up there. Way Jalon had used him from day one—even before that—and he was waiting there now. It was just too poetic to pass up! He was probably sitting behind his foolish desk in front of that giant glass wall of his with his hands folded, waiting. Master of the game. He didn't know that Tokus had changed the rules.

The elevator doors opened and Tokus stepped out. Down the hallway to the right sat the office of Way Jalon. Tokus walked quietly to the door, opened it and slipped inside. He closed the door halfway, careful to be quiet, walked over to the double doors and pushed past them, leaving the doors open behind him. Way Jalon sat behind his desk drumming his fingers impatiently.

"It's about time," he said. "Come in, Tokus. Come in."

Tokus looked from side to side, surveying the room, as he approached the desk. He was about to speak when he spotted Eva standing off to his left by the wall near the futons. She wore a tight-fitting bodysuit that made Tokus' pulse jump, despite the circumstances. Hard to believe such beauty could be so cruel. She eyed Tokus as if he were a test specimen that had failed.

"Stunning," Tokus stated.

She raised a gloved finger to her lips. Tokus turned to Way Jalon.

"Your jig is up, Way Jalon. You can't get me."

"Tokus! You sound so melodramatic. You know, niggers are known for reacting without rhyme or reason. They just come off the top of their heads, you know, a gut reaction. It really is a detriment. I know for a fact that you aren't one of those people."

Way Jalon motioned toward a chair. "Please, sit."

"I'll stand," Tokus replied, unmoved.

"Sure you will." Way grinned at him. "Okay, let's start at the beginning. One question. Answer any way you like. Who are you? I mean, look around you. It's obvious who I am but in a real sense, exactly who are you?" He looked at Tokus expectantly.

"I'm daddy's little preacher," Tokus spat. "Listen, Way Jalon, spare me the bullshit philosophies, theories and other self-injected stupidity and tell me why you did this to me. And I mean 'me' in particular. I don't care if your grandfather or great-grandfather or your uncle-cousin-nephew's brother, the great Klan Jalon discovered the joys of inbreeding. I just want answers."

"Answers, huh?" Way Jalon stared at Tokus. "The answer to your question is: I hate the Moor. Quite simple, isn't it? I mean history is my basis. This

entire country operates on that one simple concept. It's how I got to be…
me! I hate the Moor. Go back, Tokus. Go back in history. You'll find that…"

"Miss me with that shit," Tokus interrupted. "I don't care. You still haven't answered my question. Let me rephrase. Why me?"

"Don't interrupt the teacher," Way warned. "I proscribe to the theory of one of our forefathers. He said, and I quote, 'I will say in addition to this that there is a physical difference between the black and white races which I believe will forever forbid the two races living together on terms of social and political equality.' That is beautiful shit!"

Way Jalon was standing now, his face flushed with conviction. The two men faced each other across the expanse of carpet and animosity. After a moment, Tokus spoke.

"While they do remain together there must be the position of superior and inferior," Tokus recited to a stunned Way Jalon. "And I am in favor of having the superior position assigned to the white race."

Tokus paused to look Way in the eye. "Abraham Lincoln. You found an old racist to sing your theme song, huh?"

"Very good," Way responded, regaining his composure.

"No, very bad. Not only are you outdated…you're deadly. You would turn Feenin loose on this entire city, with all the other drug problems out there, and point every finger at me. Because I'm black?"

"No," Way answered. "Not just because you're a spade. A spade is a spade. Because I hate the Moor. I mean, I have the right to hate something, don't I? I hate with the heart of Iago…and you're my Othello. I hate with the lust that cursed you and your kind with the skin on your back. I'd ship you all back to Africa but you've been around good, white people so long that you don't want to go. I guess we gave you dreams."

"You are one sick bitch!" Tokus snapped.

"Well, I have a dream, too," Way yelled. "If I can't send the niggers back to the jungles, I'll bring the jungles to them."

"Feenin," Tokus stated.

"That's right," Way roared. "Feenin. I'll dope them all!"

"Not me, you won't." Tokus turned for the door.

"Tokus Stone," Way called out. "You don't actually think that you are just going to walk out that door?"

Eva stepped forward.

"Let me introduce you to Pause. She's a killer. Sometimes she goes by the name of Eva, but that's only when she relaxes." Pause reached behind her back and pulled out a star-shaped disk, its metal twinkled dully in her hand. She went into a karate stance with the disk held at shoulder height, a good throwing position, and moved closer to Tokus as Way narrated.

"I think those are called shurikens. I'm not sure, but I think they are coated with a deadly poison. She's very good, too, Tokus. She never misses."

Pause reared her arm back poised to fire the star toward Tokus when she suddenly yelled out and stumbled back against the wall. A small dart protruded from her shoulder. She looked toward the door. T'Challa stood there with the bamboo reed down by his side, and she threw the shuriken at him. The disk sliced through the air toward T'Challa, who dove out of its path but it bit into his calf, imbedding him with its poison. T'Challa rolled over to the door and looked up at Pause, who had fallen, weakly, to one knee.

"You have sixty seconds to live," he yelled.

"That's five seconds longer than you have," she screamed before struggling to her feet. T'Challa rose from the floor. They stared at each other, determined to watch the other die. They walked toward each other until they stood face-to-face in the center of the room.

Tokus saw Way Jalon had gone into his desk drawer. He covered the distance to the desk in one stride. With the second step, he launched himself toward Way. The gun swung toward Tokus while he was in midair and a shot went off. The blast of the explosion assaulted his ear as the bullet streaked past and burned into the soft flesh of his shoulder before he crashed into Way Jalon. Way had been leaning forward and the blow sent his body into the glass wall with a loud "thwack." Tokus' arm exploded in pain when he landed on it, and his body trembled in protest as he lay on the floor. He struggled to his feet, trying to push the pain down, when he saw that Way Jalon had made it to one knee, the gun swinging upward.

Pause and T'Challa stood face-to-face, inches apart, searching for death in each other's eyes. T'Challa felt his heart begin to race but his eyes showed no hint of its sequence. Beads of sweat began popping up on his forehead.

"No fear, Undamo."

A voice spoke to T'Challa. His mentor. His savior. The one who had cut away the Bug in him. He had returned. The Undamo had taken away his weak, cowardly spirit once before, in a dream of hope and renewal, and replaced it with the honor of a man. The Undamo had imbibed T'Challa with a warrior's pride and that pride, that sense of himself, helped him to stand taller.

Pause was breaking. Her face had turned an angry red. Little tremors rocked her like toy lightning as her body slightly convulsed. She seemed determined. T'Challa looked into her eyes and saw the light of life dimming from them. A flicker caught his attention and T'Challa looked deeper into Pause's eyes. The spark of light began to take shape. It pulsed and moved until the image of the Undamo appeared. Pause was a fighter but she was fighting alone. T'Challa had the Undamo.

Pause suddenly pitched forward into T'Challa's arms in an awkward, deadly embrace. Her arms went around his neck, her lips nearly touching his. She looked into his eyes before she pulled him toward her and their lips touched.

"All I ever wanted," she rasped, "was a kisssss…"

She flopped from his arms to the floor.

T'Challa looked down at her lifeless body. His fate would come calling soon. He felt death coming for him. T'Challa's vision was going gray, his brain was going soft and a fire was burning in his ear. He dragged his body over to the futon in the corner of the office and collapsed into the cushions. His hands began to shake and his vision went a shade darker, yet he had to complete his mission. With a trembling hand he reached into his pocket and pulled out the remaining dart. He felt someone walk past him and then a light invaded his gray. With pain-racked fingers, he pushed the dart into the bamboo reed.

Tokus dove as far to his right as his leg muscles would allow and the bullet missed, high and behind him. Tokus rolled into a crouch and sprinted toward the sitting area—the futons and wet bar. Way Jalon squeezed off two more shots, missing the moving target but shattering a few glasses on the bar. Tokus looked up at the huge oak doors and bolted through them. He veered hard to his right, out of the open doorway and crashed into something wooden that sent him sprawling. Electric pain shot up his arm, into his throat and he cried out in anguish.

Way called out to him.

"You're in my room! No one goes in my room! But since you did...how do you like it?"

Tokus bit down on his lip to keep from screaming. His shoulder was hot with pain. He fought it down and decided to ignore it.

Way continued ranting. "How do you like my motif?"

Tokus looked around the room for a weapon. He looked for anything of use, preferably something heavy. As his eyes adjusted to the dim light, the odd shapes in the room began to take form.

In the middle of the room was a large, canopied, four-poster bed. It was elegant. A work of art surrounded by filth and madness. The walls were decorated with chains, shackle, long-handled whips and hangman's nooses. Next to the bed in the corner was a mock theater—a balcony with two chairs enclosed behind a wooden rail. Two mannequins, a man and a woman, were seated in each chair facing a stage that stood about six feet away from them. On that stage was a surreal scene that shook Tokus to the core. A pregnant slave girl was suspended in midair from ropes that were tied to each ankle. The other ends of the ropes were tied to a pair of plastic mules who pulled them artificially taut. The slave girl's head was thrown back in agony and the unborn baby's head stuck out between her legs as it was pulled forcefully from the womb.

"It's my Lincoln menagerie," he heard Way announce. "You know it's really ironic. You see, Tokus, I'm out here reloading and I'm coming to get you. You're dead, fucker! Dead!"

Tokus looked around wildly. Directly across from him was another horror scene. An almond-toned man was spread-eagled against the wall with both of his arms pinned helplessly. Long, red streaks of blood ran the length of his bare back.

The light streamed through the open door, and Tokus heard Way Jalon lumbering toward it. Tokus reached up over his head and grabbed a whip. He uncurled the long coil and hefted the handle, his hand testing the grip. The lash of the whip seemed to be at least six feet long and it shone an angry tongue.

"As I told you before," Way's voice was getting closer. "I hate the Moor. And in your heart… you hate yourself. But it won't be much longer."

With his free hand, he pushed the door until the doorknob banged against the wall. Satisfied that Tokus wasn't hiding behind it, he reached inside for the light switch on the wall.

He spun into the room gun first. As it swung toward him, Tokus lashed out with the whip. It caught Way Jalon across the face and his finger squeezed the trigger, sending a bullet into the wall just over Tokus' head. Tokus pulled his arm back as the gun clattered to the floor and Way Jalon staggered backwards. His arm went forward and the whip caught Way Jalon across the neck. Way shrieked and dove for the gun lying on the floor. Tokus sent the lash forward again. It struck Way Jalon across the back and he bucked in pain before he turned over with the gun in his hand. He pulled the trigger before Tokus could move, but his aim was off. He set the sights on Tokus' heart, but the whipping affected his aim and the bullet grazed a bloody shoulder instead. Tokus staggered toward the door and fell through the open doorway. He got up and started running toward Way's desk. He had taken three off-balanced strides before Way Jalon appeared in the doorway.

"Why fight it?" Way Jalon was eerily calm. He rubbed the mark that streaked across his face. "You're poison."

He stepped through the door, faltered suddenly and swore. "Ooh, shit!"

A dart protruded from his neck. He pulled it out and growled before he looked down at a dying T'Challa taking his last breath—one that had launched a poison dart into Way Jalon's flesh. Tokus stood behind Way Jalon's desk with blood leaking down his arm. He looked at Way in disgust.

"You have sixty seconds to live."

Way Jalon was stunned.

"Sixty seconds! Sixty…"

Way Jalon raised his gun and fired at Tokus, missing and hitting the glass wall. Tokus hit the floor behind the desk. Way Jalon kept shooting. The glass wall didn't shatter; there were holes where the bullets went through and solid cracks reached out in every direction but it held. It wouldn't withstand a barrage of gunshots, but Way Jalon continued pulling the trigger until his mind registered the hollow clicking of metal. Tokus dared a peek over the desk. The fool was digging in his pockets and pulling out bullets to reload! Tokus cursed. He couldn't reach Way in time; his shoulder was a licking flame that flashed up his shoulder and he didn't think he could move at all. But the window! Fifteen floors up!

"What the fuck are you doing, Way?" Tokus cried.

Way shoved a bullet in the chamber and looked at Tokus. Tokus noticed that his face was getting pasty. He had already used up at least thirty seconds. He hoped that Way would fall before he blew out the window behind him. Way's legs began to tremble.

Tears began running down his face.

"I'm going…" he faltered. "To kill you." He raised the gun and opened fire. Tokus ducked under the desk as three more bullets blasted the glass behind him. He heard the sounds of Way's pounding footsteps coming directly toward the desk. He rolled to the side—away from his bad arm. Way Jalon came over the top of the desk, landed directly behind it and looked to the left. Tokus was on the right. He launched himself at Way Jalon and smashed him in the face. He knocked Way Jalon solidly into the window wall. The bullet holes screamed in protest and bounced Way back. He staggered forward with the gun raised. Tokus' arm felt paralyzed. He couldn't move it, so he jumped forward and kicked with every ounce of energy he had left. Way Jalon had the gun pointed toward him and as the kick broke his nose and sent him flying, he squeezed the trigger. Tokus never saw the gun, only a flash of metal as Way swung his free arm up. A red flash is all he would remember, dream about sometimes, in the days that followed. His brain didn't register the darkness that followed the blinding flash that careened off his left eye, shrouding it in darkness. Nor would his mind recollect Way Jalon crashing through the glass wall, falling, slowly as his heart attacked him, killing him before he splattered on the ground fifteen stories below. Tokus would only remember a burning haze that darkened half his vision.

He awoke in a hospital bed.

The African warrior from T'Challa's house; the one on the shelf—the Undamo—floated before his eyes. He sat in a field of red, black, and green while he whispered one word. "*Imandé.*" Tokus' eyes popped open. The first thing he felt…was the handcuff on his ankle.

ABOUT THE AUTHOR

Nane Quartay is a new voice in urban fiction.
He was born in upstate New York and attended Augusta College
in Augusta, Georgia. After a tour in the U.S. Navy,
he traveled extensively before returning to New York to
begin writing his first novel, *Feenin*. Nane Quartay is also
the author of *The Badness* and the upcoming novel *Come Get Some*.
He lives in the Washington, D.C. area.

Excerpt from

The Badness

by Nane Quartay
Available from Strebor Books

CHAPTER 3
Flo Jigga

D.Wayne lay on his bed, staring at the ceiling. He had a comic book spread open on his chest, happily lost in a world of his own creation, when he heard her voice break the barrier.

"Come here, boy!"

He groaned out loud and turned over on his side, facing the wall and closing his eyes in an attempt to ignore his mother. He pretended to sleep.

"Don't make me get up and come up in there, D.Wayne. If I come up there, you know that I'm gonna whoop 'em ass! I know you hear me, boy!" The drunken timbre of Joselle's speech warned him that she may have been deep inside of that bottle of vodka so it was best to go ahead and get the alcohol tricks over with. Sometimes Joselle would get really juiced up and her mind would conjure up all manner of twisted, stupid brain teasers. Games like, "who hid my bra" or "scrape the gum off the floor with a fork," and once they had played a game called "get my earring, I dropped it down the toilet." D.Wayne especially hated that one.

At other times Joselle could be real ornery and scary. Her aggressive nature sometimes burst to the fore and she would take the stance of a defiant woman against a world of manly confrontations. It was during these episodes that she would bring out the knife, her friend, Flo Jigga—bent flat and curved for a nigga. Joselle sometimes conversed with the knife as if Flo Jigga was a lifelong buddy.

"Shit!" D.Wayne groaned as he rose from his bed. His ribs were feeling much better. All that remained was a dull throb, and that was only when he moved suddenly, but the cut over his eye still felt fresh. The insistent pain hovered near the edge of his mind, steady and bothersome. He didn't bother to put his undershirt on as he plodded over to Joselle's room to see why her drunk ass was calling him.

D.Wayne wished fervently that he could have a mother that acted like a regular mother. Like the mothers he saw picking up the other kids from school, the ones he saw at football games and at the malls. He longed for the serenity that he saw everywhere…laughter, hugs, harmony…everywhere except where it mattered most—home, the place where he lay his head.

So he was an outsider. He couldn't relate to the cliques and other little groups of kids his age because he had no common interests; in essence he had no commonality at all. He often told himself that he was above the need for that particular type of group therapy, that he was strong enough to be alone, that he was a tempered steel mandingo and nothing could hurt him.

Until he met Alicia.

Alicia was special. She made him "stir" the first time that he saw her. *I wanna do that porno movie-type shit with her.* That was how he knew that he liked her…more than liked her. He casually followed her, hoping to catch her alone so that he could look at her up close. She was pretty; he could tell that from afar, but there was something there that was much better than pretty. She wore her hair short, close cropped to her skull and brushed back into finger waves. Her burnished copper skin reflected the intensity of her eyes showing hints of daring that radiated from her. D.Wayne fidgeted with fear. He couldn't wait.

As fate would have it, he didn't have to wait at all. Alicia was a loner just like he was. She was always alone, away from the crowds, separated from the mixed-up girls who were always so worried about their hair and clothes and other kiddy shit. She chose the outside. And that's just where D.Wayne resided.

They eyed each other warily—each suspicious of the invasion of their solitude, yet each open to the possibility of a loneliness shared. D.Wayne was drawn to her. Pulled by an attraction that forced him to cast his inhibitions aside, he had to investigate that stir that she had awakened in him. She was a step beyond the other girls, those silly girls who would often stop and stare at her as she walked by. She shied away from others and apparently seemed oblivious to their cold, penetrating stares.

She and D.Wayne had been moved from subtle glances to more meaningful eye contact. It signaled an attraction that would lead to its resultant physicality, and soon he found himself on the precipice. He was having magnets in his dreams. He dreamed of Alicia, imagined her flying through the air, naked and willing, with him on her tail, more than willing and ecstatic in the throes of the virginal flushes of lust. He saw her with the clarity of realness as she landed on her back in a soft field of cotton flowers. The space between her legs, her center, glistened with wetness and beckoned to the urges that engorged his suddenly swollen member. When his lips touched her softly rounded breasts he felt sensations that sent currents throughout his body and sent them to *his* center. And he heard her make sounds! A combination of breathing and moaning right next to his ear as she pulled him by the back of his head and pulled him…pulled him…pulled him. He felt liquid pleasure coming down the center of his body. Like ragged iron filings that scraped the inside of his core; only each ragged piece of metal sent molten sparks of pleasure clattering down his shaft; and Alicia controlled his polarity. He was having magnets in his dreams!

They passed each other often in the hallways at school and when their eyes met, D.Wayne would feel his heart pick up its pace. Soon he began to imagine that maybe, just maybe, he might have a chance with Alicia. But his courage would fade with the remembrance of her pretty brown eyes and her soft, full lips. *She is just too pretty*, D.Wayne rationalized.

But one day, Alicia set D.Wayne's world on fire. He was sitting outside the school, with his back against the wall during his lunch break reading a comic book. D.Wayne was caught up in the cartoon world of daredevil dandies that were saving the world from evil. He was spaced-out, oblivious to the raucous laughter of kids at play on the sprawling, well-kept fields.

The school was shaped like a humpbacked "U" and there were athletic fields on every side of the building: football fields, soccer fields and baseball diamonds, each lined perfectly for play. A soft voice spoke to D.Wayne, rousing him from his favorite superhero's dilemma.

"What you reading?" Alicia stood before him. She had on a pair of blue jeans and a pleated pink shirt. She had the prettiest eyes that D.Wayne had ever seen.

"Comics," he finally managed to gasp.

"You read them a lot, huh?"

D.Wayne fidgeted. "Yeah. They good."

An awkward moment of silence stretched out between them as D.Wayne looked at her. Alicia shifted nervously and, without a word, sat down next to him. D.Wayne's heart pounded in his chest as the warmth of her nearness heated the space between them. His mouth went dry as his mind worked furiously in an attempt to conjure up something magical to say to her. He looked over at her when she turned to face him and the sight took his breath away. His blood pounded down through his veins and he felt the distinct sensation of an erection blossoming to life. He pulled his knees up to his chest and dropped the comic book on the ground in front of him.

"I see you all the time," Alicia began. "By yourself."

"I see you, too," D.Wayne answered. "Hey, Alicia?"

She looked up at him. "You know my name?"

"Yeah. I saw you, too."

She took D.Wayne's hand and intertwined their fingers. She looked into his eyes and then suddenly bent his fingers backwards. D.Wayne yelped out in pain just in time to hear the school bell go off, signaling the end of the lunch period. It was time to go to his next class. Alicia was watching him with a wicked grin on her face.

D.Wayne was puzzled. "Why you do that?"

"Let's cut class," Alicia whispered. "Let's go over there." She pointed to the woods that were beyond the edge of the school property. "Nobody won't know. Let's go! We can have some fun."

D.Wayne looked back at the school and then at Alicia. "Come on," she urged. He jumped to his feet and they ran together to the woods. They spent the rest of the school day out there, exploring the open, deserted fields; playing semi-erotic games of hide-and-go-get, freeze touch and red-light-green-light. They found a patch of thick, plush grass surrounded by a copse of trees and they stripped down to their underwear, lying down side by side with their arms folded behind their heads while they looked up at the blazing sun. Alicea reached over and tickled D.Wayne's nose and he tickled her back, giggling. Their horseplay soon took on a more serious tone and they started on a journey of exploration, beginning with their lips, fumbling in the daytime against each other in clumsy attempts to find intimacy. D.Wayne moved over her and conjured up every image that he had memorized from the nasty books that he had hidden under the bottom of his stack of comics in his closet. He moved her bra up over the slight swell of her breast and took her nipple in his mouth. He rolled it on his tongue, marveling when he felt the small bud grow rigid as he began to suck and lick. Her moans barely reached his ears as he ran his tongue around the perimeter of her tiny breasts and then paused to look at her face. He wanted to see if she liked what he was doing. He couldn't tell. He spread her legs and wedged himself between them so that the only impediment to penetration was the fabric of the underwear that they both still wore. D.Wayne felt his hardness swell to the biggest degree that he had ever felt and he dipped his hips into her, grinding until he felt a warm friction building in his shaft. Alicia put both hands on his chest and pushed him off her and onto his back. She leaned up on one elbow, reached over and began to trace the outline of D.Wayne's raging hard-on with her fingers. She looked up at him and smiled.

"We can't do that!" she said, watching him. "But one day?" She began squeezing him through his underwear and his breath caught in his throat.

"Get here, boy!" Joselle's gruff voice snatched him away from his soft memory of Alicia's touch and right back to his present, unpleasant situation. He couldn't escape his mother; she even intruded on his memories. He stepped over to her bedroom doorway.

"What, Joselle?"

She was laid out on her stomach on the bed. She wore a skimpy pair of black underwear that barely concealed the roundness of her fat ass while she watched herself in the mirrored headboard and put on her lipstick. Joselle was so nasty. She needed to cover herself up; D.Wayne could see the imprint of her privacy through her flimsy panties. She turned toward D.Wayne and he couldn't help but notice the fullness of her bra as it strained to contain her healthy titties. She opened her mouth to say something but caught herself. Her eyes traveled downward and a wicked expression came across her face. D.Wayne followed her obvious stare and looked down to see that his cock was quite noticeably swollen, jutting against his underwear in a rage. He moved to shield himself with his hands and jumped behind the doorway to hide his shame.

"Get in here, boy!" Joselle commanded. "At least something about your ass is growing into manhood! Now get here!"

D.Wayne hesitated. He was still hard, even though he wished it to go down. It was like Little Petey had a mind of its own; some volition to exercise and the circumstances were irrelevant. Joselle was waiting.

D.Wayne stepped from behind the doorway. There was a drink on the nightstand next to Joselle's bed. A tall bottle of vodka also sat on the table next to her knife, Flo Jigga. The sharp edge of the blade gleamed in the lamplight, its menace intrusive and deep.

D.Wayne started whining. "What, Joselle? I need to get some sleep! Dag!"

Joselle rose from her bed. She shot a quick glance at Flo Jigga before turning to stare at D.Wayne. "Nigga, who you talkin' to like that? Try it again and I'll fold you." She walked over and stood in front of him, looking down at his hardness that was still jutting out. A knowing smirk crossed her face before she looked up at him. When she shifted her body, her titties strained, trying to escape the lacy bra that she wore. D.Wayne's eyes were drawn to the enticing movement of the twin mounds of flesh. Guilt clouded his vision and he quickly looked away. Joselle grunted and stretched her body to its full height and posed seductively. It was a practiced undulation that had moved many men into actions that they would later regret.

"Ma," D.Wayne exclaimed and instantly regretted it. Joselle's hand balled into a fist and he instinctively flinched from her violent reaction. Joselle had beaten him once before for calling her out of her name. Joselle had power in her fists—she had given up on using the belt on D.Wayne when he was in the seventh grade—and she had pummeled him about the chest and ribs, all the while repeating her name to him. So it had been "Joselle" from that day forward. It had been a rough beating. D.Wayne closed his eyes and waited for this one to commence.

"Say that again," Joselle commanded. "Say it!" D.Wayne opened his eyes, surprised to still be upright, and stood stock-still.

"You better not!" Joselle's eyes blazed. "Sho' nuff! Now go in the bathroom and get me that cocoa butter and bring it here."

D.Wayne scrambled into the bathroom and gratefully retrieved the lotion. When he stepped back into her bedroom Joselle was bent over, going through her dresser. Turning back to face D.Wayne, she had a full drink in her hand and the early warning signs of drunkenness were on his mother's face. Her liquored-up eyes were starting to look like bloodshot devil's orbs, and there was always evil shit in the night when Joselle got drunk up.

She stared at D.Wayne and held him motionless. "You see this." She held the glass of vodka in the air. "This," she paused for a quick sip. "This is my ho juice!" She looked at D.Wayne and mocked him, throwing his own words back at him in an off-key imitation. "Ho juice! Ho juice!" She paused to stand directly over him. D.Wayne was not a big kid; he was almost average size, but Joselle towered over him. She bought fear from up above—with a temper to match.

"You called your own mother a ho!" Her lips were mere inches from his face.

There was nothing that D.Wayne could say to defend himself. Joselle had caught him at point-blank range, on the other side of the shower curtain, so there was really no denying. He did not intend to give Joselle any further ammunition so he was definitely keeping quiet and riding this one out.

"If I'm a ho, a damn good ho! Sexy enough to be a ho if I want to," she demanded.

D.Wayne didn't know the answer to that one. He didn't know that hos had to be sexy. *But there are some sexy hos though,* he reasoned. *Some of them girls be wearin' that real sexy shit, too!* D.Wayne's nature twirled at the memory as he pulled up the images of a few of the working girls that he would see on his way home from school. He fixed them in his mental Rolodex and began to replay their fleshy movements, practiced to enticing perfection. His imagination caught on one fine-ass woman with an ass that he could only describe as perfect flesh. She liked to wear tiny mini-skirts but she didn't particularly care for underwear. D.Wayne liked to watch her walk and as her hips caught his lust in an uproar, he thought that he spied the roundness of her mound, swaying with the openness of pleasure. D.Wayne was a virgin but instinct screamed for him to put his manhood inside of her and once that mission was accomplished there would be no better place on earth. He felt his cock stiffen with the anticipation.

Joselle looked down at D.Wayne's hard-on and then back at his face.

"Look at you." She indicated his erection. "You talk that shit…but look at you!" She quickly reached down and grabbed his dick through his underwear. "That! That is the same shit that men do! Then they wanna call you a ho! You seen ho juice, boy, and look at you! You just another motha fucka." Joselle released D.Wayne and walked over to her dresser with her drink in her hand. D.Wayne fell to the floor, his knees weak with shock. Joselle had touched his privates! "Joselle," he screamed. "That's nasty! You can't touch me there! No! You can't!" Joselle turned to look at him. She tilted the drink and drained the rest of her vodka before she slammed the empty glass down and picked up her knife, Flo Jigga.

She walked back over to D.Wayne. "Get in my bed." It was a simple command spoken without question and with a quality that he had never heard before. But he was not going to get in Joselle's bed. She had to be fucking kidding.

"But Joselle…" D.Wayne began. Joselle reached down and he felt her fingers dig firmly into the flesh of his throat.

"You better not lose that hard, boy," she snarled. "Now get. In. That. Bed!"

She yanked him to his feet and threw him toward the bed. D.Wayne tumbled forward. When he regained his balance he turned back toward Joselle and was met by Flo Jigga, inches away from his throat.

"Take them draws off." Joselle had a mad glint in her eye. D.Wayne shook his head "no" furiously. In desperation he grasped the band of his underwear with both hands and pulled upwards as far as he could. He stretched them over his stomach while trying to back away from Joselle. She wrapped her hand around his throat again, squeezed and pulled, nearly lifting D.Wayne off the floor. She swung him around by his neck and slammed him on the bed. D.Wayne could smell the stink of the vodka as it rolled over his face. Suddenly, Joselle raised Flo Jigga in the air and D.Wayne froze. She reached out and grasped the band of his underwear, pulled it toward her and slashed down with the knife. She cut them straight down the middle and suddenly D.Wayne found himself naked, exposed to his mother.

"Lay on the bed!" Joselle commanded. "And you better get back that hard! Lay on the bed...and don't move!" He did as she commanded, lay there on the bed, motionless, as Joselle moved over to her dresser, poured herself another drink and tossed half of it down in one gulp. She let out a loud gasp as the liquor hit home and then she stepped out of her underwear. It was the first, real cooty cat that D.Wayne had ever seen! And it was his mother's! He closed his eyes against the sickness he felt building in his brain, his mental rejecting the transpiring reality. His eyes popped open when he felt the cold touch of Flo Jigga pressed to his neck. His erection went instantly soft. Joselle looked down.

"Oh no, nigga," she exclaimed. She took Flo Jigga and nestled the flat curve of the blade against the base of D.Wayne's cock. "Perform, nigga. Now!"

D.Wayne felt the cold, flat blade of steel press against him and tears began to well up in the back of his eyes. He willed his erection to stand tall. He envisioned all of the erotic women he had seen in his magazines. He imagined that it was his cock going in and out of their pussies and mouths, and he felt his hips try to buck in response. His fear intensified.

Joselle sat astride him and began to grind her nakedness against his thickening penis. She moved and moved...but it wasn't working. D.Wayne felt fear mounting inside of him. He knew that Joselle would cut him...she was crazy when she got all liquored up. *I gotta do this. I gotta!* He made his mind a blank. Phased out every sickening thought that threatened to invade his consciousness. Ignored the feel of the cold knife-edge that was pressed to his balls. Denied the hate that he felt for Joselle as she sat astride him, doing the bad thing that a mother is supposed to protect her child from. Focus. He felt the pressure of Joselle's weight as her sex pressed down on him. Felt the fat moistness of her pussy lips as they caught the tip of his dick. Blood flowed up inside of his cock, engorging it, and D.Wayne felt the guilty hell of pleasure as his manhood began to grow. He was invading his mother's warmth; and it was nasty. He felt the suction of her lips pulling at him and he became fully aroused. Her sex enveloped him like a fetish, an agonizing dark penchant, and a yearning heartbeat that went deeper and deeper inside of her. He felt her inner walls clench around his shaft. Joselle moaned. D.Wayne separated his mind from his body...and felt a dark stain expanding across his soul as he lost his virginity...to his mother.

CHAPTER 4
A Badness

Doin was frozen with anger, the rage in his eyes deepened by the fright that he saw in Bonita's. He stepped toward her. She shrank away from him.

"No! No! No!" Doin jumped up and down in an angry tantrum. Bonita looked back over her shoulder as she ran away from him toward Front Street. He calmed himself, facing the realization that she would never see him with the same eyes again; maybe she never had.

His stepfather stood in the doorway, watching. His face was etched with regret. All traces of alcohol seemed vacant from his red-rimmed eyes. He stepped halfway through the screen door and stood silently with an outstretched hand. A single tear rolled down his face.

Doin didn't see that drop of sorrow trail down the dark-skinned cheek. All Doin saw was the menacing devil of pain. The maker of scars. The giver of life marks. He ran his fingers across his disfiguration, the scar that tore a swath across his face, the mark of the devil who stood before him. The blotted soul who had come for Doin one cold day and altered his life forever.

Memories. Sometimes they felt like yesterday.

His stepfather kept his demon in a bottle, trapped in the watery grave called vodka. It was a thirsty little devil that couldn't be slaked, absorbing mothers and fathers, sisters and brothers, dollars and dollars until entire paychecks were consumed. Alcoholics never made enough money.

They never make good providers either so at the tender age of twelve, Doin found himself working on a farm alongside migrant workers, picking apples in order to buy his own clothes. He had managed to save over twenty-five dollars in a savings account for a pair of sneakers that had caught his eye and, with a few more dollars, they would soon be on his feet.

Doin walked into the house one evening to find his stepfather in a rage. He had been gambling and, poor gambler that he was, lost all of his drinking money. He was cursing up a storm when Doin walked in the door. He angrily summoned Doin to the kitchen.

"Boy!" he thundered and pointed at an opened letter laying on the kitchen table. It was Doin's bank statement.

"You got some money in the bank, nigga," his stepfather commanded. "We goin' to get all of that shit!"

Doin's heart sank.

"Come on!" His stepfather bustled out the front door. Doin straggled behind him, angry and scared, with unformed tears stinging his eyes. They piled into the car and his stepfather raced to the bank trying to beat the closing time.

"I know you don't like this shit, nigga!" The car roared around the corner onto Warren Street. They had ten minutes left before the doors at the bank were locked. Doin prayed that they wouldn't make it. Maybe a cop would pull them over for speeding.

"How you think I feel when you wanna eat eva' day? I got to go down in my pocket eva' time yo' black ass wanna eat!" They pulled up in front of the bank and screeched to a stop in the handicapped parking space.

His stepfather turned to him. "Now gone! Get up in there, nigga!"

Doin crawled out of the car, his heart aching, and slowly trod into the bank.

"And how much are you depositing today, young man?" The teller was a kind, gray-haired lady who always smiled at Doin when he made his weekly visits to deposit money into his account.

"I'm taking it all out," Doin said.

"Well, you'll build it back up in no time." She took his withdrawal slip.

Shortly, he emerged with a closed-out bankbook in one hand, twenty-five dollars in the other. He climbed into the front seat and held the money out to his stepfather, who snatched the cash from his grasp and stomped the gas, making a beeline to the nearest liquor store.

They pulled up to a glass storefront. His stepfather hopped out and vanished through the front door. Doin waited in the car and watched him through the store window as he strode up to the counter to pay for his drinks. Doin cursed the devil and wiped away a tear, wishing to God that he had never met this drunk-assed man. Muthafucka.

The front door swung open and his stepfather came bustling out of the package store like he had hit the number, carrying a brown bag in each hand. He tossed one back through the open window into the backseat, snatched the door open and eased his considerable bulk behind the wheel. He pulled the other bottle out of the bag he was holding—the word "vodka" was printed on the label in large letters—and twisted it open. He paused to look at Doin.

"From you to me," he cheered and raised the bottle to his lips. Huge gulps of air rushed toward the bottom of the bottle as the devil tilted the quart to the sky and toasted his demon. When the bottle came down…it was empty. Doin stared, open mouthed, as his stepfather tossed the drained bottle into the backseat and started the car. It didn't seem possible that a human being could drink that much liquor, that fast.

"That ain't nothin' but water," the devil belched before he pulled away from the curb. "Count your blessings," he sang as he stomped on the gas, burning rubber before he pulled out into traffic. "Count them one by one."

The car squealed around the corner onto Columbia Street, tires screeching, and right then, Doin knew that the devil had dues to pay.

"Count your blessings," his stepfather sang drunkenly as he swung the car onto Third Street. The tail swung out from under them, sending them into a spin. Doin screamed and tried to find something to hold onto.

"See what I have done." His stepfather's voice was tight as he battled the wheel, straightened the car out and pulled around the next corner onto Second Street. When the wheels caught traction he pressed his foot on the accelerator again. The car shot forward with such velocity that they were both thrown back in their seats. They went barreling toward Warren Street, the busiest intersection in the city, and the light facing them was red—but the devil never hesitated.

A huge, black SUV reached the crossing slightly ahead of them. His stepfather yanked the wheel to the right, avoiding impact by mere inches but he was unable to maintain control of the vehicle. The car rammed headfirst into a street lamp on the corner of Warren and Second Streets. The force of the crash flung Doin face-first through the windshield and fifteen feet through the air, crashing through the glass window of Mardell's Sporting Goods store. Baseball bats, footballs, basketballs and soccer balls came crashing back into the store with the force of the breaking glass. Doin was thrown into a sneaker display and crashed into the store counter. The pair of shoes that he had been saving to buy landed on his chest. And then...darkness.

His stepfather stumbled out of the wreckage and staggered three blocks down Warren Street and pulled the lever on a fire alarm box. He told the police that he had seen an accident and that someone may have been hurt.

Doin awoke the next day in the hospital staring into the darkness, assuming that he was dead and that this was what death looked like. He was blinded by the bandages that were wrapped around his face to cover the deep and vicious cuts that would later scar him.

The devil...his stepfather, suffered a broken hand.

That was the curse of the demon that had hit him, the one standing in the doorway, reaching out. The one who was responsible for Bonita trembling in fear from Doin's touch. The origin of misery, the pain of daily existence was the tall, dark inferno that ruined everything with his touch.

"Fuck you!" Doin felt a tear roll down his cheek. "You the bastard."

Memories of childhood held no joy for Doin. Any happiness that he might find was simply a harbinger of disaster, the yin and yang of dysfunctionality. More than anyone, his dark stepfather had colored Doin's life, shaped his development into a hard, distant thing. An entity that couldn't be reached by caring, emotion or compassion. A badness is what it was. A badness that spread through his inner self and separated him from the most basic human desire; to love someone passionately...and to be loved the same in return.

Memories.